Hard Contract

McKenna Rae

A Romance of Power, Control, and Consequence

* * *

He offered a deal she couldn't refuse.

She changed the terms.

For all the friends I forced to listen to my KDrama obsessive talk and to all those as equally obsessed. Enjoy my very own westernize biracial spin.

Chapter 1

RAYLEN

"YOU CAN DENY IT **all you want,** I know you've been aching for me to fuck you on the nearest flat surface since you saw me walk into that café." Jae-Hyun reached out and gently brushed a stray curl from my face. A shiver went down my spine at his words. I wasn't going to admit it out loud, but my body spoke volumes. I wanted him just as badly as I did all those years ago, maybe even more.

Flashes of our time together played through my head. In his room, my room, in the backseat of his beat-up little car. Anywhere we could get even the smallest amount of alone time together and we were ripping each other's clothes off. I wanted that again. I've been trying to keep my distance from him when all I could think about was letting him drive that massive dick between his legs into me repeatedly.

He didn't wait for me to respond. Jae-Hyun slipped his arm around my waist, pulling me close so my body was flush against his. He leaned in and whispered in my ear, "I still remember what you taste like, how badly do you want to feel my tongue on you again." My mouth went dry, and it suddenly felt like there was a river flowing between my legs. Why did this man have this effect on me. I should never have let this happen.

Eight years ago, I had my heart ripped out of my chest by the man that just walked in. Dark eyes, black hair, broad shoulders, and a devilish smile, just like I remembered him. You never forget someone like Jae-Hyun Park, the man who made me love him. Made me hang on every word he said and do anything he wanted just for him to walk out of my life with no explanation or any form of communication whatsoever for eight whole years.

His eyes darted around the room, searching. I knew he was looking for me, but it was like my body was frozen. I couldn't move a single muscle, that's what he did to me. What he always did to me, and I was powerless to stop it. It felt like time was moving in slow motion when he looked at me. Like suddenly the rustling of the leaves in the trees around me slowed and became deafeningly loud. My heart was beating a mile a minute and it felt like the blood was draining from my head so fast that I could lose consciousness at any moment. I couldn't seem to get any air into my lungs as he began his stride with those long legs towards the table I was sitting at.

The look on his face as he approached me was unreadable. He wore a smile but not the soft one I remembered, this one I knew was only a mask. One he wore just for show. I was so caught up in looking at his face that it took me a minute to realize he was dressed in a suit. And if I must admit it to myself, he filled it out perfectly. When I noticed the perky red head behind him, I snapped out of whatever trance he always managed to put me in and was immediately thrown into a state of confusion.

I had a million questions running through my mind, starting with why the hell was he here and ending with where the fuck had he been for the last eight years. My questions came to a screeching halt when he opened his mouth to speak.

"Ms. Clark, it's nice to meet you." *Ms. Clark?* Since when was I *Ms. Clark?* I sat up straighter in my seat and tried to process everything that was happening.

Today I was supposed to be having a meeting with a large publishing company that was interested in poaching me from the current company I'm working with to publish my new book. The plan was to meet with the head of the editing department to politely tell them I'm not interested in person since having my agent tell them through a nice email was no longer working.

Every day like clockwork my agent was receiving two phone calls and at least one email trying to schedule a meeting until finally the constant harassment from them as well as my agent's constant nagging finally wore me down and I agreed to at least meet with them. It's safe to say I was not expecting this to be the person that walked through those doors.

"My name is Jae-Hyun Yuu." He held out his hand for me to shake, but I didn't move. I just stared at it in confusion. Who the hell was Jae-Hyun *Yuu?* The man in front of me was Jae-Hyun *Park,* the man who abandoned me eight years ago. This man in front of me, this *Mr. Yuu*, he was the one badgering my agent to see me?

He cleared his throat and put his hand back at his side. Jasmine, my agent, gave me a slight nudge to get me to pay attention. She had no idea how hyper focused I already was on every word that came out of his mouth.

"Why don't we get this meeting started." Jae-Hyun and his assistant took a seat at the table across from us at the small coffee table. Jasmine and I had both decided we wanted a more casual setting for this meeting, so we opted for a quaint coffee shop instead of a stuffy office which I regretted the moment I felt his knees bump mine under the narrow table. I continued to stare at Jae-Hyun, trying to see if he would at least look me in the eyes but it seemed like he was trying his hardest not to.

I could feel my anger slowly beginning to bubble up. The more I thought about it, the angrier I got. After eight years of no contact from the man I thought I loved and who I thought loved me. The man I spent almost every day with laughing and joking, who made me forget about everything I had to deal with at home with my dad. The man who took my virginity and disappeared without a trace.

He has the nerve to want something from me and doesn't even have the decency to apologize for anything that happened.

His assistant placed a large stack of documents on the table, but I continued to stare at him. Those dark almond shaped eyes, like little bottomless pits that always sucked me right in. His jet-black hair gelled back out of his face. The years we were apart were good to him and I hated that. I wanted him to be miserable and have let himself go because he felt bad about what he did, but I guess wishing on a star didn't always work.

"As you are aware, we're very interested in buying your latest work." He spoke. "Your previous novels have produced great numbers, but we think that if you sign on with us, we can get your work out to a greater audience." The way he was talking, all business, no familiarity. Like I was a stranger, like there was never once something between us.

I wanted to scream at him, I wanted to demand answers that I probably wouldn't like but I feel like I was owed. How could he not so much as reach out to me after all this time and think that because he wants something from me that I would just do it because it was him. As if he had all the power like he always did. Well not this time, this time I had the power. He was still in the middle of his stupid speech of why the publishing company he works for was better than the one I've been with for the last six years when I cut him off.

"Let me stop you right there." I said holding up my hand successfully shutting him up. He looked a little shocked like it was the first time he had ever been interrupted or maybe it was because he never expected me to do the interrupting. "The only reason I took this meeting was to get BY Publishing to stop harassing me. I'm not interested in leaving the company I'm currently with especially for a company that has proven they have no soul."

I could hear Jasmine gasp as I got to my feet and leaned across the table. I was so close that I could practically feel his breath. His face remained unchanged, like nothing I was saying to him had fazed him. "I'd rather wait another eight years to publish than to give you the satisfaction." With that I grabbed my bag and stormed out leaving an alarmed and slightly confused agent behind.

Jae-Hyun

Raylen Clark, just as hot headed as I remembered her to be. Just as dramatic and irritatingly beautiful too. Those brown ringlets I was so used to being wild and all over her head, now a little looser and longer but still just like her personality, wild and free. Those hazel eyes with the tiny flecks of green in them seemed brighter, almost like they burned just as hot as the amount of rage she felt towards me. She wasn't alone in that feeling. Eight years is a long time, and for me it felt even longer. I had spent that entire time searching for her so I could demand to know why she did what she did, but now that she was in front of me, that feeling of missing her was even stronger. I thought my anger would make me immune to whatever power she had over me, but the memories of her and how it felt to be with her were just as prominent as ever.

A year after I left the states, she was still all I could think about. When I left without telling her, I thought it was for the best, she didn't need to be dragged into everything that I had going on with my family. I knew she had enough family issues of her own. I missed her though, and I wanted to know what happened to her after graduation.

I found one of her books online. At first, I had no idea who Levi Ray was, all I knew was that her books spoke to me. They were touching and very emotion driven, they were also supposed to be all based on fiction, but after deep diving on the internet trying to find out more about the author, I found a video of an interview that she had done.

That was when I saw her, just as gorgeous as I remembered, but this time she seemed stronger. She wasn't the shy, sweet, young girl I had fallen in love with. Now, she was a strong confident woman who knew what she wanted out of life and went for it. Just by looking at her image in that short video clip, the urge to see her, hold her, just be around her, was almost unbearable.

She talked about how all her work was loosely based on true events that had happened to her throughout her life.

I watched that interview I don't know how many times and each time it took my breath away when she talked about her passions as a writer and the things that inspired her work. It was such a turn on to hear her speak, I couldn't get enough of it.

She was the reason I chose to go into publishing and I haven't regretted it since.

I left my home in Seoul, South Korea and came back to the states as soon as I could, but it took almost six more years to track her down. She used to talk about all the places she hoped to live one day when she finally published her first book. Florida, where it was always warm. Colorado so she could do nothing but sit outside and stare at the Rocky Mountains all day while she wrote. She even mentioned California at one point, claiming she dreamed of living in the same city as all the celebrities.

Never did I imagine finding her in New York, it wasn't pure coincidence when her new manuscript landed on my desk. It shouldn't have even been there since she was already assigned to another agency, but her contract would be up soon, which meant her new work was up for grabs.

Over the last eight years, I had taken over the role as managing director of BY Publishing, a small branch in our large family conglomerate. It was known as the largest and most respected publishing and distributing company in all South Korea and now thanks to me the U.S. I made a deal with my father to let me take over the international branch in America and he could choose a shareholder to take over the reins in Korea. Raylen had no idea about my family, or the family business and I wanted to keep it that way. Now, my secret was going to work in my favor.

I expected her anger and rage, but I wouldn't let her feelings overshadow mine. I owed her an explanation, and she owed me one. I got up from my chair and stormed out of the little café after her. By the time I got outside, Raylen was just rounding a corner. I reached for her wrist to stop her. I heard her slight gasp as she turned around and tried to yank free of my hold. I hated how good it felt to be holding her again, even this small amount of skin-to-skin contact was like electricity going through my entire body.

"Let go of me" she said, still trying to pull away. I kept my grip firm. Some people stopped what they were doing to see what was going on, but I didn't care, I wouldn't budge.

"We need to talk." Her face scrunched up and she tried again to pull her arm free. "I'm not going to let ago until you calm down." She stopped struggling and dropped her head so I couldn't see her eyes anymore.

I heard a small, defeated sigh before she spoke. "What do you want Jae-Hyun? Why are you here and don't say it's for my book because you know that's not what I mean."

The way she said my name sent a shiver down my spine,

the same way it did all those years ago, but now wasn't the time for that, I wanted answers. "It's simple, you and I need to have a very long overdue conversation, do you want to have it here or go somewhere more private."

She scoffed at my comment but still didn't look up to meet my eyes. "Really?" She tried again to free her arm and this time I let her. I was expecting her to try for another escape, but she didn't, she just let her arm flop to her side still opting to find my glossy dress shoes more interesting than my face. "After eight years, now is the time you decide to make a reappearance and all because you just want to talk. Excuse me if I don't believe that excuse at all."

I took a step forward trying to reach for her but she followed my movement and took a step back folding her arms so I wouldn't try to grab for them again. "Look, I know you're angry, but-"

"Drop it Jae, there's nothing you can say right now to make up for what you did." She finally looked up to meet my eyes and it felt like my heart skipped a beat when I looked into those glistening eyes. Those breathtaking hazel eyes had me completely choking on my tongue. "You wanted to see my face, well now you've seen it. Do me a favor and fall off the face of the Earth for another eight years." She turned on her heels and, in a blink, she was gone, not even giving me a chance to stop her again.

I didn't even realize Elizabeth, my assistant was standing behind me until I heard her clear her throat. "What should we do now Mr. Yuu?" My brain was working a mile a minute.

She believed I was the only one that had explaining to do. Like she was completely absolved from any anger I might be feeling towards her. I haven't talked to her in eight years, and I want to know why.

I ground my teeth as I stared at the spot she was just standing in moments before. I would make her understand how I've felt all these years. I would turn her world upside down if it was the last thing I did.

Chapter 2

RAYLEN

"YOU'RE JOKING AREN'T YOU."** Olivia stood in the middle of the spare bedroom in my apartment that I had converted into an office space. Jet black waves hung down her back, stopping just above her waist, bright green eyes stared me down, and her slightly overlined lips hung open in shock. She had both hands on her hips which made her perky boobs stick out even more.

I rolled my eyes and spun around in my desk chair to stare back at my computer screen. I really didn't have time for her dramatics today, I had been sporting the same headache for 24 hours now and I really didn't need her making it worse.

"I'm telling you now, I'm seriously not in the mood to talk

about this. I shouldn't have even brought it up." I tossed my glasses on my desk and rubbed my eyes. I was supposed to be working on a new manuscript, but instead I've spent the last four hours staring at a blank word document. I had a deadline coming up in a couple months and I couldn't get my mind off what happened yesterday.

Jae-Hyun popping back into my life was just like him. No consideration for the pain he has caused me over the years, just doing whatever the hell he wants, just like always.

"Bitch don't play games you know damn well it would've been lights out for you if you held this secret." Olivia walked around and leaned on the edge of my desk. I didn't even bother looking up at her, I already knew what look she was giving me. "So, what are you going to do?" She asked.

"What do you mean Liv," I threw my hands up in frustration. I had resigned myself to pretending like yesterday never happened. Actually, I was pretty much hoping to pretend Jae-Hyun didn't even exist, as difficult as that would be.

"You know what I mean, are you going to tell him?" My eyes shot to her this time. I wasn't sure if she was joking or if she really believed I was willing to do that.

Based on the serious look on her face, I guess that was my answer. "Are you crazy, why the hell would I do that?"

"Raylen," She warned. I hated when she got that tone with me, we were the same age, but every time she talked to me like that it was her way of telling me I was being very childish.

"You don't understand." Olivia stared at me for a minute before she sighed and walked around my chair, leaning over it, and wrapping her arms around my neck in a hug.

"Raylen, I love you. You've been my best friend for I don't know how many years now and you know I would never want you to get hurt, but it is time you told Jae-Hyun the truth. He has a right to know." I listened to Olivia's words and deep down, I knew everything she was saying was the truth. I had to tell him the truth, if not for him, at least for Levi's sake.

Right on cue, Levi burst into my office almost knocking the door off the hinges and stumbling inside. She ran straight into Olivia's hip, wrapping her arms tightly around her waist.

"Well, if it isn't my most favorite of goddaughters." She bent down and scooped Levi into her arms. The dark brown messy bun on her head, even more of a mess than when she left home this morning for school. Hazards of having an eight-year-old, they very rarely cared about the hard work a parent puts into their appearance.

She smiled revealing the missing canine she had just lost. "TT Liv, I'm your only goddaughter." She said with a giggle.

Olivia leaned in and planted a kiss on each of her cheeks. "And that's exactly why you're my favorite." I watched Levi from my position still planted in my desk chair. She laughed and smile with Olivia, almost completely oblivious to me, but I was able to comfortably admire her.

She looked like him. Those dark, almond shaped eyes, those round cheeks. She even had parts of his personality. The stubbornness, her complete inability to believe that she was ever wrong about anything. Her intelligence, she was so freaking smart just like him, she thrived in school. It didn't matter what the subject was, math, science, art.

Levi was so beautiful and special, anyone would be lucky to know her. Could I really keep the privilege of being her father from him? Who knows if he would even want her, we were only in high school when we were together, it's not like we ever talked about having kids. I don't even know if he wants any or has any already for that matter.

"Ray?" Olivia called to me. I hadn't realized I was still staring until she waved her hand in my face. She looked back at Levi before putting her back on her feet. "Go get started on your homework, I'll come help you in a second."

Levi nodded her head, walk over to me to place a kiss on my cheek and disappeared out the door. I let out a sigh of relief when she left, the longer I looked at her face, the guiltier I was starting to feel.

"You have to tell him." She said again and all I could do this time was nod my head. I know I did. I knew at some point I would have to tell him, but after so long I didn't think I could handle having him back in our lives.

I grabbed my phone off my desk, went through my contacts and found Jasmine's number. I hit dial and she answered on the first ring.

"I'm so glad you called, I was just about to call you."

"Why? What's going on?" She sounded out of breath like she had been running.

"There was a huge package delivered here for you."

"From who?" It wasn't unusual for me to have things sent to my agent's office, a lot of my fans sent things like fan mail.

Mostly letters, sometimes small packages, but nothing big.

"The card said it's from Mr. Yuu. I wonder what he sent, I hope he isn't trying to bribe you to sign with him." I rolled my eyes, of course Jae-Hyun wouldn't give up so easily, he had to be pretty determined to ambush me at that café. I at least thought he would wait a little while to see if I would contact him first, but I guess that was something else I would be wrong about.

"I'll be there in a minute." I hung up with Jasmine and looked to Olivia who still stood in front of me anxiously waiting for me to tell her what was going on. Too bad I wanted to make her suffer a little. I got to my feet and walked out of the room, Olivia close behind me.

"What was that about?" She asked.

I ignored her question. "Can you watch Levi for me really quick, I need to run a little errand." Levi sat at the counter swinging her legs. Her backpack and all its contents were thrown all over the countertop.

"To where? Are you going to meet him now." Levi's head shot up to look at me when she heard Olivia's question.

I shot her an annoyed look and she immediately snapped her lips shut. I turned and grabbed my purse off the counter and headed towards the door. "I'll be back in an hour."

Jasmine and I looked at each other in confusion. A huge white box with a big red bow sat on the small glass table in her office, right next to a giant bouquet of bright red roses.

"Something you want to tell me?" Jasmine asked. She stared at me expectantly but I'm sure the confused look on my face hadn't changed.

"What are you asking me for?" I shrugged at her, never taking my eyes off the box.

"I've had a lot of clients over the years, but I've never seen anything like this before." She kept her eyes on the items on the table. "This is definitely more than a bribe sweetheart, so I'm asking again, something you want to tell me?" I ignored her question and instead reached for the small white envelope that sat on top of the box.

Tearing open the small envelop, I read the card.

Raylen,

I think it's time we did some catching up
If you're free tonight I would love for
you to join me for dinner.
I hope I hear from you.

-J

I couldn't help the chuckle that slipped from me when I read over the note. He wasn't serious, was he? What is wrong with him, after all these years he thinks I'm just supposed to be at his beck and call. I wanted to talk to him so I could tell him about Levi, but I was thinking a more casual setting where I could just drop that bomb on him, not a date. I crumbled up the note and threw in the trash bin next to Jasmine's desk.

"What did it say?"

"Nothing important," I stared down the crumbled-up piece

of paper that sat by itself in the trash. I stared at it so hard almost wishing the thing would burst into flames.

I ignored the suspicious look on Jasmine's face and focused all my attention on the mystery box. I pulled the bow off the box and pulled out the most gorgeous dress I had ever seen in my life. It was a bright red strapless ballgown with huge rhinestones under the sweat heart neckline, along with smaller rhinestones forming a giant, sparkling flower on the side.

"Wow" was all I could manage at that moment. "This looks way too expensive." I couldn't take my eyes off the dress, but I also couldn't help but wonder why he would spend so much on a dress for me and where the hell did he plan to take me while I wore it.

"It's beautiful," Jasmine commented "are you sure there's nothing going on between you two." Of course, there wasn't and they're never would be again.

Chapter 3

RAYLEN

"**I CAN'T BELIEVE I let you** talk me into this." It feels like I've been in a shitty mood the entire day and it's all because of Olivia and her annoying advice. After Jae-Hyun sent me that dress, Jasmine spent almost thirty minutes trying to convince me to go out to dinner with him. When I adamantly told her that wasn't going to happen, I had her contact his office and tell him that I was willing to meet up to discuss the contract. To which his response was that he wasn't willing to meet up and discuss anything unless I agreed to put on this dress and go to an industry gala with him tonight.

This was the last thing I wanted to do, but of course I made the unintelligent decision to tell Olivia about it which is why I've been sitting in this chair for almost an hour letting Olivia smack me in the face repeatedly with this huge powder brush.

After going into a long-winded rant about how I needed to look my best before dropping baby daddy news on my baby daddy, she explained what she had planned for my look and she's been going to work ever since.

"Yeah, yeah, yeah, quit complaining. We don't have much time." For some reason she insisted on doing my hair and makeup even after I told her I could just as easily go au natural. After she laughed at me for about 20 minutes, which I found vastly offensive she promised she would make me look beautiful.

Olivia worked on my makeup for what felt like forever before she claimed that she was done. My leg bounced anxiously as I sat with them both folded in my vanity chair waiting to see what she had done. I wasn't a big fan of makeup, I hardly ever wore any and I didn't want to look weird tonight especially because I was going to be with Jae-Hyun. I didn't want him to think I put in special effort just because it was him.

After she finished my makeup, she moved on to fussing with my hair. It's not a secret that curls take a lot of work and as someone with super lose beachy waves, I don't think she was completely prepared for the amount of energy and time it would take to tame my tighter ringlets.

"Are you finished yet?" I groaned. I sounded just like Levi did when she whined, even to myself but I couldn't help it, I hated sitting for this long.

"Quit crying you big baby" she replied bumping my elbow with her knee. A few minutes later Olivia sighed in relief and took a step away from me to check out her finished product.

She smiled and told me she was finished. When I tried to turn towards the mirror Olivia stopped me saying she wanted me to wait until I was completely dressed to see the final product. She stepped out of the room so I could slip the dress on.

I was surprised to find the dress fit me perfectly. How he knew what size I was I probably will never know. I looked in the mirror and my jaw nearly hit the ground. It didn't even look like me. Olivia had done an amazing job with my makeup. She gave me a grey smokey eye with a silver sparkle to it to match the rhinestones in the dress. She made my eyelashes look long and thick without using falsies which she knew I hated. She tied everything together with the bright red lip she gave me. I always thought red lipstick wouldn't look good with my complexion, I guess I was wrong.

As far as my hair, all she did was pin my hair to the side, so it draped over my shoulder, but somehow, she managed to make it look like an intricate yet elegant style.

When I stepped out of my bedroom into the living room, both Olivia and Levi stared at me with wide eyes from their seats at the counter. "Mommy, you look like a princess." Levi said before she went back to doodling in her notebook.

"Wow" Olivia said not taking her eyes off me as she got out of her seat and made her way over towards me. She looked me up and down. "If I wasn't so in love with that special part that hangs between a man's legs, I would be all over you right now." I couldn't help but laugh at her ridiculous comment.

"Yeah right, I'm way out of your league." I replied playing along.

"Oh, I could so get you if I wanted to. But" she said with a shrug. "I probably wouldn't look as good as a certain some-one in a suit" My shoulders stiffened when Jae-Hyun's face popped into my head. The memory of how he filled out that suit was enough to have me almost tripping over my own tongue.

I heard Olivia gasped and when I looked up at her she was pointing at me with this really annoying smile on her face. "What?" I looked down at my appearance, wondering what she was pointing at.

"You were picturing him naked, weren't you?" She put her hand to her mouth to try and cover her smile.

I looked away from her and began fidgeting with my hands. I didn't like feeling like I was caught doing something bad, so instead I went for the distracting route. "Did it come with a matching purse? I think this would be so cute with like a little clutch or something." I couldn't care less about a purse, and I know Olivia knew that, she decided not to call me on it though.

She walked past me into my room, digging through the box on my bed, pulling out a small silver clutch before sighing and turning back to face me. "Here," She held out her hand to me. "You know at some point I'm going to want more X-rated details." Olivia was interrupted by a knock at the door. I jumped and she narrowed her eyes at me as I practically flew out of the room to answer it.

"We *will* be finishing this conversation later." She called after me as I reached out and snatched up the clutch, she had in her hand on my way to the door. I took a deep breath looking over my shoulder to make sure Olivia took Levi to the back before I opened the door.

All the negative thoughts I had about tonight and spending any amount of time alone with Jae-Hyun immediately flew out the window once I got a look at him. Even after all these years just the sight of him did me in. My mouth dried up, my knees turned to Jell-o and I swear it felt like I was floating in my panties. That is how this man affected me and the fact that he looked absolutely mouthwateringly gorgeous in a tuxedo did not help at all.

Jae-Hyun

Is it possible for one woman to be this incredibly sexy? I ask that question every time I see her, but now with her standing in front of me wearing this incredible dress, with those smoldering hazel eyes that looked like she could see right through this suit and those sexy red lips I would really like to put to use, I could feel certain parts of my body growing rock hard.

"Jae-Hyun." She said in a voice so husky I could barely contain my groan of pleasure. I wonder if she was just as turned on as I was right now. Her eyes traveled up and down my body and the amount of space in my boxers suddenly became very limited, luckily the bouquet of red roses I was holding provided a sufficient shield.

I cleared my throat before speaking. "Raylen, you look beautiful." She blinked a few times before staring up at me with a confused expression. I watched in satisfaction as her cheeks began to darken. I was aware of the effect I had on her years ago, it's nice to know that hadn't changed. Just like my body's reaction to her hadn't changed. I was going to use that discovery to get me everything I wanted.

There was an awkward silence with Raylen staring at the floor, and me staring at her. "Well," she said finally breaking the silence. "will you look at the time." I held out the bouquet of roses for her to take. She gave me a half smile before taking them and sitting them on the small table by the door, stepping out and closing it behind her. After locking the door, I followed her to a waiting elevator that would lead us to the parking structure.

The ride on the elevator was even more awkward. I was mentally strangling myself. Why was I acting like this? I'm usually the one who's always in control. I used to be able to play it off pretty well, but after so many years apart, I guess I'm out of practice. I caught a glimpse of Raylen out of the corner of my eye and my heart rate kicked up a few notches.

Maybe it was that dress, it was drawing blood from one part of my body to another and that was messing with my mind.

I watched as she nervously fidgeted with her hands and chewed on her bottom lip, and I couldn't contain the groan this time. I really wanted to be the one nibbling on those lips. The elevator dinged signaling its arrival and the doors slid open. "Should we go?" I said holding out my arm for her after I cleared my throat to get her attention.

She looked up and gave me an awkward half smile before nodding and slipping her arm through mine. We made our way to the elevator and through the lobby doors to the car waiting for us. She stared at my car with her eyes wide and her mouth hanging open. I smirked, loving the satisfaction I get every time I catch people gawking at it. I've always had a thing for limited edition Italian sports cars, but I barely drove them, tonight however, I felt like the occasion called for something special. The sleek black sports car with the bright red strip down the middle, glistened under the fluorescent lights of the parking structure.

I reached for the doorhandle, opening the door, and waiting for her to get in. When she didn't move and instead opted to continue her staring, I had to hide my smile before speaking, "Are you coming or are you planning on wasting that gorgeous dress on random strangers that walk past?" Her cheeks darkened and she closed her mouth before taking the few steps to the car and getting in. I closed the door behind her and made my way around to the other side, climbing into the driver's seat.

Once I was settled in, I turned to look at Raylen only to see her eyes glued to her fidgeting hands. It was starting to bother me that she was avoiding my eyes. I was hoping by the end of the night that would change. I couldn't help but smile, she had no idea what I had in store for her.

Chapter 4

Jae-Hyun

THE BANQUET HALL WAS **grand.** Incredibly high cathedral ceilings. Large chandeliers hanging everywhere making the entire room seem like it was glowing. Lit candles in wall sconces lined the walls. A stage for the live band sat at the front of the room and tall circular tables took up the rest of the dance floor. It was obvious the hosts wanted this event to be as extravagant as possible and had my mind not been elsewhere maybe I would've been able to appreciate my surroundings more.

I hated coming to these things, I always felt like the vultures were circling my wallet and even I knew I wasn't anything more than a piece of meat with a checkbook to these people.

I didn't have a choice though, had to schmooze the masses for the sake of the company. At least this time, it made for a good excuse to spend some time with Raylen.

For the next hour and a half, it seemed like Raylen closed herself off more and more. Before I would at least be able to get a few words out of her, but now, all I was getting was nonverbal responses and shoulder shrugs. It was starting to drive me crazy.

I leaned into Raylen so I could whisper in her ear. "Let's talk." She seemed hesitant to agree, chewing on her lip nervously before nodding and following me through a doorway that led to a long, dark corridor. We passed a few locked doors before finding one that we could duck into. She followed me inside and I closed the door behind her.

I turned around to look at her, but she refused to face me. She had a gorgeous smooth back with beautifully tanned skin, but I would much rather look at her face, not her back. I waited to see if she would provide me with an explanation for her mood, at least an explanation besides the obvious. I was really trying here, and I know I screwed up all those years ago, but I wanted to make up for it. Not to mention it wasn't completely on me that we haven't spoken to each other in eight years. When she didn't speak, I decided that maybe I should start the conversation. Maybe now was the time she would tell me the truth about why she disappeared on me.

"Let's talk Raylen?" I could see her flinch when I spoke.

RAYLEN

"I don't want to talk." I said after a long pause. It took me a minute to compose myself enough to speak. I didn't want him to hear any weakness in my voice.

"Tell me what's wrong." I heard his shoes scrap the floor as he took a step towards me. Shortly after, I felt his hand come up to touch my bare shoulders, giving me a little push so that I would turn to face him. The moment his hands came in contact with my skin, it was like a lightning bolt shot through my entire body. The feeling was so powerful, it actually knocked the wind out of me. When I finally faced him— even in the poor lighting— I could see the way his eyes darkened, like he was feeling the same things I was.

I tried to pull away and put some distance between us so that I could clear my head, but he tightened his grip, making it impossible for me to move an inch.

"Jae-Hyun, let go of me." I saw his jaw flex before he spoke.

"Give me one good reason and I will." He pulled me in closer causing my breasts to be crushed up against his chest. I caught a whiff of his masculine smell, strong, earthy, and just the tiniest amount of spice. He smelled delicious. I licked my suddenly dry lips as I stared up at him.

Did he ask me a question? At the moment I couldn't remember. I couldn't even think straight. I know I should push him away, after all he was the one that broke my heart, left me and our daughter all alone, and I wouldn't put it past him to do it again. I know I could get hurt, but for some reason I couldn't seem to care. My eyes flickered down to his mouth as he leaned down, almost like he could hear me begging him to kiss me. He leaned in more and I could feel his breath ghosting over my face.

I couldn't take it anymore, I reached up and snaked my arms around his neck, pulling him down and crashing his lips onto mine. The moment our lips met I couldn't help the groan that escaped my body. I missed this, I missed his lips and the way he uses them to kiss me. The way his arms would pull me in and crush my small frame against his much larger one. It was heaven.

His lips moved over mine, nibbling slightly until I surrendered and opened to his skilled tongue. His hand slid down to grip my ass while his tongue slowly began to message mine. I've had one or two partners since Jae-Hyun, but it was never the same feeling I got when I was with him. They could never touch me the same way, they could never make my body burn the way he did.

Those skilled lips moved from my mouth down to my jaw and then my neck. He found that special spot right below my ear and sucked, hard. I gasped and felt myself arching into him more. Jae-Hyun was definitely going to leave a mark there, but that was something to worry about another day.

He pulled away from my neck and made his way back up to my ear, stopping there to whisper. "I want you." My body was on fire and even now with my mind clouded I knew it was a bad idea, but I wanted it anyway. His hands slid up and began fumbling with the zipper of my dress and with one swift motion, he managed to unzip it and have it pooling at my feet leaving me standing in nothing but a bra, panties, and those strangely comfortable red heels he brought me. Jae-Hyun took a few steps forward pushing me back and causing me to step out of the puddle that was my dress. He placed his hands on my waist pushing me back until the back of my knees collided with a small couch in the poorly lit room.

I sat down and he leaned into me giving me a quick kiss. I could see him giving me that sexy smirk he always gave when he was up to no good and it only succeeded in turning me on even more.

He kneeled in front of the couch, reaching up to grab the waistband of my panties. Slowly he slid them down and I shifted so that he could lift them from underneath me and toss them on the heap that use to be my dress.

I thought I knew what he had planned until he grabbed both of my ankles and pulled me until I was sitting at the very edge of the sofa, then lifted them up onto his shoulders. I gasped and tried to pull my legs away, my hands shooting down to try and cover myself. Even in the terrible lighting, I didn't want to risk that he might see something. Call me strange or even a prude but even when we were together in the past, I never let him see me like this.

The thought of being this exposed to anyone always made me hesitant. Even more so now that I've had a baby.

"What are you doing?" I asked. Out of all the things

Jae-Hyun and I had done in the past this was not one of them. He'd always offered to do it for me, but since I always told him how uncomfortable the thought of it made me, he eventually stopped asking.

He let go of my ankles only to grab my wrists and yank them out of the way leaving me completely exposed to him and said three simple words, "I'm tasting you." My heart skipped a beat and I tried again to pull away, but it was no use trying to get away. Jae-Hyun let go of one of my wrists to grab my ankle and lift it to his mouth. He placed a soft kiss on it, then another and another slowly making his way up to my knee then my thigh. "I've been wanting to do this since I saw you in that dress. I knew you would look perfect in it."

My heart skipped a beat. Jae-Hyun personally selected that dress for me, somehow that revelation turned me on even more and I could feel more moisture pooling between my legs.

I watched in silence unsure what to do while Jae-Hyun leaned in more and blew lightly on my core. A shiver went up my spin. I was wound so tight, it felt like I could come just off that alone. In the terrible lighting, I could see the smirk he gave me before he dove in. All my insecurities told me to push him away, but my body screamed for me to let him continue.

The moment I felt the first swipe of his tongue, any thoughts I had of pushing him away were completely silenced. I watched as he buried his face against my center. My back arched and I pushed further against his mouth as wave after wave of pure pleasure took over my body.

I wanted to touch him, but he seemed so far away not to mention, unlike me he was still fully clothed. As if reading my mind, he pulled my hand towards his head and placed it in his hair. With one hand on the thigh that was propped up on his shoulder and the other hand drawing small circles onto my stomach I could only imagine what we would look like to someone if they decided to walk in on us at this moment.

In the silence of the room, I could hear his groans mixing with the soft pleasured moans coming from me, almost like he was getting just as much enjoyment out of licking me as he would if I was touching him. Jae-Hyun's tongue slid along my slit and my entire body shivered.

What was this man doing to me and why didn't I let him do it years ago? His tongue flicked along the tight bundle of nerves at the very center of me. I gripped his head tighter practically smashing his face into me as the pressure began to build starting all the way from my feet.

It was like an itch that I desperately needed scratched. The pressure built and built but I just couldn't quite get there. "Jae-Hyun" I pleaded. I really didn't know what I was begging him for, but I knew that if I didn't get what I needed soon I was going to lose my mind.

Suddenly I felt the pressure of his strong, rigid finger massage my entrance before slipping inside me. That was it, that was all I needed to scratch that itch. My body tightened like a spring and all at once it released, my body stiffened but my legs shook. All the air left my lungs, and it was a struggle to catch my breath.

Jae-Hyun didn't let up, his finger continued to move inside of me, and his tongue continued to work against me, making me experience the most powerful orgasm I've ever experienced in my life.

It seemed to last forever. When I felt like my body couldn't take any more and I thought for sure I was going to pass out, Jae-Hyun pulled back. His finger slipped out of me, and his mouth disappeared from my very sensitive flesh. He kissed my thigh and then my stomach, working his way up my body. I laid there feeling like a bowl of jelly.

Finally, he made it up to my lips. He gave a quick kiss and said, "You tasted delicious."

Chapter 5

JAE-HYUN

"DUDE, YOU SERIOUSLY HANDLE **everything** ass backward. has anyone ever told you that before?" Daniel joked slapping me on the back. He took a seat on the plush grey couch in the middle of my patio while I paced in front of him and his brother Liam.

It took me a while to find a house that I really liked, but thanks to Liam who was my very own personal realtor, I found the perfect one. I needed to get out of those hotel rooms and now that I had a house, it made New York feel much more permanent. Like somewhere I could settle down and start a family with.

Speaking of families, the woman I wanted to start one

with was driving me insane. I was losing it. It had been days since that night at the banquet with Raylen and she hadn't returned any of my phone calls or texts.

Maybe I did prove to be a little more aggressive than necessary that night, but it was clear she was into it. I didn't do anything she wasn't practically begging me to do.

"It's rare we agree on anything, but I would have to say I second my lesser half." Liam pitched in. Daniel rolled his eyes at Liam before reaching over and punching him in the arm. Liam side eyed him, but chose not to retaliate, instead taking a sip from the beer bottle he was holding.

"Well what the hell else was I suppose to do, she spent the whole night avoiding me. I had to get her attention somehow." I threw my hands up in frustration. I knew what I did was not the smartest move, but that's what she does to me.

Every time I'm around Raylen, I can't think straight. Every plan I make, every thought I have, goes completely out of the window whenever she's around and after all these years, that still hadn't changed.

The girl had complete control over me and I hated everything about that.

"Well you could've tried using your mouth for something productive like talking." Liam took another sip from the beer bottle in his hands and hit me with 'duh' face.

"I don't know about that. I think what he did was a very productive use of his time." Daniel chimed in, tossing back a shot of vodka before dropping his shot glass on the small glass top table. Danny hated beer but he could drink the hell out of some vodka which is why he was doing shots at 3 o'clock in the afternoon in my backyard.

"Of course you would." Liam huffed.

These two might be twins, but they were the complete opposite of each other.

Liam was the handsome good guy who loved to wine and dine women. The realtor who took the word boujee and ran with it.

While they were identical twins, they looked so different to me. Liam had the whole golden retriever thing going on with the light brown hair he was religious about keeping dyed so he didn't look too much like Daniel and bright blue eyes.

Danny on the other hand, was the rough, and rugged tattooed biker boy mechanic with the jet black hair and the odd mix match eyes. One blue and one brown.

I met the both of them when I was in high school, around the same time I met Raylen. They were the only ones I was able to keep in touch with while I was away.

It was safe to say they were a little too eager when I told them I was coming back to the states. Imagine my surprise when they set up shop in New York just like Raylen.

"At some point you really just need to have a conversation with her." Liam, ever the voice of reason.

"Why should I be the one that has to explain anything. She was the one that ghosted me for eight years." I plopped down on the couch on the other side of Daniel.

"Now I would have to disagree with you on that one," Daniel chimed in kicking his feet up on my table like this was his house. "To be fair she wasn't the one who fled the country because mommy and daddy told her to."

I pulled back and punched Daniel in the arm with as much force as our awkward positioning would allow. He laughed and rubbed his arm.

"Come on man, you know that wasn't fair. I didn't have a choice."

Daniel shrugged. "Why are you telling me that, maybe you should tell her." He was right, I always knew that Raylen and I needed to have this talk about my family, but I never knew how to bring it up.

Maybe if she had answered any of my text messages or phone calls over the years, the opportunity would've presented itself, but now I feel like I've lost my chance.

I leaned forward placing my elbows on my knees and scrubbed my face in frustration. "I don't want to talk about this anymore."

Liam grabbed another beer bottle from the cooler on the other side of the couch. "You were the one so desperate to talk about *the one that got away*." I straight faced him before dropping my head back between my legs with a sigh.

As hard as the two of them tried to be different, they had very similar shitty personalities and I have no idea why I was even friends with them.

"Can we please talk about something else." I whined. I didn't care how childish I sounded, I couldn't think about this situation anymore, it was giving me a headache. Besides, I think I gave them enough opportunities to make fun of me for the day.

"I have a better topic of conversation." Daniel added sitting up straighter in his seat. I raised my head just enough to look at him and when I did, I immediately groaned.

"Oh god, please don't say it." I said dropping my head again.

"Say what?" He asked. His voice raised an octave which told me he knew exactly what I was talking about.

"Please don't." I begged again, but it was too late.

"Olivia." The both of them said in unison. I looked up and made eye contact with Liam. I huffed and sat back in my seat.

This was an everyday thing with him. Ever since I met them in high school. It started with Daniel having a little crush on the little Italian bombshell. Now he was practically obsessed with her.

I was 100% convinced she was the reason both of them settled down in New York instead of staying in Ohio where they were from. Every time I bring it up of course they deny deny deny, but they couldn't fool me. They were a huge help in finding Raylen after all these years. It was Olivia admitting to them that Raylen had left Toledo to start a new life in New York that led me here.

They were worse than me when it came to women trouble though. While my situation with Raylen was pretty fucked up, at least I actually had a situation with Raylen.

These two clowns have been in a one-sided unrequited love triangle for years. Daniel loud and proud—at least to me— and Liam, well Liam is a special type of stupid. He kept his crush a secret from even his own brother. All they did was make shameless sexual comments at her but never actually told her how they feel.

Liam even took it a step further and would parade half naked women around her whenever he had the chance. I could only guess to make her jealous or something hence why I say he's a very *special* type of stupid.

Honestly, the more I thought about it, the less I understood why I came to them about relationship advice in the first place, these two were terrible.

"Unless you have at least asked her on a date, what is there to talk about?"

"Don't rush me, I'm just giving it some time. This a process."

I scoffed at that. They can call me delusional all they want, but I was nothing compared to them. "How much more time do you think you need to give her? You've been chasing her longer than I've known Raylen."

"True, but it's a completely different situation." Daniel poured another shot into the small glass cup from the vodka bottle on the table.

"It's not that different."

"It is. She hasn't exactly had the best perception of me over the years if you haven't noticed. Every time I ask her out, she shoots me down. If she would ever give me an opening instead of those losers she normally goes for I wouldn't still be circling the drain the way I am." My eyes darted to Liam and I watched him shift uncomfortably in his seat.

I knew he felt the same way about the guys Olivia had been

dating over the years, he would call me long distance all the time to bitch about the latest douchebag he had spotted her out with.

Why he couldn't share this information with his twin brother, I couldn't fully understand. I think he's taken this secret crush thing a little too far.

The twins had both shared a lot of secrets with me over the years, not just about Olivia, but about numerous other things. Including their proclivity for sharing women in the bedroom.

Despite the twins bickering all the time and their total opposite personalizes they enjoyed that more often than not, but who was I to judge them. What they enjoyed behind closed doors didn't affect me, which is why it was so strange that he would keep his mouth closed about this for so long.

They were still my best friends and I wanted them to be happy which is why I was tired of them talking about Raylen's best friend. Their obsession with her started before I ever set foot in the states.

Daniel was the first friend I made when I made it to Toledo. I guess he felt bad that the foreign exchange student was going to be the most likely target of all the cliché bullying.

It wasn't long after that when he introduced me to Liam and then it was three of us against everyone. When I first saw Olivia, I thought she was gorgeous, as did a lot of the other guys in school. Everyone knew that the twins had some kind of claim on her, no matter how much Liam tried to deny it. The end result, Olivia had a very dateless high school experience.

I felt kind of bad for her. They were huge cockblocks and they didn't even make up for it by telling her how they felt.

The first time they convinced her to hang out with the three of us was the first time I met Raylen. I don't know how I never noticed her at school before, a girl that gorgeous had to have all eyes on her at all times.

I knew right away after our first conversation, she didn't know how much of a hidden gem she was. High school boys are stupid and care a lot more about the superficial things like what a girl wears than people think. The unflattering baggy clothes she aways wore were a deterrent for them, but it only drew me in and made me want to see more of what was underneath.

"It's time." I said sitting up and giving them both a serious stare. Liam looked away and pretended he was just oh so interested in the beer he had been sipping on for the last half hour. "It's been way too long, you have to tell her how you feel."

"I will." Daniel said with a huff. Liam threw his arm over the back of the couch and slouched down, trying to give the impression that he was completely calm and unbothered by this conversation, but I knew better.

"Preferably before she finds another man to marry."

"That'll never happen." Daniel shouted, jolting up in his seat. I could see the clenched jaw and the white knuckles on Liam no matter how hard he tried to hide it. Oh yeah, they had it bad.

Before I could crack a joke about his reaction to my comment, I heard the chime of my phone. I shifted my weight in my seat so I could pull the device out of my jean pocket, almost ripping them in the process. Was it just me or were phones becoming obnoxiously large.

I'm ashamed of how eager I was to see who was contacting me and I was really hoping the twins didn't notice.

I tapped the screen causing it to light up and I see the name *Elizabeth* next to the green message bubble on the screen.

I let out an annoyed sigh. Fuck. It was probably something work related.

That's what I thought anyway, until I opened the message. It was a mass invitation from Elizabeth. Her birthday was tomorrow and she was inviting the entire office out to that new club they just opened called *Trust.*

I heard about it, Liam and Daniel had been bugging me to go check it out with them, but I had been a little too preoccupied coming up with a plan for dealing with the Raylen situation that I had to admit I'd been neglecting them a little.

I wasn't much of a clubbing kind of guy anyway.

"Who is it?" Liam asked.

"Probably the woman who had her legs wrapped around his head the other day." Daniel joked, running his hand through his dark locs.

I ignored his comment and instead stuck to reading over the details on the invitation. Tomorrow night?

I didn't really feel like going. Wouldn't it be weird and super inappropriate for the boss to go out to a club with his subordinates.

Not to mention I wasn't oblivious to how Elizabeth looked at me. The woman was sexy for sure, and there was defiantly a little sexual chemistry between us, but she wasn't Raylen.

I didn't want to lead her on.

"My secretary invited me to a her birthday celebration tomorrow night at Trust."

Both the twins sat up straighter. In this moment, they looked almost identical. Like two kids ready to open up presents on Christmas.

"What's with the looks?" My head bounced back and forth between the two of the them.

"Isn't it obvious." Liam spoke. "This is the perfect opportunity for you to put some distance between you and Raylen. She wants to do her own thing, so you should too."

I scoffed. "Who says I want to put some distance between the two of us."

"She did when she chose to ignore your incessant calling for the last few days." Daniel always the one that likes to twist the knife.

"I say you go and check out your other options." Liam nodded his head.

"I agree. I've seen your assistant, she's hot. If Liv hadn't ruined me for other women, I would be all over that."

I chewed on my lip. This sounded like a horrible idea. I knew what I wanted or should I say who I wanted and that was Raylen. Why would I bother entertaining another woman.

Then again what's the harm in going out for a little fun for one night. I'm sure Raylen has been having her fill of fun for the last eight years while I was working my ass off to get back to her.

I let out a sigh, "Fine, I'll go."

"And we'll go with you." Liam said. The devious smile on his face was making me uncomfortable.

"Yeah, just to make sure you stay out of trouble." Yeah, like I was really going to believe that was the only reason. It wouldn't shock me if somehow Olivia managed to be at the same club on the same night as us.

Like I said, I knew all their games.

Chapter 6

RAYLEN

OLIVIA SAT ACROSS FROM me at the small circular glass table with a giant umbrella in the middle. This was one of our favorite little cafes to have lunch at. It was near the hospital where she worked, and the food was delicious.

I picked at the small slice of chocolate cake that sat on my plate and all the ice in my coffee had long since melted. I haven't been able to eat anything for days, everything tasted like sand in my mouth.

"Ok." Olivia said slamming her hand on the table. I jumped slightly and looked up at her. "That's like the fifth time you've sighed in the last ten minutes. I gave you almost a week to tell me what happened at that banquet thing you went to with

Mr. Baby Daddy, and you still haven't told me." The annoyance was clear in her voice. "Now you're sitting here ruining my break with this depressing energy." Her face scrunched up and she gestured toward my face. "Will you just tell me what happened that night."

"Nothing happened." I responded too fast, I know I did and unfortunately she did too.

Olivia sat up straighter in her seat, a sick smile spreading across her face. "I only have an hour for my break, and you just spent the last 30 minutes of it being all mopey, so you better talk fast."

I chewed on my lip and picked at the cake more. I wasn't sure I wanted anyone to know what happened that night between Jae and me. I was embarrassed enough as it was without Olivia making it worse. She wouldn't do it on purpose of course, but if I told her that at some point during our little outing, Jae-Hyun had stripped me naked and had my legs wrapped around his head, that would only help her entertain the idea that there was a chance for us to get back together and there was just no way in hell that was happening.

Not to mention I don't want to hear the lecture about how I demanded that Jae-Hyun take me home after and didn't even give him the opportunity to escort me back to my apartment. The moment the car stopped in the parking structure I ran out of there like a bat out of hell. In the end, I never even got to tell him about Levi which was the whole reason for me going out with him in the first place.

I took a deep breath and tried again a little slower this time.

"Nothing happened. I don't want to talk about it."

Olivia's smile dropped. "So, I'm assuming when you say nothing that includes telling him he has an eight-year-old daughter."

I shook my head, confirming her suspicions. Not telling him the other night meant that I was going to have to meet up with him again just so I could tell him. I really didn't want to see him after I allowed that to happen, but I didn't have a choice. It was better to do it sooner rather than later, but I was still working up the courage to face him again.

"You're hopeless." She said with a sigh. She lifted her arm to flag down our waiter and took one final sip of her coffee. "You know what you need."

"To tell him the truth. I know, you don't need to rub it in." I ran my fingers through my curls, fluffing them out a little. It was pretty humid today, I don't know why I thought it would be a good idea to have lunch outside. We could've just as easily ordered our things to go and ate in the cafeteria of the hospital.

All the skin I was showing thanks to this powder blue spaghetti strap tank and blue jean shorts wasn't helping to keep me cool in the slightest.

"No bitch. I mean yes, you should've but that wasn't what I was going to say." The waiter came and handed the long black book to Olivia. She slipped a couple bills into it and handed it back to him. "I was going to say you need to go out, have some fun."

I rolled my eyes back at her. "I just went out remember, I

think I'm good for a while." I got to my feet, grabbing my bag off the armrest of my chair and began following Olivia back towards the hospital.

"That doesn't count." Olivia stepped closer to me as we got ready to cross the street and threaded her arm through mine. "I'll take care of everything. Tomorrow night is Saturday, we'll get sexy, go out and get drunk, it'll be fun."

I opened my mouth to protest and tell her that I should really stay home and work on my next manuscript, but she wasn't giving me the chance. "It's just one night, you can spare it." She kissed me on the cheek and scurried off towards the hospital while I was left staring after her on the curb.

I let out a sigh of relief when I was finally able to hit save and close out the document I was working on. I had been sitting in this desk chair for the last four hours working on my new manuscript. It was such a relief to finally be getting something on paper especially since I had been in such a rut for the last few days. That night out with Jae-Hyun was reeking havoc on my psyche.

"Momma?" Levi called to me running into my office and straight into my waiting arms. She looked up at me and smiled, showing me the missing tooth. Her curly hair pulled into two mickey mouse buns on either side of her head. Her light pink and white jumper was a mess. Why I still sent her to school in light colors knowing that she loved playing outside during recess I don't know, I plead insanity.

"Hi bunny, how was school?" I couldn't be more grateful that we lived in an apartment building full of other kids that attended the same school as Levi. Some of the other mother's formed a carpooling group for drop offs and pick-ups.

They were nice enough to let Levi join, which meant on days like today where time just got away from me she wouldn't just be sitting outside of school waiting for me to pull myself away from my work.

Times like this makes me think how great it would've been if my parents were in our lives, but that ship had long since sailed. Dad was an abusive drunk and mom disowned me when I decided I wanted to have Levi and I really stuck the knife in and twisted it when I refused her attempt to put Levi up for adoption.

Levi pulled out of my hold so she could slide her backpack off her shoulders and drop it onto the floor. She rummaged around in it for a second before pulling out a giant folder and handing it to me. Inside was a work sheet, at the top it read *genetics.*

I felt a lump growing in my throat as I stared at the paper. What were the odds that her teacher would assign her something like this right around the time her father decides to make a reappearance. A sick sensation began developing in the pit of my stomach. A feeling I could only classify as pure guilt, something I wasn't feeling about the situation until now.

"Momma, Ms. Jenkins showed us this cool chart about how babies get their eye color and hair color from their mommies and daddies. She says we have to do one too." And there it was, the final nail in the coffin of this horrible situation. Levi had never asked about her father before and I never mentioned him either. I always tried my best to make her feel like she was never missing anything from life without him around, but I couldn't do that anymore. She was getting older, so it was about time she was going to start having questions. I couldn't hold off on it anymore.

"Sweetheart, why don't you go start on your homework in the living room. Mommy has to make a phone call and then I'll be right in to help you make your chart." Levi smiled at me, took the folder I held out to her, grabbed her backpack, and ran out of the room.

I turned around and grabbed my phone off my desk and opened a message thread to Jasmine.

Raylen: Hey can you send me the direct line for Mr. Yuu's office.

I took a deep breath and leaned back in my chair while I waited for her to respond. The more time that went by, the more nervous I was getting. I couldn't back out this time, I had to tell him today. It was time to rip the band aid off.

Her response came a few minutes later, in the form of a ten-digit number followed by her telling me to keep her updated on what I decided to do.

She was only saying that as my agent because she thought

this was about business, but still I was almost tempted to type back that I was going to tell him. She would have no idea what I was talking about, so I didn't.

I tapped the number, and my phone immediately began dialing. My palms began to sweat when I put the phone up to my ear.

I wondered how he would react when I told him about her. Would he be angry that I had her, or would he be excited and welcome her with open arms? Would he hate me for waiting this long to tell him or would he understand my pain after he walked out on me all those years ago?

He had to understand why I did what I did didn't he? He just disappeared one day no phone call no text, just gone and I was left to pick up the pieces of a shattered heart and navigate my surprising new role as a single mother at just 18 years old.

I had no idea where he had been all this time or what he was doing. I didn't know why he left, or why he cut off all communication with me when he did. This situation we were in now, wasn't one completely of my own making, he played his role too.

I could hear the phone ringing in one ear and the other I could hear my heart rapidly beating.

After all these years, I don't think I could bring myself to hear him telling me that he hated me for not telling him about his child. *"Hello, thank you for contacting BY Publishing. Our offices are closed for the weekend, please check back Monday at 8am. Thank you."* Well damn, so much for that idea.

Chapter 7

RAYLEN

I KNEW THIS WAS **a** bad idea when Olivia suggested it, but still I went along with it and now here I am with overwhelming regret. Olivia and I stood in front of a night club called *Trust,* which is ironic since apparently she couldn't be trusted to save her life. Standing behind her were two very tall men. One was slightly tan with dark eyes and bright red hair that he had pulled into a bun on top of his head. The other was a fair skinned blond with shocking blue eyes.

I stared her down with my arms folded across my chest because in all her talk about coming out tonight, she failed to mention the part about her bringing us dates. I thought this was a girl's night where I could go out, get drunk with my best friend, and not think about men, but I guess we were on two different pages.

Olivia smiled at me while keeping a tight hold on the red-head's hand. "Don't look so angry, I told you we were going out to have fun, and that's what we're going to do."

I reached out and grabbed Olivia's hand, pulling her away from the two men. "Excuse us, I just need to talk to my useless friend privately for a second." Before either one of them had a chance to respond, I pulled Olivia a few steps away from them.

"What's the issue, they're cute right. I got Luke for you, he's a doctor. I showed him your picture and-" I held up my hand to cut her off. I had to close my eyes and take a few deep breaths just so I wouldn't cause a scene in this public place.

When I opened them again, Olivia was staring at me expectantly, almost like she wanted me to thank her or something. "Are you fucking kidding me with this? I told you I was having guy trouble and you thought adding another guy to the mix was the best solution?"

Olivia sighed took a step towards me and placed both her hands on my shoulders. "Yes, I did." She shook my shoulders slightly before releasing them. "You've been so stressed with all this baby daddy drama, and it's been so long since you've even gone out with a guy that wasn't him. You need this."

"Nobody said you had to marry the guy, just let him buy you a few drinks and dance with him for god's sake." I stared her down, not saying a word. Right now, being here, set up on a blind date was the last place I wanted to be. I would much rather be at home watching Disney movies with my daughter.

"Will you please give it a try, for me." Those green eyes of hers bore into me, pleading with me to say yes. I tried not to let her wear me down, but I honestly didn't have the energy to argue tonight. I did want to have fun and not think about the inevitable conversation I needed to have with Jae-Hyun, so for a few hours at least, I'll give it a try.

"Fine." I dropped my shoulders, giving in. "One drink, maybe two, but I'm not making any promises."

Olivia squealed and grabbed my arm. "This is going to be so much fun, it's been forever since we've gone out." She pulled me back towards the two men, introducing me to my date Luke. I had to admit, he was incredibly attractive, but he was no Jae. I shook my head slightly, I shouldn't be comparing the two, I shouldn't even be thinking about Jae-Hyun tonight. Tonight, was about fun and that was it, everything else could wait until tomorrow.

"Ladies, shall we." The red head who's name I found out was Paul gestured for us to lead the way to the club entrance.

Luke held out his arm for me to take, pulling me towards the building and Paul grabbed Olivia's hand and began following us.

The line outside was so incredibly long, but somehow Olivia

managed to get the four of us inside immediately. It always seemed like she had so many different connections everywhere in the city.

The bouncer stamped our hands and ushered us inside. The music was blasting the moment we opened the tall, black double doors. The entire space was shrouded in darkness except for a few overhead black lights and a few bright white strobe lights. Just enough for the waitstaff and the DJ to do their jobs without incident.

The place was huge. It had to be hundreds of people on the dance floor, bodies grinding close together in time to the infectious beat coming from the speakers.

Luke grabbed my hand so I wouldn't lose the group before navigating us behind Olivia and her date towards the bar. There was so many people, it was a challenge to make it the few feet from the door to the bar.

Luckily for us there weren't that many people at the bar, most everyone here opted for grabbing their drinks and hitting the dance floor or ordering directly from the booths they reserved that were lined up against the walls.

Luke raised his arm and flagged down the bartender, a perky brunette who was wearing a shirt so low cut it left absolutely nothing to the imagination. She sported a giant butterfly tattoo on the side of her neck and when she smiled at Luke, I could see the tooth gems on her two canines sparkling when the strobe light hit it.

He leaned across the bar to tell the bartender his order and slipped her his card. While he was distracted with her, I took the time to admire his appearance. Round face, sharp nose, and nice-looking lips.

With the tight fitting clothes he was wearing, I could tell he had an incredibly good looking body. Wide shoulders, and big arms like maybe he wasn't a *gym bro,* but he still spent a decent amount of time in one.

I was so wrapped up in staring at him, I hadn't even realized he was holding a small glass out to me. My face heated up immediately and I let my eyes drop to the glass in his hands, too embarrassed to look him in the eyes again. The drink was dark pink with a strawberry garnish on top. When the strobe lights hit it, it almost looked like it shimmered a little.

I almost asked him what it was, but I decided fuck it, I wanted to come out tonight and not think about anything. The quicker I got liquor in me the better. Probably not the most responsible ideology to have, but Olivia was right, I needed this. I'll have regrets tomorrow.

Bringing the cup to my lips, I chugged the entire contents of the glass, barely registering the sweetness as it went down. I licked my lips and looked up at Luke who stared at me with wide eyes. He was holding his cup up to his mouth but hadn't even had a chance to take a sip of it. The look on his face was comical, but I'll laugh after I'm drunk.

Once the initial shock of my actions wore off, Luke gave me a small smile before following my lead and throwing his drink back as well.

When his glass was empty, he took mine out of my hands and placed them both on the counter flagging the busty bartender down again. He repeated the actions from before, leaning across the bar to tell her his order and handing her his card. This time she came back with a tray of shots, fourteen shots to be exact. I stared at the tray, my eyes getting a little big and then I looked at him.

Luke smirked at me. Oh, so this was a challenge. Sounds like just the fun I needed.

After the initial fourteen shoots Luke had ordered us, he ordered a second round and the four of us split them. The hour after however, has been a bit of a blur. Paul had gotten us a booth to sit down in so we could all have a little bit of privacy and not have to worry about the crowd of bodies if we didn't want to.

Privacy was the last thing I was interested in tonight though. I didn't want alone time with my date, I wanted to do whatever I needed to, to keep my brain turned off for as long as possible.

The moment the waitress led us to our designated booth, I immediately grabbed Luke's hand and pulled him to the dance floor, leaving Olivia and Paul to enjoy themselves.

Luke was all too eager to press his body to mine, but I didn't mind it, it felt nice. It was a warm night in New York, so I had opted to wear a simple black bodycon dress and some black strappy heels. My curls hung loose and wild on my head and

I kept a bare face except for a nice glossy lip plumper on my lips.

Luke slipped his arms around my waist pulling me in close. I could feel every hard ridge of his abs through his tight fitted shirt. My arms snaked around his neck, and I couldn't help but look at his full lips. I wonder what it felt like to kiss them. I leaned in slightly but suddenly the DJ changed the song to something with more of a bass in it and I had the urge to shake my ass.

I spun in Luke's arms, turning so my back was to his chest. His hands gripped firmly on my hips and at first, we did a little side to side sway, but as the tempo picked up so did the movement of my hips. I leaned forward slightly, pressing my ass harder into his crotch. I could feel his erection grow the more I moved.

One of his hands went to grab my neck, pulling me up so my back was pressing flat against his chest. He used one finger to guide my chin to turn and face him. Before I had time to process what he was doing, his lips were on mine. I moaned slightly at the contact. His lips moved slowly over mine, at the same time I could feel his other hand move from my hip down to my thigh. His fingers slowly slid up my thigh and then to the hem of my dress.

They kept going until they reached between my legs brushing against my panties. He gently began brushing small strokes over my pussy at the same time his tongue slipped past my lips. I could feel myself instantly getting wet. This is why I very rarely drank, it always made me so horny.

Luke pressed his lips harder against mine, massaging my tongue with his. I was enjoying the kiss so much it caught me completely off guard when I felt a huge hand wrap around my arm and yank me out of Luke's hold.

I gasped from the force of being pulled away from Luke's amazing hands on my body. The alcohol was impairing my vision too much for me to be able to focus on who was actually pulling me through the crowd of people. The stranger weaved us through the crowd and through a couple of double doors at the back of the building. It took me a second to realize the stranger had led us through the emergency exit into a small dimly lit hallway.

He turned around and my heart skipped a beat when I looked into those dark eyes. Shit, Jae-Hyun.

Chapter 8

JAE-HYUN

THE AMOUNT OF RAGE I was feeling right now I don't think I could even begin to put into words. Raylen was out with some guy letting him touch her, kiss her, after she was just out with me a few days ago. Who the fuck was that and why was she with him?

Was she with someone this entire time and she just chose not to tell me? I pushed her shoulders until her back hit the wall behind her. I wanted to rip her head off but by the way she was stumbling around I knew she was far from sober so maybe her actions weren't completely her fault.

"Jae," she slurred my name, but it still sent tingles down my spine when she said it. When I think about the hold this woman had on me, it makes me even angrier that I just caught her in the arms of another man.

I still had her shoulders held firmly in place against the wall, so she lifted her arms at the elbow and lightly brushed my arms with her fingertips. That touch was like fire against my skin. When I looked at her face, her eyes were glazed over slightly telling me just how under the influence she was. She smiled at me and licked her glossy lips.

I remember what those felt like on mine just a few days ago. I wanted them again, but they were on another man tonight, so I wouldn't be falling for her little seduction tricks this time.

"Who the fuck was that?" I asked, not letting the anger slip from my face.

Her face switched to one of confusion and she turned her head to look in the direction of the doors we had just walked through. "Luke?" she questioned.

"Yes *Luke,* who is he? Your boyfriend?" Raylen turned her head back towards me and burst out laughing. I was finding it really hard to see what was actually funny. Drunk or not, it was obvious that I was angry about her being here with him.

She's been ignoring my attempts to get in contact with her for days so we could talk about what happened the other night. Now here she was drunk off her ass, barely dressed and making out with another guy on the dance floor. I couldn't even get a proper date out of her. Did what we have years ago mean absolutely nothing to her? Clearly, I was the only one that did all the missing these last eight years we were apart.

"What's so funny?" Her face straightened and her smile disappeared. She reached up again but this time instead of touching my arms, she put both her hands flat on my chest. She pushed, making me release the hold I had on her shoulders.

Raylen rubbed one shoulder and then another. I hadn't realized how tight I was holding her or thought about the fact that I was maybe hurting her. All I could think about was how I felt when I saw her with that guy. When she looked back at me, I couldn't read the expression on her face, so I just wait for her to answer my question.

"You're acting just like a jealous baby daddy." My face scrunched up in confusion. What the hell was she talking about. Without another word, she turned and started heading back toward the door. I grabbed her arm and pulled her back to me.

Snatching her arm away, she turned to face me, rage written on her face. I wasn't sure if it was the alcohol or how angry she was, but even in this crappy lighting, I could see her cheeks tinting pink. "Don't touch me, you only have one child and I'm not her. I don't need a babysitter."

I let out a sigh and tried to grab again. She was clearly a lot drunker than I thought she was. There was no way I could let her go back out there, I needed to make sure she made it home safely.

"Raylen, you're not making any sense. You're drunk, let me take you home."

"No!" She shouted taking a step back from me. "You lost the right to worry about me when you abandoned us years ago."

The more she talked, the less sense she was making. 'I didn't abandon you, and who is us?"

Her bottom lip began to tremble, and I could see the tears start to form in her eyes. First, she was trying to seduce me, then she thought everything I said was funny, and now she's crying?"

"How could you leave her to grow up without her father. Do you know how difficult it's been to do this by myself?" A lone tear slid down her cheeks, but I couldn't even register it really. There was suddenly a loud ringing in my ears, and I suddenly felt a sharp pain in both my stomach and my throat, almost like at any moment I would throw up.

I took a step towards Raylen, but she matched my movement and took a step back. "Raylen, what are you saying?"

She folded her arms across her chest and looked away. I wanted to scream at her and snatch her up. Force her to tell me if anything she was saying was the truth or nothing but her drunk ramblings. Was she really saying that she had a baby? No, not a baby anymore. It's been eight years, did she really keep my child from me this entire time?

"Raylen, tell me the truth." I tried to breathe through my words. I needed to keep my temper in check. She was drunk and yelling at her wasn't going to help this situation. "Do I have a kid?"

She shoved a frustrated hand through her curly hair, still

not making eye contact. "No, she's my daughter. You lost the right to call her yours when you abandoned us." Before I had a chance to say anything else, Raylen turned her back to me and disappeared through the double doors, probably back to her date.

I felt dizzy and sick to my stomach. I had a kid, a daughter. Raylen had my baby eight years ago and chose to keep her from me. Why did she lie to me? Why did she keep her from me? Did she really hate me that much?

A million questions were running though my head right now, but I couldn't seem to make sense of any of it. I leaned against the wall and tried to make the spinning stop.

I couldn't figure out what was up and what was down, I needed to talk to Raylen. I took a deep breath and pushed off the wall, bursting through the double doors. A sea of people dancing and grinding on each other stood in front of me. There was no way I would be able to find Raylen in this group again, that's if she decided to go back to dancing and not just leave all together.

I didn't feel like trying to find Liam and Daniel in the crowd and knowing that Olivia was probably here too, I could only imagine what they had gotten into. I didn't have the mental to deal with anything other than getting out of this building right now.

Instead of attempting to make my way through the crowd of people, I hung a left and headed toward the front door, before I could even step through them, I felt a hand on my shoulder.

I turned and came face to face with the striking green eyes of my secretary Elizabeth. She had gotten a booth in the far corner for our group from the office, but that was all the way on the other side of the club. How did she even find me in this large group of ass shaking people I wasn't sure.

Before all this, I was having a pretty decent time listening to the music and having a drink or two. Finally getting my mind off Raylen for a few hours, that is until I saw that knockoff male model mauling her on the dance floor.

"Where are you going?" She asked. I pulled my arm from her grip. I wasn't in the mood to be touched right now.

"I'm calling it for tonight." I said turning towards the door.

"Wait." She grabbed my arm again and narrowed her eyes at me. "Can you take me home?" The way she was looking at me, I knew what she was getting at. Part of me knew it was a bad idea, the other part didn't care. The twin's words flashed in my head and I've never thought they were more right until this very moment, I was hurt and furious and I *needed* a distraction.

It didn't take us long to make it back to Elizabeth's apartment. Considering it was around the corner from the club she decided to have her celebration at. I had texted the twins to tell them not to look for me and that I would catch up with them later.

I licked my lips and let my eyes roam over her luscious body. The tiny, emerald, green dress clung to her body in the most delicious way and made her matching green eyes stand out even more. The thin straps helped to keep her breasts hidden from my view, but just barely. On the walk back to her place, to keep myself distracted, I had been wondering what would happen if a strong gust of wind came along. Would the fragile fabric stand a chance or would it give way and let me enjoy the spoils.

Elizabeth leaned against the doorframe to her apartment. Her hair was swept back away from her face, held in place by a few pins on one side. She chewed on her bottom lip, running her long red painted fingernails up her thigh, lifting her dress slightly. Her eyes roamed over my body the same way my eyes did hers.

"I don't know about you, but I'm not tired at all."

I folded my arms across my chest, causing my biceps to bulge. Her eyes immediately zeroed in on the action. I wasn't stupid, I knew where this night was leading when I agreed to walk her home. If I had any doubts about it, the way she had been looking at me all night combined with how often she would find some kind of excuse to lean into me on the walk, pressing her chest into my arm, that was all the confirmation I needed.

I reached out to brush my hand across her cheek. Her eyes narrowed and I saw her entire body shiver. She was just as ready for this as I was, so there was no need to drag this out. She wasn't my woman, and we weren't in love. A nice hard fuck was just what we both needed. I pulled my hand back and before she had a chance to miss it, I slipped my hands around her waist, crushing my lips to hers before she had a chance to let out that surprised yelp I knew was coming. Her lips were thin but soft. I could taste the cherry from the thick gloss she had smeared all over her lips.

I swallowed every moan she let out, not caring to hear them, all I wanted was to see if she knew how to use these lips of hers. I took a step forward, pushing her back into the apartment, kicking the door shut behind me.

She pulled away from me and took a step back. Giving me her best attempt at a seductive smirk, she grabbed the straps of her dress and pulled them down. Her breasts bounced free. Pulling the dress the rest of the way down, she wasn't wearing any panties either. That was fine with me, I didn't need to waste any time undressing her. She reached out and grabbed my wrist, pulling me to the couch.

Once she had me seated on the coach, she made quick work of getting my pants undone. If I didn't know any better, I would say I am not the first man she has lured into her little den of sin. That works out perfectly for me. I didn't need some inexperienced girl that I had to be gentle with. The last time I had that was eight years ago and that same girl ripped my heart out and lied to me.

I shook my head slightly to clear my thoughts, now wasn't the time to be thinking of her. Except this wasn't a new occurrence. In the last eight years since we had been apart, every time I tried to be with another woman, I couldn't help but compare them to her. The way the shape of their hips could never compare to the dip of hers. The way her soft, full tits fit perfectly in my palms. The delicious shade of chocolate of those suckable nipples. Even the amazing feel of her firm but soft ass when it bounced on my lap. Nobody could compare. Nobody had been able to take my mind off her.

Her moans, the claw marks she left on my back, the tiny gasp she made when I first enter her, even the sweet taste of her juices. Elizabeth by every form of the word was considerably sexy. She would be any guy's wet dream with her long red hair and her perfectly tan skin, even the way she expertly devoured my dick pass those gloss covered lips.

I looked down at her, her head bobbing up and down but never breaking eye contact with me. This should be one of the sexiest things in the world, but still all my mind could focus on was the caramel skin and the hazel eyes of Raylen.

I closed my eyes and imagined her face and just like that I started feeling the first tingles of my orgasm. The tingles started in my toes but before I knew it, I could feel my balls draw up tight. The urge to shoot my load down her throat was so overwhelming, I didn't even have time to warn her. All I could do was sit there with a tight grip on the leather couch and ride out the continuous waves of unending pleasure.

Elizabeth swallowed everything I gave her like a champ, no gagging, no chocking. My heart pounded in my ears but still my eyes stayed closed, Raylen's face running rampant in my head.

Elizabeth continued sucking until she got every drop before letting my still semi erect dick slip from her mouth. She climbed on top of me, wrapping her arms around my neck. Aligning her core with my dick, she pressed down engulfing my dick in her warm, wet center.

Man did she feel good. Not as tight as Raylen, but if I closed my eyes, it was close enough that I could still imagine it was her body riding me. Treating me like I was there just for her pleasure and nothing else. If I had to admit it to myself, that was all I wanted. To do whatever it took to make her happy. It was too late for that now though. We may have had our little fun the other night, but that was all it was. The pain from the past and the decisions we made, sealed the deal on any chances of rekindling anything.

That was something I was going to have to deal with, but what I wouldn't deal with was being kept from my kid.

Elizabeth leaned forward so she could whisper in my ear. "You like that baby?" Her words snapped me from the little world I created in my head. It also made me realize, I was no longer interested in what we were doing, and I wanted it to be over as fast as possible so I could get out of here.

I reached up and grabbed Elizabeth by the hips, forcing her further down on my dick. She let out a yelp but held me tighter. I used the leverage I had on her hips to pound into her harder, smashing her pelvis into mine.

Moan after moan slipped past her lips the faster my movements got. Part of me felt bad with the amount of aggression I was using to fuck her, but the other part was just anxious for this to be over.

Elizabeth let out one final shout, her body seizing, trying it's hardest to milk me to completion, but it didn't work. I didn't feel the least bit like coming. When her body finally stopped it's convulsing, she collapsed in my arms. I stroked her hair for a few minutes before I heard the soft snore that told me she had fallen asleep.

Gently rolling her off me so her head laid on the back of the couch, I stuffed my still semi-hard dick back into my pants and as quietly as I could, I got the hell out of there.

The overwhelming irritation was starting to set in. I didn't come or more like I couldn't come. The last time something like this had happened was during the first two years Raylen and I were apart. I had tried with multiple different women to get hard but I couldn't do it. It wasn't until I started imagining her face on theirs that I could get an erection but coming definitely was not in the cards. I thought it would be like that forever but one day that just wasn't the case.

Years later and I'm back in the same boat I was then, only being able to come if it's Raylen. I was so turned on the other night just licking that sweet pussy of hers, I almost exploded right there in my pants without ever being touched.

I should be turned off by her, I should hate her for keeping something so important from me. But past the rage I was feeling towards her, I was happy and grateful that of all the women in the world I could be tied to for the rest of my life, it was the one woman I could never get off my mind.

Right there standing in the elevator heading back down to the lobby, I had made up my mind. No matter what, I would get Raylen back in my bed. The three of us would be a family.

Chapter 9

RAYLEN

I T TOOK ME A **full** day to remember what happened that night at the club. The amount of liquor I consumed should've been enough for three people and I wasn't even sure how I made it home.

Jae-Hyun knew about Levi. I actually told him and thanks to the alcohol I didn't do it anywhere close to how I wanted to. There was so much screaming and anger, mostly from my end, which wasn't fair. It technically wasn't his fault, and he didn't technically abandon Levi. He did however abandon me which in my book was the same thing.

All the anger I had been feeling towards him over the years just came spilling out once I was drunk off my ass. Or maybe it was the fresh anger I felt at the fact that he thought he had some kind of claim on me to demand I tell him about Luke. He lost the right to concern himself with any romantic relationships I have when he left me behind eight years ago.

I was laid out on the couch, arms behind my head, staring at the ceiling. I've been rocking the same pjs and messy bun combo for two days. Jasmine has been blowing up my phone for God knows what reason and so has Olivia. She kept bugging me about what my hurry was to leave that night. It wasn't that I didn't want to tell her, I was just too embarrassed to tell anybody about what happened.

It was the same when it came to the night at the banquet with Jae-Hyun. Why was it that every encounter I had with him made me feel too embarrassed to talk to anybody about? He was like my secret shame, and I didn't want to think of him like that because what did that make Levi. I absolutely could never be ashamed of her.

A knock on my door pulled me from my thoughts. I turned my head slightly to look at it like somehow the door would tell me who was behind it so I wouldn't have to get up and actually check myself. My phone sat on my chest, I picked it up to check the time. 1:25pm. It was too early for Levi to be back from school, and this wasn't the normal time Olivia would take her break from work.

I heard the knock again and let out a sigh. I guess I had no choice but to answer it. My bare feet hit the cold wooden floor and I did a little stretch before I got to my feet.

The moment I checked the peephole on the door, I suddenly felt like answering the door in what I was currently wearing was not the smartest idea, but there was no time to change.

I tried to smooth the imaginary wrinkles of my pajama shorts. I took a deep breath and opened the door to the shimmering blonde hair and bright blue eyes of Luke standing outside my door.

He smiled at me the moment his eyes landed on mine and held out a bouquet of yellow tulips for me to take from him. I took them giving them a little sniff before asking the most obvious question. "Luke, how did you figure out where I lived?"

Luke's smile grew wider and raked a hand through his hair. It looked thick, I wonder if it's soft too. Did I have my hands in his hair the other night? I remember a really heated kiss between the two of us on the dance floor, but not much more than that.

"I guess that answers my first question of if you remember what happened the other night. I'm the one that made sure you made it home." Of course, he was the one who saw me down four more shots after my encounter with Jae-Hyun and then proceed to trip and stumble over nothing but air.

"Of course, you did." I took a step back and gestured for him to come in. I closed the door and turned to face him, that gorgeous smile on full display as he stared at me. I had to admit, he had damn near perfect teeth which should be a good thing, but in reality, kind of made him look like a Ken doll.

I pasted a smile on my face to try to hide the disappointment that I wish wasn't there when I saw who it was and set the bouquet on the counter. I stared at him waiting for him to tell me what he was doing here, but at the same time I waited for the fluttering feeling I was sure I got when we were together the other night, but nothing.

I felt nothing with him standing here in front of me. No flutter, no shortened breath, not even my heart raced when I was in his arms. All the things that happened whenever I was in Jae-Hyun's presence. He didn't even have to touch me.

Luke took a step towards me and held out his arms. I picked up the que and stepped into his hold giving him a hug. I felt awkward being around him. Was it because I got sloppy drunk and did who knows what with him while I was under the influence. Was it because my ex showed up and ruined our date or was it just because I desperately wished that I felt the same kind of heat I felt for Jae-Hyun with someone like Luke.

"I just wanted to check to see how you were. That whole thing with that guy was pretty strange." Luke said as he loosened his grip on the hug long enough for me to step out of his hold. Why did I feel so much more relieved once there was distance between us?

"Yeah, an unexpected visit from an ex is never ideal." I gave him a small shrug not really wanting to tell him much more than that. I didn't really know Luke that well especially to give him every detail of the tragedy that was my relationship with Jae-Hyun.

Luke grabbed both of my hands and pulled me close to him. "Before he showed up, I thought we were having a pretty good time." He smirked at me and leaned down, placing a small kiss on my cheek. "I was hoping we could make a second attempt." I felt horrible that my immediate response was to tell him *no that was never going to happen.* Or to tell him that the only reason anything happened with us that night was because of the alcohol and nothing more, but that's not what I said.

Instead, I just smiled and nodded like an idiot. What else could I really do, I led him on the other night and now he was standing here in my apartment asking me for a real date.

Between all the drama with Jae-Hyun, being a mother to Levi and making sure I keep up with my deadlines, I really didn't have any time for dating. I should just turn him down. I opened my mouth to tell him the truth, but before I could he reached up and brushed the side of my cheek with the back of his hand.

"Are you okay?" He asked. "You seem out of it." I stepped out of his embrace, walking around him to lean against the island that sat in the middle of my kitchen.

My apartment was small, with the living room, dining room and kitchen all being in one area. Even knowing the size of the room we were in was small, it felt even smaller being with Luke.

"I'm fine, it's just been a long week." Was I being too obvious that I wanted this interaction to be over?

Luke dropped his head. He ran a hand through his hair

before shoving it into his pockets. I didn't realize until now, he was wearing scrubs. Did he waste his break to come all the way here just to see me. The hospital wasn't that close and if you include the afternoon New York traffic, he had to have used most of his break just to get here.

That only made me feel worse. "I'm sorry my mood isn't the greatest right now, I just have a lot on my mind. I would love to go out with you again." Luke looked back at me and smiled. The excitement on his face was a little shocking. I really didn't leave that great of a first impression the first time we went out, so why he was excited to hang out with me again I wasn't sure.

"Great, how's Friday?" I smile and give him a small head nod. He was sweet, so what would it hurt to hang out with him one more time. The sexual tension might not be there, but that doesn't mean we couldn't be friends.

Luke smiled back at me and headed to the door. I followed close behind him. He gave me another small hug before walking out the door and down the hallway. The attraction wasn't there yet, but who knows, he could be just the thing I needed to get my mind and my heart off Jae-Hyun for good.

Chapter 10

Jae-Hyun

SHE WAS SEEING SOMEONE, **and** they were playing house with my child. That's all I could think about. The whole inter-action played over and over in my head.

I decided to hire someone to do a background check on Raylen. She spent the last eight years hiding a child from me, what else was she hiding. How many men was she involved with, just the one from the other night, or were there more than that. Was she only the mother of my kid or did she have more children by other men? I wanted to know how much the woman I fell in love with all those years ago changed.

I wanted her to be in my life, but I couldn't go into this blind like I did when I scheduled that meeting with her and her agent.

I was aware that I was probably spirialing a little after her little confession, and maybe I should've taken a moment to really think things through, but I didn't do that.

Instead, I chose to go the extreme route. I could only imagine what Liam would say if he knew what I had done. Probably tell me that I was being a creepy stalker, then again that would be rich coming from one of the two guys that ran off any man that came within twenty feet of a woman they had no romantic relationship with.

Daniel was the one more likely to be on my side. He would probably agree that I needed to do whatever it took to get what I wanted just like Raylen did.

I sighed and sat back in my seat. They had been trying to call me since the other night, but I hadn't answered any of them. How would I even begin to tell them what happened that night?

I was hoping when I hired that P.I., all my fears would be unfounded, but after the he came back with an envelope full of pictures, I knew they weren't. There were pictures of the same guy she was with the other night. Shitty lighting and a little alcohol wouldn't make me forget that asshole's face or the way he touched the body that belonged to me.

He was leaving her apartment with a shit eating grin on his face and in one of the pictures, I could see her in the background in pjs. Did he sleep there? Did he sleep with her?

I crumbled the picture in my hand and pulled the next one from the vanilla envelop in the passenger seat of my car. My eyes instantly got wide and I sat up straighter in my chair. It was another picture of Raylen, but this time she was dressed in a lose-fitted bright blue dress. Her curls blowing all over her head with the help of the wind. Next to her holding tightly to her hand, was a little girl.

Looking at her was like looking in a mirror. She had my eyes, my dark hair, just much curlier, just like her mother. There was no denying she was mine.

The more I played the night that Raylen told me out in my head the more enraged I became. If my daughter saw me out on the street, she would look at me like she had no idea who I was, like I was a stranger. That's because that's exactly who I was to her, nothing but a stranger. Raylen had done that to us. Raylen had kept my daughter from me for all these years and now I was nobody to her. I didn't even know her name.

Did she call that other man dad when that's what she should be calling me? Did Raylen tell him that she was his child? Did they pick out her name together? Watch her first steps, hear her first words? All of this without me.

Who the hell was he anyway? Her boyfriend, her husband? There was no way she would let what happened between us happen if she had a husband waiting for her at home. Then again, eight years is a long time. People change, I know I have. I'm not the same boy that had to do what everyone else told him too. Now, I'm the type who does whatever it took to get what he wants or in this case who he wants. Right now, what I want is my family and I would get them by any means.

Any resolve I had about following through with the plan I

had come up with earlier had completely disappeared. I was going to be a part of my daughter's life, even if that meant invading every part of Raylen's life piece by piece. I walked into the small office I had built in my new home, tossing my keys on the couch before I took my seat behind my desk.

The stack of papers sat in the same spot I had left. A contract. The same one I had offered her and her agent before, but with a little amendment in it.

Now the contract read that in exchange for 25% ownership and royalties for her current book and the next four, she would get full creative control as well as $2.5 million dollar signing bonus. It almost sounded like a contract that was too good to be true.

But of course, what kind of businessman would I be if I didn't get a little bit more than a few royalties out of it. At the very bottom it stated that this contract would only be valid if we married within 4 months of signing and stayed married throughout the fulfillment of the contract. Making Raylen my wife meant I would have full access to my kid whenever I wanted, no arguments from my wife.

Raylen wouldn't be able to take my kid and run off whenever she felt like it and once we were married, she wouldn't be able to change the terms of our agreement until the contract was over. A normal custody agreement she could bend how she wanted, but this marriage would be completely in my control with the added bonus being that she couldn't screw the man pretending to be the father of my child anymore.

The sudden relief I was feeling in my chest at that thought, didn't escape my notice but I was trying my hardest to ignore it. It didn't matter anyway, soon he would be a nonfactor.

This contract stated in so many words that once she signed this contract, she had 4 months to marry me and she had to stay married to me until the fourth book under the contract was completed. I felt probably much smugger than I should as I stared down at the words on the page.

This would basically be a form of blackmail, she either signed with my agency and agreed to marry me or I would file for full custody of my daughter and her career was over. I didn't want to go this route, but she wasn't giving me many options. It was only fair to level the playing field, at least I was hoping that's how she saw it.

I sent a copy of the contract to Elizabeth marked as confidential for her to have a carrier deliver it straight to Raylen and not her agent. I wanted her to read it first, she could tell her agent whatever she wanted to once she made her decision.

I had only been at the office for about two hours before I heard the yelling. I couldn't make out a lot of what was said, but one of the very few words I could make out was the word *bastard*.

I couldn't help the slow smile that spread across my face as I sat back in my chair and laced my fingers together. I had just gotten comfortable when the office door flew open and in walked an extremely angry but still incredibly sexy Raylen.

My smile slipped from my face and my heart skipped a beat when I saw her. Her hair hung loose and wild around her shoulders. I always did love it when she wore her curls down. She wore an off the shoulder white sundress that was snug fitting and left little to the imagination and when the sun streaming in through the large windows behind me hit her, she looked just like the goddess I remember.

Elizabeth stumbled in behind her looking flustered, but I just waved her off giving her a slight head nod so she would know I could handle this myself. She nodded back at me and slipped back through the door, closing it behind her.

"You sick son of a bitch."

She was fuming. I could see her chest heaving and the small droplets of sweat on her forehead when she burst through the wooden double doors of my study. I expected this reaction after receiving the revised contract, but I must admit to myself I was more than satisfied that I had gotten under her skin.

"I see you got the new contract." I sat back in my chair, elbows propped up on the armrest, fingers laced together, with a huge ass smile on my face.

"You mean this bullshit stack of papers you're using to try to buy me." She tossed the contract at me, but the flimsy staple couldn't keep the pages together. The packet burst open, and the pages scattered, flying in every direction.

"Buying? That would imply you're for sale and I would never

suggest that." I got up from my seat, walking around my desk to stand it front of her. She took a step away from me trying to keep the distance between us and that only made my smile grow even bigger. I could tell she hated me knowing the effect I had on her.

I leaned back against my desk and kicked my feet out in front of me. "I take it there was something not to your liking about it?"

"Do you really expect me to justify that with an answer?" I gave a little shrug. "You think that you can buy me in exchange for my career and my daughter?" I held up my hand, stopping her.

"Don't you mean *our* daughter." I could practically hear her grinding her teeth. Too bad, I wasn't budging on this, she had already cost me enough time getting to know my child. "And I don't think anything. I was just offering up an option to advance your career and give you a much more comfortable life for the both of you. But as a businessman, of course I would expect something out of it as well, don't you agree that's fair?"

RAYLEN

Why was he talking like this? He was making it seem like this was something small and trivial. He wanted me to marry him, if I agreed to it, would he really only view it as some type of business transaction and not something more intimate.

What would that mean for Levi. How would I explain things to her? What was his game? I didn't want to think that the sweet and loving boy I fell in love with all those years ago would resort to something like this, then again, it's been proven that this is not the same boy from back then.

This man in front of me whose been doing a really good job of not letting me know what he's really thinking, this man who thought it was a good idea to write up a whole contract just so I would marry him. I don't know this man.

I took a deep breath and tried to reel in my rage. "I won't sign this contract or any other contract that you decide to send. I hope it finally gets through to you that I don't want anything to do with you anymore." Jae-Hyun's expression remained unchanged, but I decided I didn't care anymore, actions speak louder than words and if he wanted proof that this thing he thought he was starting between us was going nowhere, I could show him better than I could tell him.

I took a deep breath and turned on my heels, heading back toward the door. This conversation was pointless, and I was done having it.

I couldn't make it further than putting my hand on the doorknob when I felt a shadow looming over me. Before I had a chance to turn around, Jae-Hyun grabbed my arm and spun me around, pressing my back against the wall, effectively trapping me in place.

I stared into his eyes, those beautiful brown eyes that always made my knees turn to jelly. His proximity made breathing anything but his delicious aftershave damn near impossible. Keep it together Raylen. I put my hands on his chest and pushed, but he didn't budge. Instead, he took a step closer, closing the already small space between us even more.

"Let's think about the facts shall we." He spoke. His face inching closer to mine. I turned slightly so our lips wouldn't touch, but once his lips brush my cheek, I knew this wasn't that much better of an option.

"Your career is at a standstill with that little company you're so insistent on staying with. I have the power to make your career really take off or I can end it with a simple phone call." He gently brushed a finger down my cheek and underneath my chin. A shiver went down my spine. Everywhere he touched felt like fire.

"You kept my daughter from me Raylen, and now you're playing house with another man. How do you think your little adoring fans will react to that news. Can you see the scandalous headline *New York Time's Bestselling author keeps lovechild a secret from their father.*" I turned my head more, trying to get his hand off me, but it didn't work. "I'll blackball your career. No publishing in the world will want to touch anything with your name attached after I'm done. The way I see it, the choice is obvious. Sign the contract and marry me or I take my daughter and tank your career."

"And what makes you think I care about my career more than I do her. You don't know me anymore Jae-Hyun, I'm not the same person I was back then."

Jae-Hyun brushed his nose against my cheek before dropping his head down low and inhaling deeply when he got to my neck. "Oh, trust me, I'm probably the only person that truly knows who you are, but that's okay I don't need you to admit to anything. Just sign the contract." Jae-Hyun pressed his lips to the side of my neck giving me a gentle kiss that made it feel like the temperature in this room seem to spike ten degrees.

I tried again to push against his chest and this time he let me, and I couldn't feel more relieved about it. I knew if we stayed in that position any longer, I was going to once again be sucked into doing something I know I shouldn't and I couldn't have him clouding my judgement anymore.

Jae-Hyun took a few steps back and the smile that was there just a few minutes ago was completely gone. "I don't know what your obsession is with getting me to be a writer for your company, but marriage is a whole separate issue. I don't think I need to tell you that what you saw the other night was exactly what it seemed like. I'm with someone and the sooner you accept that fact, the better." I was lying through my teeth, he didn't know that was the first time I had ever met Luke but he didn't need to.

He looked at me, his eyes roaming my body, like that day in that office when we had nothing but time to explore each other's bodies. To remember what it felt like to be together all those years ago. That time was different though, that time I thought I was being touched by an inexperienced boy with softer features who had no idea the inner workings of a woman. Now, he was a man with a firmer body and sure hands. I wonder how many women made him the way he is today.

"The guy from the club," His voice was firm when he spoke but the look on his face remained neutral. I knew he was annoyed that there was someone else in my life, no matter how hard he tried to hide it. "Does he know that you spread your legs for me or that we both know you'll do it again?" My heart skipped a beat, and I clenched my jaw. The urge to slap him returning tenfold.

When I didn't respond, he just smiled. "I'll take that as a no." He shrugged then bent down scooping up some of the papers from the floor and holding them out to me. "I can't force you to sign this contract, but I will be part of my daughter's life. Whether that involves you or not is up to you." When I didn't take the papers from him, he turned his back towards me and tossed them on his desk. "We had something good at one point and you can't deny that. When you think about it, it's a win-win situation, there's really no way for you to lose. All you have to do is say yes."

"Why are you doing this?" I stared down at the white strappy heels on my feet. I had planned to spend the day in the park enjoying the nice weather and getting some writing done, but the moment I opened my apartment door, I came face to face with the carrier he'd hired to deliver this stupid contract. Today started out to be promising, I thought after telling Jae-Hyun about Levi that it would scare him enough to get out of my life permanently. I guess I was wrong.

"I told you already didn't I." Jae-Hyun never turned to face me which I'm glad for, I didn't need him to see how much I was hanging on his every word. He didn't need to know he had that kind of power over me. "I'm doing this because it's you and I have a right to what's mine." That was all he said before he walked around his desk and sat back in his seat.

"The choice is yours Raylen, I told you where I stand but the question is where do you?" How do I answer that? "I'll give you until the end of the week to make your final decision."

My mouth dropped open, and my eyes shot to him. "You're giving me two days to decide if I want to accept a marriage proposal?" The pitch in my voice was annoying even to my ears, but this was ridiculous, how could he expect me to decide something like this in such a short amount of time.

"If you're the same Raylen I remember, then this should be an easy choice." That was easy for him to say, what did he have to lose.

Chapter 11

RAYLEN

SITTING ON THE PARK **bench**, I breathed in all the smells of the fresh air around me. Listening to the rustling of the tree leaves as the wind blew through them. The bright, hot sun shining on my face. The laughter of the children playing on the jungle gym in front of me. The things that had brought me comfort for so many years before, now they did nothing to keep me from replaying the events of yesterday repeatedly in my head.

What Jae-Hyun was offering was ridiculous, but I was still oddly compelled to accept them. He was offering to take me to new heights in my career, something that I had been dreaming about since I first discovered my love of writing.

Levi would have her father in her life, and I would have the man I thought I would spend my life with. I should be happy, he was handing it to me on a silver platter. Well, maybe not a silver platter because all I had to do was change my entire life and that of my daughters. Was that even a fair trade off? He wasn't giving me a chance to back out or change my mind because of what happened in the past. I should be happy about that shouldn't I?

It seemed like this deal was made so I had everything to lose, and he had everything to gain.

"Momma, did you see me on the monkey bars?" At the sound of Levi's voice, I looked up to see her running towards me. Her beautiful dark hair blowing in the wind as she ran as fast as she could to reach me.

Her smile was infectious, and I couldn't help but smile back. It must be nice to be that age, without a care in the world. To be able to be free to run around and play with your friends. No drama, no responsibilities, no difficult decisions. To let someone else think things through for me and all I would have to do is go along with it.

"Of course my love, you're getting so strong. Pretty soon you'll be strong enough to lift a car." She ran into my open arms, and I pulled her close, burying my face in her hair.

I had to do this didn't I? I had to accept Jae-Hyun's offer so that I could give her the future she deserved. Or was that just an excuse to do what I know deep down I really wanted and that was to be with Jae-Hyun again. I wanted him and I knew I couldn't keep denying it, but I also knew he could never be trusted.

"What's wrong momma?" Levi asked me.

I let her slip from my hold, and I looked into those beautiful brown eyes of hers. Tucking a lose curl behind her ear, I pulled her into me, so she was sitting on my lap. "Do you remember the project you had from school before?" I asked.

She thought about it for a few seconds before recognition shown in her eyes and she nodded her head. "The one about genes. It showed why babies look like mommies and daddies."

I laughed and kissed the top of her head. "Yes baby, that's the one."

"Yes, I remember." She looked down at her fingernails and began picking at the chipped polish.

"How would you feel if your daddy could play with you just like your school friends and their daddies?" Levi didn't respond with words, instead all she gave me was a slight shrug of the shoulders and that's it.

I was expecting more questions from her, like where had he been this entire time or why didn't he come to play with her before now. Was I expecting more of a reaction from a child that didn't see the world the way I did, or maybe I'm just nervous that I completely ruined her interest in even having a father in the first place?

I couldn't help how relieved I felt that she didn't want me to answer any questions because honestly, I wasn't sure how I would answer them.

Hey Levi, your daddy wants to meet you. He's been God knows where for the last eight years of your life because before I could tell him you existed, he decided it would just be much easier to abandon us. Now, he's back for whatever reason and he wants to be a part of your life. Aren't you just so happy he showed up? Smiley face. Eight years old is not young enough to buy that load of bullshit.

I squeezed her tighter and leaned back on the bench, trying to enjoy the peace I was sharing with her because I knew this was probably the last time I would get it. He wanted to meet her, today. I couldn't put it off any longer. It was the next logical step after I told him she existed.

He wouldn't tell me where he was taking her or what they would be doing, but I had to trust that she would be safe with him, he was her father after all. He might've been careless with me and my feelings, but I couldn't put my fears of that onto her. Who knows maybe he would treat her with more care than me since she was his daughter.

I didn't have a chance to play all the scenarios of what could happen out in my head before Levi pulled out of my hold. She looked at a spot over my shoulder and my spine instantly went rigid. I didn't even need to turn around to know that he was walking up behind us. I stared into Levi's eyes, but she never took her eyes off him. I tried my hardest to hold back the tears. I didn't want this. I didn't want our relationship to change.

Call me selfish, but for eight years of her life, it was just me and her. I didn't have to worry about sharing her moments with anyone else, but after today that was all changing and I wasn't sure I was ready for that.

I watched Levi lift her hand to wave at him and I took a deep breath before pushing her back a little so I could get to my feet and turn to face him. There he was, wearing a white button up shirt with the first few buttons left undone, light wash jeans and white sneakers. His hair was slightly tussled like he had been nervously running his fingers through it all day. He was waving his hand at Levi but the moment he met my eyes, he dropped his arm.

I blinked a few times, trying again to hold back my tears. I grabbed Levi's little hand and her multicolored unicorn backpack off the bench, walking around it to stand in front of Jae-Hyun. Jae-Hyun kept his eyes on Levi. What do I say? How do I even introduce them? I chewed on my lip for a second and decided to just go for it.

Dropping down to her level, I kissed her fingers before redirecting her attention to him. "Bunny, this is Jae-Hyun." I gestured toward him, and he followed my lead crouching down as well. "He's..." What do I call him? I opened my mouth to speak, but no words came out. Levi stared at me expectantly and suddenly it felt like my heart was racing a mile a minute and I was finding it increasingly difficult to pull air into my lungs.

"I'm a friend of your mom." Jae-Hyun interrupted, holding his hand out to Levi. I looked at him, but he kept his eyes on her. He bailed me out, instead of letting me crash and burn in front of our daughter?

Levi took a step towards him and grabbed his hand. Her

hand looked so much smaller in his. A sharp pain went through my chest when I thought about how many years of her life he had missed out on.

"My name is Levi. Nice to meet you Mr. Jae-Hyunny." Levi shook his hand enthusiastically. I wonder if she was aware of who he really was and just played along or if she really just thought he was a friend to me.

Jae-Hyun hesitated before speaking and I thought for a second he was just going to tell her that he was her dad, but instead he kept up the pretense, and instead said, "You can call me Jae, it is very nice to meet you Levi. That's a really pretty name."

Levi smiled brightly at the compliment. It was done, Jae-Hyun had met his daughter and now it was time for me to give them their space. I got to my feet and held out Levi's backpack to him. He stared at it in confusion before standing up as well.

"Bunny, Jae is going to take you somewhere fun for a little while." Levi turned to face me, the same confused look on her face. In this moment, they looked almost identical. There would never be any denying he was her father. "I'll see you later."

When Jae-Hyun didn't take the bag from my hand, I held it out to Levi. She took the bag and slipped her arms through the straps. I leaned down to place a kiss on her forehead and turned to leave the two of them alone, not giving Jae-Hyun a second look.

I didn't get very far before I felt a hand on my arm and I

was yanked back, smacking into his hard chest. I looked up at him and for a second I could swear I saw concern on his face, but that couldn't be right.

Jae-Hyun only cared about getting his way, he wanted my daughter, and he wanted my career nothing else. The only reason he's shown me any interest since coming back into my life was just to continue the same sick mind games he played on me years ago. I wouldn't fall for it this time.

Once I had my balance back, I pulled out of his hold and snatched my arm back. For my own sanity, I couldn't have his hands on me.

When I looked at him, there was a brief moment where it seemed like I hurt his feelings by pulling away, but just as quickly as it was there, it was gone. "Where are you going?" He asked.

"It's obvious, I'm leaving you alone to get to know her, that's what you wanted isn't it." He reached out to grab me again, but when I looked at his hand, he stopped and dropped it back down to his side.

"I thought you would come with us." Come with them? Like a family outing, we weren't a family though. We were just two people who just so happened to have a child together. He was going to get the same amount of alone time with her as I was. I never agreed to spending that time with them.

I let out a sigh. I wasn't sure what his end goal was, but I was too emotionally drained for the day. "Jae, you wanted to have a day with your daughter, I'm giving you that. What more do you want from me?"

"I just told you, I want to spend it together, the three of us."

"Why?" I folded my arms across my chest and eyed him suspiciously.

He huffed and if I didn't know any better, I would say he was pretty close to rolling his eyes at my attitude, but I didn't care. "Because I asked you to marry me, that's why." He took a step closer to me and lowered his voice so Levi couldn't hear him. "Now come with us so Levi doesn't think mommy and daddy are fighting already."

The headache I was already feeling forming right between my eyes intensified and I bit my bottom lip. He knew what he was doing by putting me in that situation. There was no way I could say no now. A day as a family it is.

Chapter 12

RAYLEN

I WAS IMMEDIATELY REGRETTING my decision to go along with this whole family day thing. I stood in front of the big amusement park arch with the creepy ass clown overhead smiling down at me. My arms were folded across my chest, and I couldn't keep the annoyed look off my face.

Levi bounced up and down next to me, her excitement too much to contain. On the other side of her Jae-Hyun stood looking way too proud of himself just to come up with the idea of a day at an amusement park.

"This is what you wanted me to be a part of?" I asked. I couldn't take my eyes off the clown in front of me. Anybody who knew me knew clowns scared the crap out of me, but then again Jae-Hyun didn't really know me did he?

"Come on it'll be fun." Jae-Hyun held out his hand for Levi to take. Her small hand slipped into his and the two of them rushed off toward the entrance. I groaned and rubbed my hand across my face before following after them.

Jae-Hyun paid for our tickets and let Levi drag him off towards the rides. Why was I even here, they didn't look like they would even notice if I went home right now. The first ride Levi dragged him too was the merry-go-round. Lucky for them, since it was later in the day on a Thursday, the lines weren't long.

Levi stood on her tiptoes trying to see over the few adults in front of her. Jae-Hyun noticed Levi and without hesitation, he scooped her up and placed her on his shoulders. He was a natural. Being her father came easy to him. I almost robbed him of that, and that thought combined with the scene in front of me made me sick to my stomach.

Levi turned to face me, a huge smile on her face. She lifted her arm high and waved it back and forth at me. I smiled and waved back. She looked so happy, and I loved seeing her that way. I sat down on the bench across from the line queue where I could have a good view of the two of them on the ride. Part of me wanted to take out my phone so I could capture this moment, but the other just wanted to sit and enjoy it.

The line moved forward, and the crowd filed in. I watch Levi pick the brown horse with the bright pink and white bridle. Jae-Hyun picked her up and sat her on the horse, grabbing the golden bar sticking out of its back and standing next to her. The loud music began playing and the ride started its rotation. I zoned out watching them, so many thoughts in my head. Was this our lives now, family outings where I was left to watch the two of them bond while I sat on the sidelines?

Was the attention we were getting now permanent, or would he turn out to be the type that prioritized his job. Afterall, that was how all this started wasn't it. He only blew back into our lives just for the sole purpose of getting me to sign with the company he works for. Even going as far as trying to get me to sign an exclusivity contract with him. Was that so he could be in Levi's life, or did he just want to expand his roster of writers that bad?

"Hey, why didn't you join us?" Jae-Hyun jogged towards me, Levi in tow. I hadn't even realized they got off the ride.

I looked down at Levi and smiled. I didn't want her to know how uncomfortable I was with this entire situation. "Are you having fun bunny?" I ignored Jae-Hyun's question, I didn't feel like it needed an answer.

"Momma, Hyunny said I could get cotton candy." I didn't think it was possible, but her smile grew tenfold.

I gave Jae-Hyun a side look. "Hyunny?" I asked.

He shrugged. "I don't mind it, it's much easier to say than my actual name."

"Sure bunny, I'll get you some cotton candy. Wait right here." The cotton candy stall was right next to the merry-go-round. The sweat old lady behind the counter smiled at me when I ordered two cotton candies.

I slipped her the bills and she handed me the sweet treats. When I turned to head back toward Levi and Jae-Hyun, I almost collided right into him. I slipped and almost fell on my ass. Jae-Hyun reached out and slipped a hand around my waist, holding my weight and pulled me so I didn't fall.

"What the hell?" I asked when I was finally able to catch my breath.

"I didn't mean to scare you." He stared into my eyes and squeezed me a little tighter. He smelled delicious and his lips were just so close. If I wanted to, I could just lean forward a little and I would be touching them. They would feel so good on me right now. I wonder if he would push me away if I tried to kiss him.

"I was just coming to ask you if you were feeling ok?" His words snapped me out of the trance I was in. I pulled out of his hold and took a step back. He almost had me again.

"I'm fine." I wasn't fine, I was far from fine, but I wasn't his concern. He should focus on building his relationship with Levi and Levi only. I was just the girl he accidentally impregnated.

"You're clearly not fine, will you just tell me what's wrong already." My temper was getting the best of me in this moment. I can't believe he would ask me something like that, like he didn't know full well what my mood was about. Less than 24hours ago, he was threatening to ruin my career and take my daughter from me if I didn't agree to marry him and now here, he was trying to get me to play house with him like we were just one big happy family. We weren't, and he couldn't force us to be.

"Look, you're here to spend time with Levi, don't worry about me. I don't even know why you invited me along in the first place. What do you want from me Jae?"

He opened his mouth to respond, but something over his shoulder caught my immediate attention. The park bench where I had been sitting moments before while Levi and Jae-Hyun road the merry-go-round was empty. When I say empty, I mean Levi was nowhere to be seen.

I pushed past Jae-Hyun, dropping the two sticks of cotton candy on the ground as I did. My walk quickly turned into a jogged the closer I got to the bench. Her colorful backpack sat on the bench but where the hell was she? I turned to look at Jae-Hyun expecting him to answer the question I hadn't asked but should have been so obvious. When he didn't respond quick enough and instead stood there staring at me in confusion, I voiced my concern.

"Where the hell is my daughter?" Jae-Hyun's eyes grew wide, and he looked over my shoulder at the empty bench, almost like he was expecting Levi to suddenly appear. He looked around from left to right before his eyes finally landed back on mines.

His mouth opened, but no words came out. I didn't have time for this, I looked to my right at the path that led further into the park and took off running. I didn't even bother to look behind me to see if Jae-Hyun was following.

Honestly, I couldn't care less if he was. This was his fault. He wanted to meet her, be a part of her life and instead of doing what a parent should and keeping an eye on her, he took the first opportunity he had to concern himself with things that weren't relevant anymore.

He didn't like my mood? That's bullshit, if he didn't like the energy I was bringing to their daddy daughter time, he could've just stuck to the original plan of him spending the day with Levi alone. Then again, it's a good thing I was here if he was going to be this irresponsible.

I ran past the swing ride. Smiling children sat in the metal seats, the bar placed firmly in their laps. They laughed and swung their legs just as the ride began to lift into the air. None of them were the child I was looking for though. Next was the giant spaceship ride. There was a pretty long line for that ride, mostly adults. That ride was known for spinning people around in a circle at an unnecessarily high speed until they inevitably got sick, but there was a height limit to that ride, so she couldn't be there.

"Wait!" I heard Jae-Hyun yell after me before he grabbed my arm. I didn't even turn around, I just snatched my arm away and tried to run off again. This time however, he was quicker than I was. He grabbed my arm again, stopping me in my tracks.

"What?" I shouted at him, drawing the eyes of everyone standing in line at the spaceship ride. I didn't mean to scream that loud, but I was panicking, and he was slowing me down.

"We can't just keep running around the park looking for her, there's too many people. We need a better plan then that." I chewed on my bottom lip. Rationally, I knew he was right, but I couldn't seem to get my brain to stop running all the possible scenarios of what happened to her.

The only thing that I could get my mind to focus on was the rage I was feeling right now and the person I was most angry with, just so happened to be standing in front of me right now.

"This is your fault." I said balling my fist up and launching it into his chest. He stumbled back slightly, but it barely seemed like he felt it. "Why didn't you keep an eye on her. What kind of father are you." Jae-Hyun flinched at my comment and by the time I was done shouting, I was out of breath, and I had a sharp shooting pain in my head.

"Momma!" My heart skipped a beat when I heard that voice. I looked around to see where it was coming from. "Momma!" I heard again and turned around, my eyes immediately snapping toward the small ride right behind the spaceship ride. There sitting in a bright blue bumper car was Levi. She waved her hand excitedly, completely oblivious to the amount of stress and terror she had put me through in the last 5 minutes.

I breathe a sigh of relief and pulled away from Jae-Hyun once again, running in the direction of the bumper cars. Jae-Hyun was close behind me. By the time I made it to the attraction, Levi was coming out of the exit gate. I scooped her in my arms and squeezed her tight. All the fears and anxiety I had Just experienced disappeared almost immediately once I had her in my arms. I could see Jae-Hyun stare at the two of us, his face was pale, and I could read the emotion on his face loud and clear. Guilt. I wasn't in a place to comfort him though, how was I supposed to trust him with her again after this.

Chapter 13

RAYLEN

"SO YOU'RE REALLY GOING **through** with this?" Olivia laid on her side on my couch, watching me scramble around getting ready for my date.

"Why wouldn't I, he asked." I ran into my bedroom to grab the black clutch I had left on my bed and started tossing all the items on my bed into it. Lip gloss, gum, small bottle of perfume, keys and of course my phone. "How do I look?" I turned to face Olivia, smoothing down the black faux leather skirt I was wearing.

Olivia got to her feet and look me up and down. It was a little cold out tonight, so I decided on a black skirt, a short sleeve black turtleneck, and black thigh-high boots. I slicked my hair into a high bun with a few curls left out to frame my face. Tossed on my small gold chain with the letters, L.E.V.I written in cursive with matching gold hoops and I thought I looked good. Olivia looked me over, making a few circles around me.

I huffed at how long it was taking her to respond, she was doing a lot for no reason. I knew she wasn't the happiest that I was going on this date, but I didn't know why. She was the one that set me up with Luke in the first place, so what was the issue with us giving a date a real shot.

Finally, she stopped in front of me and gave me one last up and down before rolling her eyes and returning to her place on the couch. "You're cute I guess."

"You guess? That's all I get?" Her mood was putting me in a bad headspace before my date. "What's your problem, why don't you want me to go out with him?"

"Bitch are you serious." She looked at me like that was the stupidest question anyone has ever asked in the history of questions. "Why would I support you going out with him when you have all this chaos going on with Mr. Baby daddy."

I let out a sigh and grabbed the red and black tweed pea-coat off the back of the couch. Why we were even talking about this right now, I had no idea. I told Olivia about what happened yesterday at that stupid amusement park. Why would she even think I wanted to have anything to do with Jae-Hyun after that? He can't be trusted with Levi so how was I supposed to be comfortable allowing him to be around either of us.

"Look, I'm done talking about this. I think you have enough on your plate with those sexy twins following you every-where, maybe you should worry about that." I didn't have to look at Olivia to know that she was less than happy about my comment.

I don't know what her issue with them were, but she avoid-ed all their attempts at pursuing her like the plague, so who was she to judge me for giving a guy who clearly likes me a chance. She should be cheering me on.

"We are not talking about them or me. This is about you, you know this is a mistake." Of course like always, avoiding that topic.

"Why are you even taking up for him, he threatened to take me to court for full custody of Levi."

"And you believe he would really do something like that?" I never thought the Jae-Hyun I knew would ever put me through something like that, but then again, it's been proven time and time again, that this isn't the same Jae-Hyun I use to know. He could take me to court just because I hurt his feelings yesterday and then what would I do besides tell the judge that he lost our daughter.

A custody battle between the two of us would get ugly in-credibly fast and I really didn't want to put Levi through that. At some point I would have a conversation with him about how this whole *sharing a child thing* would work between the two of us, but there was no way in hell I was signing that contract or thinking about him and his stupid feelings tonight.

Tonight, I was going to go out with a cute guy and try to see if there really is a spark between the two of us or if it was only the alcohol talking that night.

I chose not to answer her question. Instead, I checked the time on my phone. 8:45pm. Luke and I agreed to meet up at 9 at a cute little restaurant around the corner from my apartment. I had just enough time to get downstairs and to the restaurant. "Thanks for babysitting for me." I didn't wait for Olivia's response, I just headed out the door and down the hallway to the elevator.

Living on the fifth meant it took no time at all for me to reach the busy New York streets. I pulled the long overcoat tighter around me when a strong gust of wind hit me and picked up my pace.

I made it to the restaurant in five minutes and immediately saw Luke standing in front of the building with a huge bouquet of red roses. He wore a black leather jacket and dark slacks. His blonde hair wild all over his head from the wind, my heart skipped a beat. Not for the obvious reason, the nervous excitement one would feel when they go on a date with someone new, but because for a split second I wished it was someone else standing there.

I plastered a smile on my face and crossed the street to the restaurant. The moment Luke saw me coming, a huge smile spread across his face.

"I hope you didn't wait too long."

"It doesn't matter, you're worth waiting for." He held out the flowers to me and I took them, giving them a sniff. This was the second bouquet of flowers I've gotten from Luke. The first I had thrown away almost immediately after he left. I felt bad about that now, but at that moment I didn't feel like I had a reason to keep them, I had no intention of seeing him again.

Luke held out his elbow for me to take and led me into the restaurant. It was a quaint little restaurant. Small enough that I could see the backdoor that led to the kitchen from the door, but still large enough that it didn't seem like none of the tables were right on top of each other. There was a decent amount of people inside, but it wasn't overly crowded.

Luke led us to the podium where the host was waiting to check our reservation. He gave them his name and they led us to a table right in the center. He pulled out my chair for me while I took off my jacket.

"Wow, we didn't even have to wait. I'm impressed." Luke chuckled and took his seat across from me, throwing his jacket over the back of his seat.

"The doctor card helps sometimes. Coming here almost every week helps the rest." Luke picked up his menu and began flipping through it. I wasn't sure if he meant to make that last comment, so I decided to tease him about it a little.

I leaned forward and placed one elbow on the table, leaning my face on it and gave a small gasp. "You're telling me I'm not your first?" He dropped the menu to look at me and I gave him my best sad face, but I couldn't hold it for long before the both of us burst into a fit of laughter.

"Does this mean you're feeling better after the other

night?" He asked. My laughter subsided but I tried not to let my smile drop completely. I grabbed the cloth napkin off the table and placed it across my lap, gently smoothing it out. I didn't want to think about what happened the other night because all it would remind me of is Jae-Hyun's face when I told him he was a father.

"Yeah, I'm feeling much better. It was just a long week at work, and I needed to blow off some steam." I knew he was referring to Jae-Hyun snatching me off the dance floor but that wasn't something I wanted to talk about especially not with him and definitely not on our date.

"Olivia told me you're a writer, is that right?" He asked. "Anything I've read?"

I looked up at him and smiled. "It depends, I would have to know what you like to determine if it's your cup of tea." The waiter chose that moment to come to the table and take our orders. I hadn't had a chance to look over the menu yet, so I let Luke pick out something he thought I would like.

For the amount of people here and the size of the restaurant, the food came surprisingly fast. We ate in silence, the occasional joke here and there but overall, just like I feared it was pretty awkward. It's been a while since I've been on a date, so I wasn't sure if maybe I just didn't know how to do it anymore, or if there really was just no spark between the two of us.

The rest of the meal went by in a little bit of a blur. We got to know each other, I found out he's the oldest of three other siblings, a younger sister and two younger brothers. When he wasn't working at the hospital, he loved working out and hiking. He asked me all the right questions about myself and even seemed 100% interested in everything I said. Luke was the epitome of the handsome, sweet, boy next door. I just wasn't sure if he was the one for me.

Luke and I stood outside my apartment building, me awkwardly staring at my shoes and him staring at the top of my head. I had a feeling he wanted me to invite him upstairs, but I didn't think it was fair to lead him on any more than I had.

Olivia was right, going on this date was a bad idea. I knew there would be nothing more than a friendship between the two of us, but I was so determined to prove that I could have a relationship with anyone other than Jae-Hyun, that I played with Luke's feelings.

I stood in front of the heavy wooden door with the giant glass window in the middle, nervously fidgeting with the stems of the roses Luke had given me. He stared me down and I felt bad that I wasn't going to say to him what I knew he wanted me to.

"I had fun tonight." I said trying to fill the awkward silence.

Luke smiled and nodded his head. "Maybe we could do it again sometime."

I looked down at the flowers not wanting to see any signs of disappointment on his face. "Yeah, maybe we could." Luke took a step forward and leaned in for a kiss. My mind raced trying to determine if I was going to let him kiss me on not. Maybe I should, just so I could see if I felt something.

Right when his lips were coming down on to mine, my body

moved on its own and I turned my head sideways. Luke's lips landed on my cheek, and it was like the cold temperature around us had multiplied. I could feel the immediate shift in Luke's attitude when he pulled away.

I expected to look at him and see his same smile or maybe since I rejected his kiss, a little bit of sadness, but I didn't see either of those things. Instead, he looked annoyed and frustrated, like not kissing him was something so far out of the realm of possibility.

"Sorry I-" Luke cut me off immediately with a groan. He ran his hands through his blonde hair in frustration.

"So, you've just been playing me this whole time?" His voice got deeper, but louder. I looked around at all the people walking past us on the street.

"Keep your voice down." There was no way he was really going to make a scene in front of my apartment building, was he? "No one is playing you, I just don't think I feel that way about you."

Luke gave me a dry laugh and snatched the bouquet out of my hands, tossing it on the wet ground. "I think we were feeling each other just fine the other night. Olivia told me about all your *baby daddy* trouble. Is that why you won't kiss me." The way he used the phrase *baby daddy* set my teeth on edge.

The on and off headache I had been feeling for the last couple of weeks came back in full force. I shocked myself with the amount of rage I was feeling so quickly. Not just at him but at Olivia too for telling him my business, but I would deal with her later. Right now, it was time to put Luke in his place, nobody talked to me like that.

"First of all, I don't want to kiss you because I just don't want to kiss you and there's nothing else to it. Now, if you want to read more into it, we could just say that you didn't wow me on our date, and it has nothing to do with anything else." Luke scoffed like he didn't believe what I was saying, but I didn't give him a chance to cut me off.

"Second, what I have going on in my private life is my business and considering I won't be seeing you again, it's far from something you should be worrying about in the future."

I turned my back to him, opening the door to the building and slipping inside, letting the door slam close behind me. I can't believe him, that date was a complete waste of time. I wish I would've known he was a tool before I even agreed to go out with him, I could've stayed home and spent the night with Levi.

The elevator ride up to my apartment seemed longer than normal more than likely because without the distraction of Luke, I didn't have anything else to think about but Jae-Hyun. I let out a sigh of relief when the elevator dinged signaling it had arrived at my floor.

It was almost midnight, Levi should be sleep which meant I could grab some wine out of the fridge... maybe something a little stronger and drown my sorrows while watching a movie. That sounded like the perfect end to a shitty night.

That's how I thought I would spend my night, but I guess the forces of the universe had other ideas. I flicked the light on the moment I walked through my apartment door and there sitting on my couch staring at me with the biggest frown known to man on his face was Jae-Hyun. I almost jumped out of my skin when I saw him. What the fuck? How the hell did he get in here?

"Enjoy your date?"

Chapter 14

RAYLEN

"**H**OW THE FUCK DID **you** get in my house." I threw my purse on the couch next to him and my jacket on the back of it.

"Are you really in a position to be asking questions like that right now?" Jae-Hyun got to his feet and walked around the couch, backing me into the wall. It wasn't until this very moment that I realized he was shirtless, nothing but a pair of black sweatpants on.

He placed both hands on either side of my head, effectively trapping me in place and leaned in close. My eyes dropped to his bare chest. "Who did you go out with?" I took a deep breath which I realized was a huge mistake when I inhaled his delicious scent. He smelled cleaned like he had just taken a shower but with just a hint of mint. Did he shower here? Was he in my shower? Naked, water dripping down every inch-. "Are you going to keep staring or are you going to answer the question."

I turned my head to the side so I wouldn't keep staring at him. "You must be slow or something. What makes you think I owe you an explanation for anything I do." Jae-Hyun grabbed my chin and snapped my head back to look at him.

"It was the guy you were with the other day, wasn't it?" I jerked my chin out of his grip and slipped under his arm. I didn't even bother turning around to face him, instead I headed down the hall past Levi's room to mine. I needed to put as much distance between us as I could. I didn't want to talk about my date with Luke especially with Jae-Hyun. Who by the way has yet to answer my question about why he was here and where the hell Olivia was.

I walked into the bathroom that was connected to my bedroom and slipped the turtleneck over my head. The zipper to my skirt came next followed by turning on the faucet to the shower. I just wanted a nice hot shower some wine and a movie. I really feel like I wasn't asking for too much.

When the mirror over the sink began to steam up, I tried to close the bathroom door, but Jae-Hyun held out his head to stop me. "You're really not going to answer my question?" He asked. I rolled my eyes and turned my back to him reaching for the scrunchy holding my bun in place. The moment I tugged it out, my hair burst free from the restraints and fell down my back. I threw the band on the counter by the sink and gently massaged my scalp, hoping to lesson some of the tension. It only helped relieve the headache a little, but Jae-Hyun standing here throwing question after question at me that had nothing to do with him, was not helping.

"I'm not leaving." He said again and honestly at this point I didn't care. I wasn't in the mood to have another altercation with another man that insisted on acting like they were entitled to anything from me tonight. I didn't need any loud noises like an argument waking my daughter up in the middle of the night either.

"Do whatever you want Jae, just like you always do." I pulled the zipper on my skirt down the rest of the way and let the material slip and fall to the cold tiled floor, pooling around my feet. Underneath my clothes I was wearing a black lacy bra and matching panties. Maybe I was feeling optimistic tonight that my date with Luke would go well and we would've ended up back at his place, thank God that didn't happen.

I started fidgeting with the clamps on my bra next, it took me just a second to unsnap the hooks and slip the straps from my shoulders. I hated to admit it, but I was highly aware that Jae-Hyun's eyes were on me. Even though my back was to him it was like I could feel his eyes traveling all over my body and it made the already steam-filled bathroom even hotter.

Maybe if I ignored him long enough, he would just go away. Not likely, but it was still a nice thought. "Are you just going to stand there or are you going to get out. I have nothing to say to you, so you-" I couldn't even finish my sentence before Jae-Hyun had me slammed into the glass side of the shower. My breasts and stomach pressed flat against the cold glass. I gasped from the cold contact but also the hot, smooth skin pressed into my back.

Jae-Hyun leaned down by my ear. "Was this your plan, to make me angry and then seduce me?"

I let out a nervous laugh, I didn't know where he was going with this. I would believe he was really angry if it wasn't for the fact that I could feel the hot, hard outline of his dick pressed against my ass. It was satisfying to know that I could still get him like this, but I couldn't let anything happen between us. That would only end badly, at least for me it would.

"I didn't have a plan, you weren't even supposed to be here." He reached up and threaded his fingers through my hair.

Getting a nice fistful, he pulled, jerking my head back slightly. He leaned in and brushed the tip of his nose against my neck, inhaling deeply.

"Then are you saying you wore these panties for another man? Are you trying to piss me off?" The deep, rough tone of his voice mixed with the feel of his erection on me was doing crazy things to my body. His hand slipped around my waist and past the band of my panties until it reached the center between my legs. I adjusted my stance to spread my legs just a little further apart. I shouldn't want him to touch me at all, but my body wasn't listening to my head and my head wasn't taking too kindly to my heart either.

"Maybe you like it when I'm pissed." The first contact his fingers made with my pussy, my hips jerked forward on their own. I wanted more. "She sure likes it when I'm pissed. You're soaking my fingers." I could feel him smile against my neck before he stuck out his tongue and licked the side of it all the way up to my ear and then pulled the lobe between his lips sucking lightly.

I gasped and a shiver ran down my spine. It was hard not to moan but I didn't want to give him the satisfaction. "Does she want to see how mad I really am?" He asked.

I licked my suddenly dry lips before I spoke. "Kiss my ass Jae."

He chuckled and pulled back. "I plan to." He spun me around, so my back was against the steamy shower. I looked him up and down before my eyes landed on the large tent in the front of his pants. I licked my lips again. I forgot how big he was.

"Lose the panties." He commanded.

My eyes shot back to his. "What?"

"You're taking a shower, right? Lose them."

I folded my arms across my chest and up until this point I had forgotten my boobs were on full display for his eyes. "Get out."

Jae-Hyun smiled and mimicked my movement folding his arms across his chest. "In your dreams."

I rolled my eyes. Fine if that was how he wanted to play

it. I turned back around so I was facing the shower, hooked my fingers into the thin straps of my panties and pulled. The fabric fell to the floor, and I stepped out of them and right into the shower. I tried to close the door behind me, but Jae-Hyun grabbed the door and snatched it back open. When I turned around to face him the black sweatpants he had been wearing before were gone. Either he was never wearing underwear, or he got rid of them just as quick as he got rid of the sweats.

He stepped in pushing on my chest until my back hit the shower wall, closing the door behind him. He gave me no chance to protest, because the next second his lips were on mine. He pressed his body firmly into mine, letting me feel every hard line and ridge of him.

I missed these lips, every time they were on me, it felt like my body was coming alive for the first time. Why did he have this power over me?

The kiss wasn't slow and gentle like we were getting to know each other again after being apart for so long. It was hungry and urgent like we hadn't lost anytime, but so much in the same instance. Jae-Hyun slanted his head slightly to deepen the kiss, his tongue slipping past my lips.

He lifted my leg up and hitched it on his hip. He pulled back long enough to look between us, lining his dick up with my pussy. "You ready to take me love?"

I didn't respond, I was too mesmerized by those lips that were just on me, and I would say whatever to get them on me again. I nodded my head.

"Hands on my shoulders." He commanded and I obeyed immediately. The next second Jae-Hyun pushed inside of me to the hilt. I gasped and dug my nails into his skin.

My knee buckled and if I didn't have such a good grip on his shoulders I would've fallen in the shower. "Fuck you're tight. This was almost over before it even started."

Jae-Hyun grabbed my other leg and lifted it forcing me to wrap them around his waist. That first snap of his hips into me forced the groan from my lips.

Jae-Hyun moaned, pulled almost all the way out and snapped his hips forward again. "Fuck Raylen." He leaned down by my ear and groaned. "You feel amazing." The way he whispered in my ear before licking the shell of my ear had the muscles in my pussy clenching. If he kept that up, I wasn't going to last long.

The pace of his hips increased and so did the force of them until he was practically fucking me into the shower wall. I was loving every second of it.

He was hitting all the right spots which no one else but him had ever been able to do. It was like he knew how to scratch all my itches in just the right way to have me climbing the walls.

The first tingles of my orgasm began in my belly, but it built so fast I had no time to try to slow it down. I locked my ankles around Jae-Hyun's waist and wrapped my arms around his neck, clawing at his back and trying to catch my breath.

"Jae." I moaned out. "Jae, I can't hold it anymore." My entire body started to seize up.

I couldn't control the next moan that left me a little too loudly, so I did the next best thing. I leaned forward and bit into Jae-Hyun's shoulder. He grunted and began moving his hips even faster.

"That's right love let it out. I'll take it all for you." Like a tightly coiled spring that just couldn't take anymore, my control snapped. The orgasm consumed me and almost drowned me. I bit down harder on his shoulder. It was surprising to me that I didn't draw blood.

Just as fast as it hit me, it was gone, and I felt completely boneless. Jae-Hyun pumped into me a few more times, digging his fingers into my thighs before he let out the sexiest moan I've ever heard, and I felt his hot come spray inside of me. It was almost enough to send me into a second orgasm.

He kissed me on the cheek before he leaned back slightly to look at me. "I'm not done with you yet. I'll make you remember who you belong to one way or another."

Chapter 15

RAYLEN

I **WAS WEARING A hole** in the carpeting of my living room floor. Levi had woken me up this morning and thank God by the time she did, Jae-Hyun was already gone. I don't know when he left or how he managed to do it without me hearing him leave, what I do know is that he left me a note on my dresser saying that we needed to talk and that he would be back later. I can guess what he wants to talk about.

I can't believe I let last night happen. I can't even remember how many times we went at it, first the shower then the bathroom counter and then a few times in the bed. I passed out at some point during the night and woke up completely naked under the blanket with the urge to take another shower.

It was so good, I wished I regretted it more than I did. Honestly, I haven't had that many orgasms in my entire life. Of course, it just had to be with the one man I hated more than anything.

A knock at the door stopped my pacing. Looking over my shoulder, I could see Levi's bedroom door closed which I was thankful for I didn't really need her to be a part of this conversation and I didn't know what excuse I would give her to close it myself.

I scrambled to the door, nervously rubbing my hands on my sweatpants before I turned the knob, what was I going to say to him? Did he expect me to sign his stupid little contract after what happened last night? Before I was so sure I would never do that, but now my feelings about it were all over the place.

I didn't have the door all the way open before Olivia burst through it and pushed it the rest of the way open. I took a step back so I wouldn't get hit in the face with the door.

"What happened on your date last night?" She asked tossing her bag on the couch. I took a deep breath closing the door and turning to look at her. I owe her an ass whopping for telling Luke my business and for letting Jae-Hyun into my apartment. She was really fumbling on the best friend front.

When I turned to face her, it almost looked like she was angry at me which was odd because she was the one so very in the wrong here.

"What the hell is your problem?" I folded my arms across my chest and stared her down.

She narrowed her eyes at me. "Did you sleep with Luke?"

I can't be the only one that has to take a second to fix their face before they speak because your first initial reaction when someone says something so outrageous is to be completely disrespectful.

I know the look on my face had to be one of pure disgust. That she would even ask me a stupid question like that was pretty offensive, that I went out with him at all or even admitted to finding him attractive was stupid on my part.

"Are you slow or something, why would I go anywhere near that douche's dick?" Yeah, I should've took more than a second before I responded. To bed fair the guy tried to embarrass me in front of my apartment last night after a subpar date and a failed attempt at getting a kiss out of me.

"Well then why did he tell me you did?" This time there was no holding back the disrespect.

"And you believe that roid raged, ass munching loser over me telling you I didn't." I still consider that comment holding back from what I really wanted to say about him. "And while we're on the topic of communication, how the hell did Jae-Hyun get into my apartment last night and where were you?"

Olivia actually had the common sense to look a little guilty about my comment. I guess she thought she was just going to come over here and check me about a lie her garbage human of a coworker told her, and I wasn't going to address the fact that she left my kid with the person who just the day before lost her in an amusement park.

"Look, I know you're mad," She held up her hands in surrender. "But he made a very compelling argument."

"And what the hell kind of *compelling argument* could he have made to you to convince you to leave him in my apartment alone with my daughter?"

"The most obvious one, he's her father." There was a long stretch of silence where we both just stared each other down not saying a word. Olivia kept her hands in the air, and I kept mine folded across my chest.

We both stared at each other unblinkingly for what seemed like forever until finally, I gave up. I sighed and dropped my arms to my side. I didn't have the energy to fight her, and it wasn't like she could have really stopped Jae-Hyun from wanting to see his daughter last night. Him staying and making her leave and then spending the night however, was completely avoidable. That was something I would be discussing with him though.

"Fine, whatever. I have other things on my mind right now anyway."

I plopped down in the stool at the counter and Olivia took the seat next to me. "Is this about your date, what happened?" I rolled my eyes. I really wish I could forget I ever went out with Luke. Better yet, I wish I could forget he ever existed.

"The date was just as garbage as he was, but my problem was what happened after I got home from the date."

Olivia sucked her teeth. "How angry was Jae-Hyun when he found out about the date? He kept bugging me about where you went, but all I told him was that you would be back in a few hours."

So that's what happened. Knowing Jae-Hyun, he probably got frustrated with her because she wouldn't tell him every single detail of my whereabouts and made her leave out of spite, just like a child. He probably just made an educated guess when I came back so late. The way I was dressed might've given him an idea I'd been out with a guy.

"He was angry alright." The look on Olivia's face when I told her that Jae-Hyun and I had spent the entire night having this amazing, mind-blowing sex, might've been funny if I wasn't so disappointed in myself.

By the time I was done telling her every single freaky detail of what happened with the exception of his dick size, which she wouldn't shut up about, Olivia was on her feet and pacing in the exact same spot I was just in. I feel bad for that part of the carpet, there would be a giant hole in it before my life finally settled down.

"So, does that mean you're going to sign the contract he gave you? I mean you might as well if you guys are back to smashing and it would be good for Levi."

I chewed on my bottom lip. On one hand she had a point, last night changed something between the two of us and it would be beneficial to Levi to have both of her parents in her life, at least that's what I hoped was true. On the other hand, I think last night was a one-time thing. Despite what Jae-Hyun said last night, I think it's safe to say the two of us just needed to get it out of our system and now that we have, it shouldn't happen again.

"I don't think I have another choice. It's clear he isn't going to let this go and it would be nice for Levi to have her father in her life. At least with the marriage part of the contract, I won't have to worry about him disappearing on her again."

Olivia nodded in agreement, I guess that settles it then. When I talk to Jae-Hyun, I'll be telling him that I agree to the terms of his contract.

"So, you're going through with this?" After calling Jasmine to let her know my plans to sign with Jae-Hyun's company, she contacted his assistant and had it sent over by carrier to my apartment. The giant stack of papers sat in front of me and every time I tried to flip through it, I got a massive migraine. It looked to be the exact same contract that Jae-Hyun had sent me before, the one that included tanking my career and taking Levi from me.

Part of me was still feeling spiteful and not at all interested in signing a contract with those threats in it, but the other part knew that in the long run making sure Jae-Hyun couldn't duck out on his responsibilities as a father was much more important.

Olivia sat on the couch behind me with her legs propped up on the armrest. She had agreed to stay with me while I signed the paperwork for moral support. Levi had gone to one of her friend's apartments to play on the floor above us. I was grateful for that, I didn't want her here while I was sipping wine and signing away my freedom.

"I don't have a choice, it's what's best for Levi." I flipped to the last page where a couple sections required my initials and at the bottom my signature.

Olivia thought about it for a second then clicked her teeth before sitting up straight. "This is a really crazy contract, are you sure you don't want to have a lawyer look it over?"

"I can't do that. It's a contract signing my work over to an entirely new company, I don't want my agency to catch wind of it until after everything is finalized. Besides that, it was embarrassing enough to let you read it, there's no way I want anyone else to know this thing exists and that I'm going to sign it."

I couldn't believe I was going to sign it myself, so I could only imagine someone else's reaction to this. "I don't like that he's making you feel like this is your only option. I wanted you to tell him about Levi because it was the right thing to do and he owed you an explanation, but this contract is ridiculous."

She was right and I knew that, but what choice did I really have. It was clear that he had the means to ruin my life if I didn't do what he wanted. How could I jeopardize anything when it came to Levi. He could take her from me, or worse he could abandon her all together if he thinks I'm being too difficult when it comes to his relationship with her.

Letting out a sigh, I leaned forward, picked up the pen and let out one final sigh. My shoulders slumped a little, but I knew what needed to be done. Signing my name right on the dotted line, I had to accept my fate. If I had to sacrifice for my child, then that's what I was going to do.

Chapter 16

RAYLEN

I'VE HAD A SINKING **feeling** in the pit of my stomach ever since I signed on the dotted line. Olivia left a little while after I finished signing the contract, to give Jae-Hyun and I space to talk about it when he came back over. Part of me thought maybe telling him in an office setting would be better since this was meant to be all business, but another part of me knew that this wouldn't be that at all.

The more I thought about it the more I was already regretting accepting Jae-Hyun's offer. If we took this to court, there was no way he could win. Afterall Levi had spent her entire life with me. She didn't know Jae-Hyun. Not to mention what happened the other day at the amusement part was not putting him in a good light. A judge had to see that as the only parent she had known her entire life, it was best that she stay with me and stayed away from Jae-Hyun.

I barely had a chance to finish the thought when I heard somebody knock at the door. I took a deep breath and squared my shoulders. I needed to look confident and not like someone who was losing a battle to the enemy. Reaching for the doorknob, I looked down at my appearance one final time. I wasn't wearing anything special, just a pair of skinny jeans and an off the shoulders white top with a few ruffles.

Would he consider this dressed up? I wouldn't want him to think I put in extra effort for him. It's too late to change now, time to face the music.

One final brush of imaginary lint from my pants leg, and I yanked the door open. I gasped when I saw who was at the door because I thought last night was the last time I would ever see this person.

Luke rushed in past me before slamming the door behind him. I stood there stunned with my mouth hanging open because this was not the person I was expecting to see right now. He aimed an angry stare at me and folded his arms across his chest.

"Luke, what are you doing here?" I asked. I took a step back as he approached me. My heart was racing but I wouldn't let him see the fear I was feeling, so I opted to match the same amount of anger that was rolling off of him in waves.

"I'm only going to ask you this one time and one time only so don't lie." His voice was deep, but he spoke softly which made him all the more intimidating. "The guy who showed up at the club the other night. The one you told me not to worry about, did you fuck him last night?"

I tried swallowing the lump that instantly began forming in my throat. He knew, but how is that possible. The fear I was feeling before only doubled with the knowledge that he had somehow figured out what happened last night between Jae-Hyun and I. There was no way Olivia told him something like that. Not only did I just tell her, and she hadn't had enough time to pass the message along to him, but she wouldn't betray me like that, regardless of what she told him before about Jae-Hyun and I's relationship.

That could only mean one thing, Luke had been watching me.

Did he just stake out my apartment to see who was coming and going? I was beginning to wonder if he was actually the one that brought me home from the club that night or if he just followed me until he figured out where I lived. I never actually asked Olivia how I got home, I just took his word for it that he was the sweet guy that just wanted to make sure his date made it safely home.

It was creepy enough that he was going around his job telling anyone who would listen that we had sex at the end of our date instead of what actually happened which was me telling him to suck it.

"What are you ta-"

"Don't lie to me!" He shouted. I flinched and took another step back. He wasn't even this angry last night when I turned him down. The look on his face seemed a little unhinged and with there being no witnesses around unlike on the streets outside my building, who knows what he was going to do. Right now, I was extremely glad that Levi wasn't here.

"I'm not trying to lie to you," I held up my hands trying to get him to calm down but at the same time still taking small steps away from him. I needed to figure out a way to either get him out of my apartment or get to my phone.

"Did you have sex with him last night?"

My heart skipped a beat, but I tried to keep my composure. "I don't know what you heard Luke, but what I do and who I do it with is none of your business." I held my hands up higher hoping that if he saw I was at his mercy, he would calm down. The look on his face never softened. On the contrary, it looked like the red that was already present on his pale skin had darkened significantly. "Luke, let's just t-"

"No!" He shouted. Luke turned and swiped everything off the island counter. Glass cups and plates shattered on the floor. The metal cutlery made a loud booming noise when it hit the wooden floor, echoing in the deafening silent apartment.

I flinched and stumbled back until I was pressed against the wall. Luke rushed me, reaching out and wrapping his hand firmly around my throat. He leaned in so his nose was touching mine. "I saw him leave this morning. He was here all night."

"You've been playing me this whole time haven't you." He clenched his teeth when he spoke. "You think you can play me like I'm stupid and then have your rich boyfriend swoop in to make me look worse."

I clawed at his hands gasping for air. I couldn't respond to his accusations even if I wanted to, so instead I was forced to stand there and listen to every delusion he had developed. "What is it that you wanted from me?" He yelled. I continued clawing at his hands unable to speak. "Do you two do this a lot, find some unsuspecting guy to humiliate just to get your rocks off? You two are sick and you're going to pay for playing with my feelings."

He tightened his grip and a tiny squeak escaped from me. I tried everything I could to get him to release me. Clawing at his hands, his neck, his face, anything I could get my hands on, but he was like an unmoving statue. Nothing phased him. Luke was going to kill me, and it would be my own fault for hurting his feelings.

A loud cracking noise could be heard ripping throughout the small apartment. Luke was snatched away from me and pushed against the back of the sofa. He stumbled and fell over it. A loud thump could be heard as his head struck the corner of the coffee table.

I crumbled to the ground, my knees feeling like jelly. My lungs filled with much needed air. I reached up and touched my tender neck, trying to will the tremors in my body to stop.

"Raylen, are you ok?" Someone called out to me, and I felt a gentle hand on my shoulder. My vision was fuzzy so I could barely make out who it was. "Answer me, are you hurt anywhere?" I tried talking but my throat felt so scratchy, anything I said came as very painful croaks.

The hand on my shoulder disappeared and I watched the figure stand up and make their way over to a stumbling and disoriented Luke. I watched as they shoved them through the open door and out into the hallway. After a few shouted words, Luke disappeared.

Slowly my vision began to clear. A pair of black, shiny dress shoes stepped in front of me. My eyes traveled up the length of his legs, then his torso and neck until I looked into the deep brown eyes of the man who gifted me Levi eight years ago. Jae-Hyun.

He grabbed my elbow and helped me to my feet, running his eyes over my entire body as he did. "How do you feel?" He asked.

I pulled my arm out of his hold and chose to lean against the counter instead. "I'm fine." The rough tone of my voice wasn't fooling anyone.

"What the hell was that? Do you make it a habit of letting random men put their hands on you like that? Have they ever done that to my daughter?" His rapid-fire questions were making the pounding headache I had even worse.

I clutched my head. "Will you stop shouting, you're overre-acting."

"I'm overreacting? Are you-" Jae-Hyun paused and took a few deep breaths to calm down before he spoke again. "How many times has he done this before?"

I leaned into the counter more before answering. "He's never done this before, I honestly don't know what happened."

Jae-Hyun stared me down before sighing and reaching for my hand again. I tried pulling away, but this time he wouldn't let me. He pulled me over to the couch and sat me down. I couldn't lie, getting off my unstable feet might've been just what I needed. The fog in my head cleared and even though my vision was still a little blurred, I could remember what I was doing before Luke got here. I looked at Jae-Hyun and I could recognize the evident concern on his face, but was it concern for me or was he selfishly thinking of what he would say to Levi to explain my death.

"How did you know what was happening?" I asked.

He turned and pointed to the shattered dishes on the floor. "I heard the smashing when I knocked, and when you didn't answer I broke in." Looking at the front door, I hadn't even noticed until now that it was hanging slanted off the hinges. So that's what that loud splintering noise was.

"Don't worry about anything, I'll hire some security for you just in case he decides to do something stupid like come back." Jae-Hyun got to his feet and looked around. "You know, better idea I should just find you somewhere else to stay all together. I could find us something so much better than this little apartment."

Here he goes again, just the same as all those years ago, always trying to control things. I should've known nothing had changed. He was the kind of man that loved to make decisions all on his own and not consider those around him. It was his decision to leave me and our unborn child and never look back, just like it was his decision to swoop in now and play the hero while he made me look like the bad guy.

I might need him to help me advance my career and I might want him to be a part of Levi's life, but I didn't need him for anything else. I had been doing just find all these years and I do not need his help.

"Jae-Hyun, what makes you think I have any intentions on moving anywhere with you or because you say so?"

Jae-Hyun tore his eyes away from the ceiling to look at me. "What do you mean, isn't it obvious."

"What's obvious?" The more he talked, the more my face scrunched up in confusion.

"If we're going to be married of course we would live to-gether in the same house as a family. This apartment isn't big enough for the three of us. Our daughter needs a place with a yard so she can run around and play, just like a normal kid."

I shot to my feet, the rage too much to stay seated. "What the fuck do you know about what a normal child needs?"

Jae-Hyun shot me with an equally angry look. "I know enough."

"You don't know shit. You think after all these years, you can come in here and play father of the year. You abandoned us!"

"I abandoned you? You kept my kid from me for eight years." Jae-Hyun took a step toward me until we were almost nose to nose. "You think it's right to keep a father from his daughter?" His voice sounded almost as menacing as Luke's voice, so much so that I actually flinched, taking a step back, but I wouldn't let him think he could intimidate me. I wasn't the same little push over I was all those years ago.

"And how the hell did you expect me to tell you anything when you up and disappear without so much as a fucking note. What happened all those years ago is your fault, so don't blame me for all the time you missed out on." Before he had a chance to come up with any more excuses, I held up my hand to stop him from talking.

"It doesn't matter now, I asked you to come here so I could tell you I signed the contract, but I have my own stipulations. One being that just because I'll be your wife does not mean I want to live with you. I'm not a hooker so buying my work in exchange for sexual favors is just not going to happen. If that is a problem for you, we can forget about this whole thing." I folded my arms across my chest and waited for him to tell me all the ways in which my terms were unreasonable.

He didn't say anything even though I could tell how much it was killing him not to. Instead, he just plopped down on the couch. I sat down next to him, unsure if I wanted to make eye contact with him.

The embarrassment of what he had just walked in on was finally starting to set in. Luke didn't seem like the violent type, but after last night I knew something was off. To see his switch flip like that and he attack me to the point I thought I was going to die. Then to make it worse, it had happened when Jae-Hyun had a front row seat.

"What about tonight, the two of you can't stay here tonight.

You don't even have a door." I sighed. He was right, there was glass and wood splinters all over the floor. I could clean up the mess, but there was no way I could get that door repaired this late. I would never let Jae-Hyun play the hero of my story, I didn't need him.

"We'll be fine, we can stay with my mom." I lied. He didn't know about my relationship with my mom, but I would rather take my daughter and stay at a hotel then stay with him. I got to my feet, reaching for my phone that had slid off the couch and onto the floor. I was just barely able to reach it without completely tipping over and falling face first on the floor.

"You can just stay with me, at least until repairs can be made to your apartment." I looked up at Jae-Hyun he hadn't moved from his spot on the couch and the look on his face told me he was determined to get me to say yes.

I huffed. "Did you not just hear-"

"It wouldn't be permanent, just for a night or two. We're going to be married, I can at least do this much. Besides think of Levi"

I really didn't have the energy to fight with him about this and staying at a hotel wasn't ideal especially with Levi after what just happened. What if Luke followed us there and tried to hurt us, then what. I guess the wolf was finally getting his chance to lure in the lamb.

Chapter 17

OLIVIA

I DON'T KNOW HOW **many** times I was going to apologize to Raylen before I felt better about what happened with Luke. Every couple of minutes I was looking over my shoulder trying to get a peek at her. Just to make sure she was ok.

"I can feel you staring at me." She said keeping her back to me. "Please knock that shit off." I stopped pretending like I was really folding her clothes. I hadn't put one piece of clothing into the empty suitcase sitting in front of me for at least an hour.

"I'm so sorry." What did that make eighteen times at his point in the last three hours. I couldn't help it, my heart had nearly jumped out of my chest when she called and told me what happened. I had just left her apartment.

Her running theory was that Luke had been sitting outside her apartment, watching her. So did that mean he waiting until I left and that's when he decided to attack. The thought of him watching me leaving Raylen's apartment with the knowledge that she was there with just Levi sent a shudder down my spine.

"I heard you the first million times, you don't have to keep saying that." Raylen stood up pulling down her lounge shorts that had ridden up while she was squatting on the floor. "I told you, you don't have to be sorry. You didn't know the douche would be a humongous psycho."

I got to my feet too, plopping down on the end of her bed and folding my legs in front of me. "I should've though. I mean I've worked with the guy for years now and I had no idea."

"I know you wouldn't have tried to set me up with him if you did, so don't worry I'm not mad." I let out a sigh. She might not be mad, but I was kicking the shit out of myself for not vetting the guy better before I set him up with my best friend.

"Now you know," She said smirking at me. "no more blind dates."

I snorted and threw myself back on her bed. "Of course not. You have Mr. Sexy captain save a hoe what do you need a blind date for." Right on cue Jae-Hyun came strolling through the door carrying a couple flattened cardboard boxes under his arm.

"Raylen, the guys just got here." He announced before he

looked up and saw me. He eyes grew wide when I sat up and immediately my eyes flew to her.

As soon as I snapped my head in her direction, her head jerked up to the ceiling. "What guys?" I asked narrowing my eyes at her.

She looked at Jae-Hyun when I asked my question, looking for help. "What guys?" I asked again, gritting my teeth. It was like I could see the water droplet emoji by the side of Raylen's head when she gave me an awkward laugh.

"I could've sworn I told you..." She trailed off.

"You didn't tell me shit. So spill, are the twins coming." I asked. The Bennett twins, specifically Danny Bennett had been the bane of my existence since second year of middle school. They both picked on me relentlessly and then when we got to high school they made it their ultimate mission to derail any relationship I found myself in.

Even after we graduated, they took some type of sick joy in these weird subliminal sexual jokes I could barely under-stand. Especially Liam, who acted like he hated me any time it was just the two of us but said the most out of this world raunchy stuff whenever his brother was in earshot.

I don't know what I did to deserve their dislike, but after all these years the feelings were now mutual.

Raylen knew how I felt about the twins which is why in high school she tried to limit the amount of group activities we had. She knew wherever Jae-Hyun went, the twins wouldn't be far behind.

She fidgeted from side to side, not making eye contact with

me. Traitor.

"I can't believe you." I jumped to my feet. I wasn't sure if I wanted to attack her, or just leave. On one hand I knew she could kick my ass, on the other I would feel bad leaving her when I promised to help her pack up her apartment as an apology for the whole Luke situation.

"Hello gorgeous." My head snapped in the direction of the voice to see Danny Bennett standing in the doorway just behind Jae-Hyun.

I watched as his eyes drifted down from my face to my bare legs and then to my bare feet. I wanted to be comfortable while I helped Raylen pack, so I opted for lounge shorts as well. I was massively regretting that decision at the moment.

"Those shorts should be a crime." He joked never taking his eyes off my legs. I turned and snatched the throw off the bottom of Raylen's bed and wrapped it around my waist.

As much as I couldn't stand him and he clearly couldn't stand me, something about the way he looked at me always made this tingling feeling erupt in my stomach. Like he could see straight through what I was wearing. It made me feel warm and like I might do something stupid.

I hated that feeling, which made me hate him even more.

"Ok." Jae-Hyun said clapping his hands together to get everyones attention. "Let's save all this awkwardness for another time." He dropped the flattened boxes he had under his arm onto the floor before picking up one and putting it together.

I kept my eyes on Danny, tightening my grip on the blanket

around my waist. He smiled at me, giving me a wink before disappearing back through the door.

"See that wasn't so bad." Raylen joked. Yeah, that's it. Even if she could kick my ass, first chance I got I would be seeking my revenge.

Another hour went by at what felt like a snail's pace. Raylen stuffed clothes for both her and Levi in to a few empty boxes and I packed up her office, making sure to box up any documents she needed for her current manuscript to work on while she was away.

The guys spent most of their time draping plastic tarps across every piece of furniture. Jae-Hyun said it could take a few weeks to fix the damage to the apartment and according to Raylen he claimed he was in talks with the property managers about getting better security for the building.

I wasn't sure what kind of money an editor made, but the way it seemed like he was throwing it around, it had to be a significant amount.

"Ok." Raylen said as she walked into the living room from her bedroom carrying another box. That had to be at least number five. For someone that swears this is just a temporary situation, she sure was packing like it was permanent.

"How about we take a break and get some food." I looked around at all the clutter still left to be packed. Between the five of us, we could probably be done in maybe another hour then again, we would still need to load everything up into the pick-up truck Jae-Hyun rented and then help them unload at his house.

Out of the corner of my eye I could see Daniel plopped down on the plastic covered couch. He crossed one leg over the other and sat back with his arms folded behind his head. He had pulled his hair back into a tiny ponytail. His hair had gotten so long, I wondered if he had any plans to cut it. The twins always seemed like they went out of their way to do things that made them look completely different from each other.

They could only do so much though, it wasn't like they could change their faces. Besides the hair and the extra tattoos Daniel had, the only real way to tell them apart was their eyes.

Those mix match eyes Daniel had, one brown and one blue were so incredibly easy to get lost in. It was how I almost fell for his bullshit flirting a few times over the years and why it was best I kept as much distance between us as possible or I would do something I would absolutely regret.

I watched as he stretched slightly and the black t-shirt he was wearing pulled taut giving me an eyeful of those sexy ab muscles. My mouth was practically watering at the sight. I couldn't stand him, that didn't mean I couldn't appreciate how incredibly sexy he was.

On the other side of me, Liam leaned against the island. He wore a matching fitted v neck that rose up slightly when he placed an elbow on the countertop. Between that messy brown hair that he usually kept so well maintained and uni-formed for his day job and that extra defined "V" that disap-peared below the waistband of his jeans, he was walking sex.

Fuck, watching them lifting and moving boxes for the last few hours, their muscles straining against their clothes had been brutal and had made me so incredibly horny.

I couldn't be around them for much longer.

I cleared my throated and silently prayed my voice didn't come out sounding hoarse. "We're almost done, we might as well power through." I plastered a smile on my face, hoping they couldn't all see how desperate I was for them to agree. The sooner we were done with this and I could put some distance between the twins and I the better.

This whole situation only made it that much more appar-ent that it's been a while since I've been good and fucked. The last guy I went out with, Paul, he was sweet and really sexy, but just like always the twins miraculously showed up that night and ruined everything. The way they surrounded us, it was no wonder I hadn't heard from him since.

I was really starting to wonder if they somehow put a tracker on my phone or something, because how they hell did they always know where I was. It was always when I was hanging out with a guy too. The whole thing was a little more than suspicious if you ask me.

Excluding Paul, I cant remember the last time I had a good tumble in the sheets and I was really feeling deprived at the moment.

I looked at Raylen silently pleading with her, hoping that she would catch onto the situation. In the corner of my eye, I saw Liam lift his head and look behind me. There was a strange look on his face and then he smirked. I turned my head slightly and saw a similar expression on Daniel's face.

They were plotting something. Something I don't think I want to be involved in.

I looked at Raylen just as she opened her mouth to speak. Before she could get a word out, Jae-Hyun stepped next to her and threw his arm around her shoulders, pulling her in close. He was smiling at Daniel.

Oh, so they were all scheming. Noted. We'll see the next time I vouched for Jae-Hyun's shitty behavior with Raylen.

"I think a break sounds like a great idea." Liam chimed in.

"But-" I tried again, but Daniel cut me off.

"How about this. You two go get the food and," Daniel got to his feet, walked over and patted Jae-Hyun on the shoulder. "We'll stay here and keep packing." I could feel my eyes bugging out of my head.

There was no way in hell they were going to leave me here alone with them.

"No I-" Daniel cut me off again, pushing Jae-Hyun and Raylen towards the door.

"My stomach is literally touching my back. I don't think I can work anymore without any food."

The closer they got to the door, Liam made his way around them, lifting up the "caution" tape that was now supposed to be considered the door. "I'll come with you guys, there's no way you can carry all that food back yourselves." Oh hell no, now it was just going to be me and Danny? "Don't worry about them. By the time we come back, all this will be completely cleaned up."

Raylen tried to turn around, but Jae-Hyun pushed her under the caution tape. "They're right Raylen. I can hear your stomach growling already, we'll hurry back."

I stood there with my mouth hanging open, my shoulders slumped and my hands just hanging at my side while I watched the twins stand in the hallway waving the two off. "I'll meet you guys down there." I couldn't believe it, the three of them had set me up and now I had no excuse to leave.

My eyes darted toward the hallway. Raylen's office was the last room that still needed to be finished up. I might have to be stuck here with Danny, but I didn't have to be in the same room as him. As long as I stayed away from him until Jae-Hyun, Raylen, and Liam came back with the food, I might just make it out of this in one piece.

I turned on my heels and made a beeline for the back, but I wasn't quick enough. A strong slightly tanned and deliciously veiny forearm snaked around my waist.

"And where are you running off too gorgeous?" Daniel asked as he hauled me off my feet. I gasped at the change in altitude and squirmed trying to get him to release me.

"Put me the hell down?" He leaned down by my ear and inhaled sharply causing a shiver to run down my spine.

"Why would I do that, I'm enjoying the way you're rubbing your body against me." My body froze completely stiff. "Aww, you're such a party pooper." He whispered in my ear.

"Daniel, put me down." I repeated through clenched teeth. My heart rate was kicking up at an alarming speed. Fuck, I needed to get out of here. I could already feel the sweat building on my forehead from his body heat.

"I don't know. Hey Liam, what are you thinking?" He called over his shoulder. A few seconds later, Liam stood in front of me. His arms folded across his chest, biceps bulging. He stared at me with a sick smirk on his face that made my palms instantly begin to sweat and the space between my legs flood with moisture.

"Well I just don't know either Danny. Do you think she ever learned her lesson for going out with that tool the other night?" He asked, his eyes never leaving mine. I rolled my eyes at his comment. I really wish they would get over whatever claim they think they had over me. I didn't belong to either of them and I could date and fuck whoever the hell I wanted.

Daniel hummed behind me. "That is such a good point dear brother. Liv baby, have you learned your lesson?"

"Don't call me that." I hated when they called me Liv, the way they said it was like a gentle carrass against me, it made me feel like they had some type of affection for me and I knew that wasn't true in my head, but my heart liked to beat to a different drum so to speak.

I looked at Daniel just in time to see him give me a pathetic attempt at a wounded look. "Doesn't sound like she did to me."

Liam huffed. "Well I guess we'll just have to fix that now won't we." Without saying another word Liam headed down the hall toward Raylen's empty bedroom. Daniel followed closely behind, carrying me with him.

I tried again to get him to put me down, but he was way too strong for me. I really needed to hit the gym. In between manuscripts, Raylen would go to the gym religiously, saying things like that body didn't just happened. I guess when you really thought about it, it made sense how she stayed in shape, she had horrible eating habits when she went on those writing benders where she didn't leave her office for an entire day.

Thank god she had me for a best friend or Levi would starve. I kept telling her I would start going with her, but everytime it came down to it, I would always make up an excuse not to go, feeling entirely too lazy on the rare off days I had from the hospital.

I regretted it every time I looked in the mirror and saw the love handles I had begun forming getting bigger and bigger. I was regetting it even more when I couldn't fight off this behemoth of a man.

When we walked through the doorway, Liam was standing in the middle of the room. That cocky look still plastered on his face. There was still things on top of Raylen's dresser, but the drawers were empty.

We didn't need to pack up her bed or the covers on top of it, the guys just settled for throwing a plastic tarp on top of the entire thing.

Without warning Daniel tossed me onto the bed and I plopped down ungracefully right in the middle of it, landing on my stomach. I scrambled to turn around and face them. The two of them towering over me menacingly had me scrambling back toward the headboard.

"You guys are really funny." I said trying to keep the quiver out of my voice. Not taking my eyes off of them, I scooted to the edge of the bed throwing my legs over it. A quick glance at the door and then back at them, told me I wouldn't make it there before they caught me.

"I don't have time for the games, we have work to do."

Daniel's face lit up. "That is one thing we can agree on."

Liam nodded his head. "Absolutely. Danny, would you like to go first. After all you did call dibs first, it's only fair." The smile on Daniel's face only got wider as he closed the distance between him and the edge of the bed. He leaned forward and placed both hands flat on the bed and narrowed his eyes at me.

"Oh this is going to be fun."

Chapter 18

RAYLEN

STARING AT ALL THE **items in** the fully stocked fridge but not actually seeing them, all the events of the night played out in my head. I'm not sure why I was under the impression that I would be able to get some sleep after all that.

I shifted from one foot to the other on the cold hardwood floor. All I had on was a t- shirt and a pair of panties. Jae-Hyun was so eager to get me out of that apartment, he didn't even have everything set up for us at his house.

He claimed he had everything I would need which was clearly a lie considering there was no guest room made up, at least not one with a bed big enough for both Levi and I to share. He expected me to share a bed with him and because of that, I was now standing in front of an open fridge, staring off into space, trying to avoid laying next to him for as long as I could.

I let out a sigh before finally closing the door when I heard the impatient clearing of Jae-Hyun's throat. I looked at him then immediately turned away to look at the dark oakwood cabinets when I realized he wasn't wearing anything but a pair of boxers.

What was wrong with me? I was a grown woman who has had sex with Jae-Hyun numerous times so why now was I too shy to even look at his bare chest. Maybe it was because when we had sex eight years ago, his chest didn't look like that. A chest that was now a lot tanner and with much more defined abs.

"How long are you planning on staying up?" He asked. I looked at him out of the corner of my eye and watched his muscles bulge as he folded his arms across his chest.

"I'm hungry, I'll go to bed after I'm done." Jae-Hyun sighed again. Dropping his arms to his side, he came over to the fridge and gently pushed me out of the way.

"What are you hungry for?" He asked, swinging the fridge door open. When I didn't respond, he gave me a shrug and started grabbing several Tupperware containers of all different sizes and sat them on the middle of the kitchen island, kicking the door closed with his bare foot behind him.

The moment he started popping open the different lids, my nose was instantly filled with a bunch of different smells. Smells that made my stomach seize from hunger. We hadn't finished moving everything until almost midnight. Between that and getting Levi settled in, it's been hours since I've had any food.

Taking a few steps closer, I peeked over his shoulder and saw an array of different dishes, some I could immediately tell were spicy others not so much, none of it were things I could actually recognize.

"What is all this?" Jae-Hyun smirked but didn't take his eyes off the food.

"Perks of a Korean mother. She always sends me a little something homecooked. Have a seat." Jae-Hyun pointed to one of the stools on the other side of the bar.

I followed his orders, never taking my eyes off the food. Jae-Hyun had never been too interested in telling me about his family before. I never even got around to learning about his Korean culture, but I guess since it's also Levi's culture, it's time I learned something even if it's from the man that I least wanted to be around.

Jae-Hyun slid a dish over to me, it smelled spicy but also a little pungent. It was bright red with a thick red paste smeared everywhere.

"What is it?" I asked. I loved spicy food, but it made me incredibly nervous that I couldn't name one thing in the dish.

"You still like spice right, it's called kimchi. Try it, I promise you'll like it." I stared at Jae-Hyun before staring back at the dish. Jae-Hyun reached out and handed me two metal chopsticks. As hesitant as I was, I was also incredibly curious, and that curiosity won in the end.

I took the chopsticks from him, secretly grateful for all those late-night sushi runs so I wouldn't have to embarrass myself in front of him. I picked up a piece of the kimchi, examining it probably much closer than I needed to. The closer I looked at it, the more it looked like part of an onion, but it didn't smell that way.

"Will you just eat it already." I stared at it for a few seconds longer before taking a deep breath and closing my eyes. I shoved it in my mouth and began chewing, bracing for whatever horrible taste that was about to hit my tongue.

That wasn't what happened, the first crunch was surprising but once the different spices hit my tongue, I realized how delicious it actually was. I looked up at him only to see a huge grin spread wide across his face.

"Delicious right?" He asked and all I could do was nod my head in response. I grabbed another piece then another until my mouth was practically stuff with the spicy vegetable.

I didn't stop eating until Jae-Hyun snatched the bowl from me. I looked up and reach out ready to take it back, but he pulled it further out of my reach.

"This is not meant to be a main dish, it's a side." He put the lid back on and slid it off to the side. "I'm glad you like it though."

He opened another lid and slid the container over to me. This time I was able to immediately recognize what it was. "Bean sprouts?" I asked. I picked up one bean sprout and looked at it closely. I wasn't sure what expression I had on my face, but I know it probably wasn't the most enthusiastic.

I dropped the bean sprout back into the dish and slid it back across the table. "No thank you." I said folding my arms. I've tried bean sprouts in the past and was less than impressed. I guess the best way to describe it was just plain disgusting and I wasn't really interested in reliving the experience.

"You didn't even try it." He argued pushing it back toward me.

"Don't need to, I'm good."

Jae-Hyun looked at me, then at the container of bean sprouts and sighed. "Just as stubborn as you were all those years ago, aren't you."

The annoyingly condescending smirk that I've grown to hate, made an appearance on his face. I could feel my body temperature rising as I felt the full-on rage completely take over my body. There he goes again treating me like a spoiled child instead of the grown woman who has spent the last eight years raising his child all by myself.

I got out of my seat and walked around the island. I had to stand on my tippy toes just to get remotely close to eye- level with him. I am not the same girl you abandoned all those years ago. Get that through-"

I couldn't even finish the thought before Jae-Hyun wrapped his arms around my waist crushing my body to his. His lips smashing to mine before I even had a chance to make a sound.

He slanted his lips over mine, gently stroking his tongue over my bottom lip. Just like I always had before, I surrendered to his assault. Why did it have to feel so good to be in this man's strong arms. I hated this man for what he did to me and my daughter, but why was I having such a hard time holding on to my anger at the moment?

Jae-Hyun slid one hand down my back and over my ass, gripping a good handful before lifting me up, giving me no choice but to wrap my legs around his waist. Jae-Hyun broke the kiss just long enough to slide the dishes on the island to the side, lifting me up and propping me in their place.

He leaned in again, recapturing my lips and effectively forcing me to lie back on the marbled surface. I wrapped my arms around his neck and my legs around his waist locking my ankles. I wanted him to have no choice but to stay right where he was, making my body feel like it was on fire.

Jae-Hyun pulled away from the kiss just enough to kiss the side of my neck and before I even had a chance to register what he was doing, he had grabbed the edges of the oversize t- shirt I was wearing and pulled it up over my head. I was left lying there in nothing but a pair of pink panties.

He reached down and grabbed the edges of my panties attempting to slide them down, but I grabbed both of his hands attempting to stop him. Call it temporary clarity, but the thought of being exposed to his hungry eyes in the bright lighting was making me question if this was a good idea or not. Anybody could walk in on us, including Levi.

"Maybe we shouldn't be doing this." I voiced my concerns. I half expected him to pull away now that I had basically thrown a bucket of cold water on our heated exchange, but instead his eyes slowly roamed over my body, taking in every inch of it. He leaned in until his lips were just barely touching mine.

"You can deny it all you want. I know you've been aching for me to fuck you again on the nearest flat surface since the other night in your shower." Jae-Hyun reached up and gently brushed a stray curl from my face. A shiver went down my spine at his words. I wasn't going to admit it out loud, but my body spoke volumes. I wanted him just as badly as I did the other night, maybe even more.

Flashes of our time together played through my head. In his room, my room, in the backseat of his beat-up little car and more recently, in an office at that banquet and in my shower. Anywhere we could get even the smallest amount of alone time together and we were ripping each other's clothes off then and it seemed like it would be the same now. I wanted that again. I've been trying to keep my distance from him when all I could think about was letting him drive that massive dick between his legs into me repeatedly.

He didn't wait for me to respond. Jae-Hyun slipped his arm around my waist, pulling me close so my body was flush against his. He leaned in and whispered in my ears. "I still remember what you taste like, how badly do you want to feel my tongue on you again." My mouth went dry, and it suddenly felt like there was a river flowing between my legs. Why did this man have this effect on me. I should never have let this happen, but it was too late now, I was too far gone.

I slipped my hands around Jae-Hyun's neck pulling him in

for another kiss. I could kiss these soft, delicious lips all day if he would let me. Jae-Hyun removed my hands from his neck, pulling away and standing up straight. He took hold of my panties once more, ripping them from my body before I had any chance of further protests.

He let the shredded material slip from his fingers, a sadistic smirk on his face. Jae-Hyun grabbed my hips and flipped me over on my stomach earning him a surprised squeak from me.

"What are you doing?" I questioned, leaning up on my elbows trying to get a better view of what he was doing behind me. He pulled my hips further down so my ass was pointing straight up toward the ceiling.

"I'm taking what's mine." He leaned in and pressed his face right to my core, lapping away at the juices that flowed freely. My body quivered and moan after moan bubbled up in my chest. He wrapped his arms around my lower back and pulled me in close, and at the same time I pressed back into his waiting mouth, enjoying the feel of his tongue flicking at my clit.

Jae-Hyun was playing with my body like an expert, like he just knew all the right ways I liked to be touch. Even some ways I wasn't aware of myself.

My orgasm hit me so fast, it knocked the wind out of me and from the position Jae-Hyun had me in, I was incapable of moving so all I could do was let the force of it completely consume me. The flicks of his tongue slowed but never fully stopped, making it seem like it was lasting forever. I was starting to feel a little lightheaded from the strength of it.

Jae-Hyun pulled back, letting go of my waist. I collapsed onto my elbows as a result. My eyes closed and my face enjoyed the effects of the cool marble countertop. I could hear rustling coming from behind me, but I didn't have the strength to lift my head and find out what was going on.

It wasn't until I felt Jae-Hyun put his hands back on my waist and I felt the scorching head of his rock-hard dick pressing against my slit that I knew what he was up to.

I flinched but didn't have the energy to pull away, I honestly don't know if I would've even if I did have the strength to. Jae-Hyun tightened his grip and pressed forward, stuffing me full of him, inch by delicious inch. The satisfying burn at the initial invasion was gone in a flash, immediately followed by overwhelming pleasure. The way he was going, he was going to make me a slave to it.

Chapter 19

JAE-HYUN

IT DIDN'T MATTER HOW **many** times we did this, I couldn't get enough. I let out a groan when her tight muscles clamped down around my dick. This pussy of hers was enough to bring any man to their knees and that's just what she was about to do to me. My knees buckled slightly and I clenched my teeth and took a few deep breaths to prevent myself from coming. Fuck, just sliding into her almost made me lose it, I didn't want this to be over yet.

Raylen looked so sexy in this dim kitchen lighting. Her body glistening from the sweat she just worked up when I was eating that delicious pussy. On her stomach, her ass in the air to do with whatever I wanted. The flushed satisfied look on her face that quickly changed to one of pure ecstasy when I slid inside of her. Her eyes closed, her mouth opened in a silent scream, what man wouldn't love this image of the one they've been in love with since high school.

It took a minute or two for me to collect myself enough to move, but once I did, I was practically salivating to fuck her unconscious, just like I did last night. I had climbed onto the counter as well so I could get a better angle. The granite was cold on my knees, but it was completely overshadowed by the fire raging throughout the rest of my body. I took a handful of Raylen's ass in both hands, making sure to give those plump cheeks a hard squeeze. I know how much she liked it rough, she would never admit it, but her body couldn't lie to me.

She moaned again and threw her hips back into me, almost knocking the wind out of me. No other woman's body could ever compare to hers. Everything about it fit me perfectly.

"Jae." She moaned out. "I need it." I licked my suddenly dry lips. She wasn't the only one, that's for sure. I pulled my hips back so my dick slipped almost completely out of her and slammed them forward again. My pelvis slapped against her juicy ass, making it jiggle slightly and make a sound that had my balls drawing up slightly. Fuck I wanted this to last longer, but it didn't look like I was going to be able to make that happen tonight. My only choice was to make sure she enjoyed this to the fullest.

I repeated my previous actions, but this time Raylen screamed out. I snaked my arms around her waist, never slowing the pace of my hips. Her pussy felt phenomenal, like I could stay in it for the rest of my life. Unfortunately, we didn't have that kind of time, I would hate to traumatize Levi by letting her walk in on mommy and daddy fucking on the kitchen counter.

Pulling Raylen up so her back was flush against my chest, I slipped one arm up to grab a handful of her gorgeous breast and the other went up to cover her mouth. As much as I enjoyed her sexy screams, we would have to put a pin in that for when we were really alone.

Raylen reached back and gripped my hips pulling me in tighter. My pace doubled and I watched as her breasts bounced from the force. Her moans grew louder and by the way her tight muscles were clamping down around my swollen dick, I could tell she was close. That's good, because I don't think I could hold off much longer. I leaned down by her ear, licking the shell of it.

"Are you finally ready to admit who you belong to?" I whispered into her ear and at the same time I tightened the grip I had on her breast. She moaned and I felt her entire body shiver.

"Go ahead and tell me." She shook her head no. Just as stubborn as always. I pumped a few more times and right when I felt her body tremble again, I stopped.

I held her body firmly against mine and didn't move an inch. It wasn't long before she began trying to move her hips back onto me, but every time she did, I pulled my hips back even further. Her hips started moving in a circle and then came the begging. I moved my hand from her mouth so I could hear every sweet plea.

"Jae, what are you doing?" She gasped out. "Don't stop." She probably didn't realize, the whining was turning me on even more. "Please." He hips rotated and she tried once more to scoot back on me, but I wouldn't let her.

I leaned into her neck and sunk my teeth into the sensitive skin right below her ear. Not hard enough to draw blood, but just enough to make this wet pussy of hers clench down on me. Her body was begging for more, but I wouldn't give it to her until she told me what I wanted to hear.

Raylen moaned when I bit down harder before I pulled back and licked the spot to soothe it. "You know what I want to hear. Let me hear it and I'll let you come."

She tightened the grip she had on my hips and tried to pull me forward, but I didn't budge. "I can't here you." I growled low and kissed her cheek. She was practically panting now and I knew I had her right where I wanted her.

"You." She whispered.

"Louder love, I can't here you."

Raylen whimpered slightly and spoke again, this time much louder. "You. I belong to you." I couldn't help the smile that spread across my face. I loved the sound of that. When her brain wasn't so lust filled, I would make sure she remembered she said that.

"Good girl." I pulled back and pushed her forward so she was on all fours on the counter. Getting a good grip on her hips, I pulled my hips back and snapped them forward over and over unrelentingly. Giving her everything she wanted.

I could feel my own orgasm building in my balls, but there was no way in hell I was going to come before she did. I reached out where our bodies connected, the sight so sexy, it made me want to come right then and there.

Using the juices that were flowing from her body, I got my fingers nice and slick before gliding it down until I reached that sensitive bundle of nerves. I pressed down, her hips jerked and she shouted out.

"Jae." She gasped. "Fuck! I'm so close." I pressed the bundle again and then gave it a little tweak. Just like that, Raylen came completely undone. Her entire body shook violently and her inner muscles clamped down so hard around me, I didn't have any other choice but to follow her over the edge.

I let out a roar as she milked me dry, taking everything I had to give her. A shudder went through me and for just a second I swear I saw something bright and white behind my eyelids. When I finally had nothing left to give, I pulled out of her and collapsed on the cool countertop next to her. Raylen fell over after me, her ass falling perfectly into the curve of my lap. I wrapped my arm around her and pulled her close enjoying the drastic difference of the sticky hot skin against me versus the cool smooth texture of the granite.

We laid there silently trying to catch our breath, but it wasn't until I started feeling the first signs of exhaustion kicking in that I realized it was time to get up. While it would be nice and a little funny to just lay on the kitchen counter for the entire night butt ass naked, there was no way we could do that with Levi in the house.

I climbed off the counter, grabbed Raylen by her legs and pulled her down to the edge. She barely reacted to the action, if it wasn't for the soft snores coming from her, I might actually be concerned. It was a nice boost to my ego that I was able to wear her out this way.

I scooped Raylen into my arms, ignoring the pile of clothes on the floor and the few knocked over containers of food that had fallen off the counter in the midst of all our tumbling, I would come back for those later.

Down the hall and to the left, my bedroom door stood open. I laid Raylen right in the center of the bed before going into the connecting bathroom and grabbing a washcloth with warm soap and water. She groaned in protest when I wiped her body down with the cloth. When I was done she rolled to her side and curled into a ball, continuing her sound sleeping.

I went back to the bathroom and did the same to myself before climbing into bed right next to her, pulling her close. I brushed the curls from her neck and gave her a soft kiss there. I was tired but it took a second before I could fall asleep, too many thoughts running through my head.

Why was Raylen so resistant to us being together? I know she was upset about me leaving eight years ago, but it's not like I didn't try to contact her that entire time I was gone. Matter of fact, I reached out a few times and she never once returned any of my messages, not even to tell me I had a daughter.

If anyone has a right to be angry with the other, it's me. I'm the one that had to miss out on eight years of my daughter's life because she just chose not to tell me. If I hadn't come back to look for her, I probably would never know.

Since finding out about Levi, we haven't actually had a serious conversation about what happened all those years ago, I had my secrets, and it was clear she had hers. I think it's time she knew the truth, I couldn't keep lying to her and she owed me the same in return.

Chapter 20

RAYLEN

"**I DON'T UNDERSTAND. WHY** jump through all those hoops if you were just going to sign with him anyway and why keep it from me?" Jasmine leaned forward in her seat and placed both of her elbows on her desk. "He didn't seem so bad plus this isn't about him, this is about advancing your career and if he can help then I really don't see the harm in it."

After all these years that I've known Jasmine, she had no idea about my history. I had never told her the things that went on with my family and I especially have never told her about the sexy Asian stud that ripped my heart out and stomped on it just for the hell of it.

It wasn't that I didn't trust her, it was just something I wasn't too enthusiastic to talk about. Now that he was back and it didn't look like he was going anywhere, maybe it was time she knew how much of a heartless bastard he was.

She sighed. "Do you two have history or something?"

I sat forward in my seat and reached up tugging on the ponytail holder in my head. After a few tugs my curls came tumbling lose and I breathe a sigh of relief that the headache I developed the moment I put it in, immediately began to wane. "What makes you think we have history?"

"Don't play dumb with me. I saw the way your face turned six shades lighter when you saw him walk through that cafe door. Then you made me jump through all those hoops to make it very clear, that we would not be doing any business with him whatsoever. Now you're telling me you signed that contract after all." I didn't respond, I settled for staring at the designs on the giant rug she had in the middle of her office.

Jasmine sighed. "You have to tell me something. This isn't just about your career. After all these years together, I thought we were friends, and I would appreciate if you took into consideration how this would affect me as well."

She was right. It was wrong and selfish of me to not at least tell her why getting in bed with Jae-Hyun *Yuu* wasn't my best decision, for either of us.

"Almost ten years ago," My voice came out a little squeaky shocking both of us. "I was in my junior year of high school when I met Jae-Hyun Park." I looked up at Jasmine's face. I was expecting to see a shocked reaction but oddly I didn't.

Maybe my reaction to seeing him was all she needed to figure out we had a past. I cleared my throat before I began talking again. "He had just transferred in and as you can imagine, immediately I thought he was gorgeous and completely out of my league."

"Park?" She questioned. I couldn't blame her, I was confused when he told me his name was Yuu. I still didn't know why he lied about it.

"That was the name he went by when we met in high school." I said with a sigh.

"Ok, so you guys dated in the past, what's the big deal?" She said with a shrug. I wish it was that simple. I wish that all we had was a little high school romance, but it was so much more than that, or at least that's what I thought at the time. Maybe it was different for him and that's why things happened the way they did.

"We spent two years together. He was the one that started it all. He asked me out and for those two short years of high school, we were inseparable. Towards the end of senior year, he started to act differently." The lump in my throat began to expand and my eyes began to sting. I wasn't going to cry anymore, not over him. I had already shed all the tears I would ever shed over this guy. He wasn't getting anymore.

"Around the time he started becoming distant toward me, we had just had sex for the first time. Imagine that," I made a weird noise that sounded like a cross between a laugh and a choke. The anger I felt over the years came back in full force. "An 18-year-old high school boy dates a girl, takes her virginity, and then ditches her. Sounds like every corny teen movie ever written right?" I hated seeing the pitying look on Jasmine's face, so I decided to focus on the wall behind her head.

"After graduation, he disappeared. No text, no phone call, nothing. That day in the café was the first time I'd heard from him since then."

"I'm sorry Ray, I didn't know." Jasmine got to her feet and came around the desk to stand in front of me. She tried to touch my shoulder, but I flinched away from her. "That's not the end of our little fairy tale." I could feel the tears building in the corners of my eyes.

Clenching my teeth, I opened my mouth and just let the words flow, "It was six weeks later when I found out I was pregnant." The loud gasp that came from Jasmine filled the quiet room and didn't surprise me at all. No one ever expected little Ms. Good girl to get knocked up fresh out of high school, but like I said I thought I was in love.

Jasmine dropped to her knees in front of me. "Don't tell me." She spoke. I didn't meet her eyes. All I could do was shake my head as one painful tear slid down my face. I wiped at it angrily. After all these years, I thought I had finally buried these feelings, but I guess it doesn't matter how much time has passed, this kind of pain never goes away.

"Levi is his daughter and I've been responsible for raising her alone this entire time." Jasmine tried to reach out to me again and this time I let her. She wrapped her arms around me and pulled me in close.

"I'm so sorry that happened to you." She gave me a squeeze. "What did he say when you told him?"

I wiped at my face before answering with a shrug. "He was angry at me, but I couldn't understand how he felt like he had the right to be."

"What do you mean, of course he would be. You had his child all this time and didn't tell him about her."

I rolled my eyes and got to my feet pushing past her. "And exactly how the hell was I supposed to tell him she existed. He left me out of the blue with no way of contacting him. What was I supposed to do hire Harry Potter's owl to deliver the message?"

"I guess you have a point there, but maybe-" I turned to face Jasmine and held up my hand to stop her from talking.

"If you're going to tell me that he probably had a good reason, I don't want to hear it. There is literally nothing he could tell me that would make me forgive him for what he did to me. Any time he missed out on with Levi is 100% his fault and he was going to have to live with that."

Jasmine sighed and her shoulders slumped. "Fine, but if you feel that way why did you end up signing that contract?"

"Because he threatened to tank my career and try to sue for full custody of Levi. He didn't give me much choice." I don't think I've ever seen someone's face get so red so fast.

"He did what?" She shouted. I quickly crossed the room to her, shushing her and looking over my shoulder at her office door that was cracked open. I didn't need the rest of the office knowing my business.

If I was being honest, I held off as long as I could when it came to telling her. I wish I could've waited longer or maybe not have to tell her at all, but once I signed that contract, there was no way I couldn't tell my agent. As my friend I knew she would want to know the backstory of Jae-Hyun and I, especially after I have been dodging the question of Levi's father for years now.

"Keep your voice down."

"What do you mean *keep my voice down.* He threatened to take your child away from you, one that he abandoned in the first place all so you would sign a contract to work with him. Why are you not angrier?"

"I was at first, but what else can I do, he is her father. Plus, it might benefit Levi to have her father in her life." That's what I was greatly hoping was the case.

"And what if it only hurts the both of you in the end?" I really wish she wouldn't have asked that question, because honestly, I really didn't have an answer. Jasmine could be right, and I could be completely wrong. Jae-Hyun could break Levi's heart and disappear on her just like he did me and then what was I supposed to tell her.

I shrugged my shoulders and gave her the truth. "I honestly don't know, I guess I will just have to deal with that if it happens." There was one thing I could say with absolute certainty. If Jae-Hyun hurt Levi, I would move heaven and Earth to make sure he lived to regret every breath he ever takes again.

Chapter 21

RAYLEN

I **DUG THROUGH MY suitcase,** tossing clothes left and right over my shoulders. I hated having to live out of my suitcase, but Jae-Hyun said the door to my apartment wasn't fixed yet, so who knows how long it would take before we could move back in. He offered me half of his closet, but I didn't want to get too comfortable and have him thinking this was a permanent thing. He was already super unhappy with me taking all my valuables that I didn't want to leave behind and putting them in a storage unit instead of moving them into his home

Married or not, there was no way I was living with him. I wasn't stupid—I knew the only reason he even wanted this marriage had nothing to do with love. It was all about control. And while he might've had a little bit of an upper hand over me, I wasn't going to let him completely have his way.

A few hours ago, right when I had a really good flow going with my writing—Levi at school, absolutely no distractions—here comes Jae-Hyun being a distraction. He texted me, telling me to pick out something sexy to wear because when he got home, he wanted to take me out for dinner. When I told him to kiss my ass because there was no way that was happening and tried to get back to my writing, he chose that moment to call me.

It took five minutes of back-and-forth—me telling him no, and him saying he wasn't going to leave me alone—before I finally broke down and reluctantly told him yes. He said he'd get a babysitter for Levi, so I didn't have any other excuse to not go out with him tonight.

Why Jae-Hyun randomly wanted to take me out on a Tuesday, I had no idea. I've made it clear multiple times that this marriage he was so insistent on was nothing more than us signing a piece of paper and sharing a child. Nothing else.

Yes, I'd made the mistake of sleeping with him a few times, but it was nothing but sex between the two of us, no emotions whatsoever. There was no future for us besides raising our daughter together.

Now I was crouched down on the floor of the bedroom, clothes scattered all around me as I tried to find something to wear, but I was quickly realizing I didn't have anything. Everything I brought with me was casual loungewear—things

I could wear around the house. Dressing up for Jae-Hyun was the last thing on my mind when it came to packing up Levi and me to move almost an hour away from our home.

I sighed when I tossed the last t-shirt out of my bag and was left staring at the shiny inner lining of my suitcase. Now what was I supposed to do? I looked over at the digital clock on the bedside table. It read 2 p.m. Levi would be getting picked up by the babysitter straight from school, so I should have just enough time to go out and find something to wear. I shoved the clothes back into the suitcase and headed out into the living room.

My purse and the spare set of keys for Jae-Hyun's second car—a black 2025 BMW XM—sat on the couch. He did say I could use it whenever I wanted, so why not? I grabbed both and headed for the side door that connected to the garage. I couldn't even make it fully inside when I heard the chime from the front door. I let out a frustrated grunt before closing the garage door and turning toward the front.

The two glass panels on each side of the door showed a distorted dark figure. I couldn't make out who it was, but it could be somebody important to Jae-Hyun, so I couldn't just leave them out there.

I dropped my purse on the small table next to the door and opened it.

A young girl stood there—she couldn't be more than eighteen or nineteen. She was Asian, with fair skin, a round face, big eyes, and long dark hair.

She was incredibly pretty, like she belonged on a television screen and not on Jae-Hyun's front porch. I smiled at her, and watched her eyes examine me closely from the top of my head all the way to the bottom of my feet. When she looked back up, the expression on her face could only be described as complete disinterest—like I was some insignificant human whose sole purpose was to annoy her.

"Can I help you?" I asked. This stare-off wasn't getting us anywhere, and it didn't look like she planned on saying anything anytime soon.

"Oh yes." Her voice was soft, but the broken English was loud and clear. "You can grab my bags." She slipped past me, bumping her shoulder against mine as she walked right into the house.

I looked down—and sure enough, there were two large suitcases sitting on the porch. I'd been so focused on her appearance that I hadn't even noticed the fact that the rude little princess came with baggage.

I closed the door, leaving her bags sitting right there, because since I had no idea who the hell she was or why she was barging into people's houses, there was no way I was going to act like her servant. I turned to face her. She had her back to me and her head tilted toward the ceiling, taking in as much of the house as she could.

"Small," I heard her mumble.

She called this giant two-bedroom house small?

I folded my arms. She was really starting to piss me off—coming into someone else's home and insulting it.

"Excuse me? Who are you?"

She spun around, looked me up and down again—probably deciding whether or not I was worth answering—then folded her arms and shifted her weight to one hip.

"Where is oppa?"

I know my face must have gone through six different emotions before finally settling on relief.

The girl had the wrong house.

"Oh, I'm sorry, sweetheart, you've got the wrong house. There's no one here by that name." I stepped aside and gestured toward the door, hoping she'd take the hint.

She rolled her eyes and didn't move an inch.

I took a deep breath and reminded myself she was someone who didn't have English as her first language. Despite the attitude written all over her face, she probably didn't understand me.

"Would you like me to call somebody for you or something?"

Her eyes narrowed as she crossed the distance between us. For a second, I thought she was going to leave, but instead of heading to the door, she stopped right in front of me.

She walked a slow circle around me.

Enough. Before I could say anything, she beat me to it.

"Why would oppa hire a maid like you?"

"Maid?" Okay, she's lost it, and it's time for her to leave. "First of all, I'm not the maid. Second, I don't know who this oppa is you keep referring to, but as you can see, they aren't here." I opened the front door.

Just like a light switch, her whole face lit up. She squealed. "Oppa!"

She ran straight into the arms of Jae-Hyun.

WHAT. THE. FUCK.

"So... is she like your little sister or something? Because I distinctly remember you telling me you were an only child."

I don't think my face could have gotten any more scrunched up. I was more than a little annoyed that I had no idea what was going on. And after all his speeches about starting over and being a family, he was still a complete liar. Just like I thought—I couldn't trust him.

I leaned against the kitchen counter with my hands on my hips as I waited for him to explain. Jae-Hyun paced the kitchen floor in front of me, anxiously running his hands through his hair over and over. If I listened closely enough, I could hear him mumbling under his breath—but from the sounds of it, he wasn't speaking English.

How strange. In all the time I'd known him, I knew English wasn't his first language, but I'd never heard him speak Korean. Normally I would've found it interesting... if I wasn't so irritated that it felt like he was ignoring me.

"Hello? Jae-Hyun, I'm talking to you." I clapped my hands sharply. He flinched and looked up at me like he'd forgotten I existed.

"Tell me what the hell is going on. Who is she?"

"Jeonun geu-ui yakhonnyeo imnida."

(I'm his fiancée.)

Her voice came from the archway leading into the kitchen. I guess she didn't understand what the word privacy meant. Whatever she said, I couldn't understand.

Jae-Hyun's head snapped in her direction, anger written clearly across his face. He sucked his teeth at her, and her lips clamped shut immediately.

My eyes darted between the two of them.

I let out a frustrated grunt and headed for the archway, making sure to bump his shoulder as I passed. "Where are you going?" he shouted.

I ignored him and made my way to the bedroom. Luckily, I had just repacked my suitcase before all this bullshit unfolded.

His footsteps followed. I bent down to grab the handle of my suitcase before he reached out, grabbed my arm, and yanked me toward him.

I almost collided with his chest but caught myself and shoved him away. "Don't touch me." I crouched down again to zip up my bag.

"Where are you going?" he asked.

"I think it's pretty obvious. I'm packing me and my daughter's things so we can go home. Clearly, we're in the way."

He stepped around me so he could see my face. I kept my expression neutral. If he wanted to keep secrets, then he could wonder what I was thinking too.

"You can't just leave."

I smiled. I loved a good dare. "Wanna bet?"

His Adam's apple bobbed as he swallowed. His eyes darted. His mind was moving fast.

"We're supposed to be getting married."

"Are we?" This conversation was going nowhere fast. I grabbed the handle of my suitcase and turned.

"Okay!" he shouted.

I stopped and looked over my shoulder.

"I was going to tell you when I had the chance."

I scoffed. "We both know that's a lie. So speak up. Who is she?"

"You'll leave if I tell you. You have to let me explain."

He looked... defeated. Shoulders slumped. Worry lines deep.

I refused to fall for it.

"I'm leaving if you don't tell me. So talk fast."

Jae-Hyun took a deep breath.

"She's... my fiancée."

Chapter 22

RAYLEN

I DON'T THINK I'VE **ever** moved that fast before in my life. I had my phone opened to the rideshare app before I even made it down the hall and to the front door. I heard Jae-Hyun's footsteps as he followed behind me and I even heard him trying to explain, but every word he said was being drowned out by the ringing in my ears. I hated the fact that I felt like crying right now.

It was my own fault for thinking I could trust him for even a second. This sick son of a bitch disappeared for eight years and had the nerve to come back with a fiancée in tow and then what the hell would that make me, the other woman, or just the idiot he knocked up.

"Raylen, please will you just stop and listen to me." I kept walking, that is until I got to the front door and came face to face with 'Miss Fiancée' herself.

She smiled at me sweetly before she spoke. "*Oppa, nae-e daehae geunyeoege mal haesseoya haesseo.*"

(Oppa you should've told her about me.)

"*Joyonghi hae.*"

(Be quiet.)

"*Jeoneun geunyeoga hanyeoin jul arasseoyo. Oppaegeneun bujokhaeyo.*"

(I thought she was the maid. She's not good enough for you oppa.)

"Min So-Hee!" Jae-Hyun shouted at her. The girl's face scrunched in frustration and for a second her face looked a little red. When her eyes landed back on me, she tried to wipe the sour look off her face and show me a smile. She held out her hand for me to shake but I just stared at it in confusion.

"I'm So-Hee. Jae-Hyun *oppa* is being nice, but he already has a fiancée."

"Min So-Hee!" Jae-Hyun shouted again. I swatted her hand away and pushed her shoulder so she would move from in front of the door.

Instead of simply stepping to the side like I thought she would, the girl tripped and fell to the ground much harder than was necessary. I stared at her with wide eyes not because I was worried that she was hurt because let's face it, her acting skills were horrible, and that fall was obviously fake. I stared at her in shock because I couldn't believe she was actually acting like this.

She was wearing a rather short linen skirt and matching jacket and the moment she hit the marble floor, she immediately grabbed her knee and began whining.

"*Oppa* did you see her push me. Are you going to let her treat me like this?" Pushed her? She couldn't be serious, I barely touched her. I wasn't even going to wait around for Jae-Hyun to try and bite my head off for touching her at all. After all I fully expected him to come to the rescue of his poor precious fiancée.

"*Eorin-ae-cheoreom gulji maseyo. Geuraeseo yakhon-eul chisohesseoyo.*"

(*Stop acting like a child. This is why I called off the engagement.*)

I wasn't sure what he said to her, but whatever it was I could see real tears forming in the corners of her eyes. Instead of getting off the floor, she dropped her eyes and sat there quietly.

Jae-Hyun turned his eyes on me. "Please, will you just hear me out for a second."

I looked him up and down. He wasn't the same put together guy that walked through the front door an hour ago or even the same one that confidently walked into that café weeks ago. Now his clothes were rumpled, and his hair was all over the place from running his fingers through it so much. He looked stressed and desperate. As much as I didn't want to, something was compelling me to hear him out.

"What could you possibly say to explain this situation away?"

His shoulders slumped and I could see the obvious relief written all over his face. "Will you please come sit down so we can talk."

I looked at the girl So-Hee still sitting on the floor. Was she waiting for someone to help her up or was she planning to sit there and pout all day. She reminded me a lot of Levi right now and it made me wonder how it was possible for someone so young to be Jae-Hyun's fiancée. "What about her?" I nodded my head in her direction.

Jae-Hyun looked at her. I don't think annoyance would be the right emotion to describe the look on his face.

"Hanggongpyeon yeyakhaetda. Oneul bam Hangug-euro dor-aga."

(I'm booking you a flight. You're going back to Korea tonight.)

So-Hee's head shot up, shock written all over it. *"An dwae!"*

"Ganda."

Jae-Hyun turned his back to her without another word and headed into the living room. I left my suitcase by the door and with a lot of reluctance followed Jae-Hyun. He sat on the black leather sofa and patted the spot next to him. I chose to sit at the other end of the sectional. He had a bad habit of getting his way when he was in too close proximity of me.

He sighed and I folded my arms across my chest waiting for him to start explaining. I half expected So-Hee to follow us in here and continue with her intrusions, but whatever he said to her made her stay exactly where she was. I really need to learn Korean, at least for Levi's sake, it was part of her culture, and it would be nice if one day she could speak it too.

"I don't even know where to start."

"Talk fast Jae, I would like to go get my daughter so we can go home."

He rubbed his pants leg nervously. His nervousness only made me even more anxious to leave. I don't think I wanted to hear what he had to say, but I needed to.

"So-Hee and I grew up together. At least up until I came to America for high school." He started. His comment shocked me, she looked so young, I thought she couldn't be no older than maybe 19. "Our parents thought we would make a good match and it would be good for both of our family businesses, so they paired us off."

I scoffed. "An arranged marriage? You really expect me to believe that?" What century were we in that he thought I would believe something like an arranged marriage was something people still did these days. He must really think I'm stupid.

He shook his head. "You don't have to believe me, but it's the truth. It's not that uncommon in my culture."

The look on his face was so serious, but the claim was so outrageous, I didn't know what to believe. "Ok, so say I believe you. Why would you give me that stupid contract? If you say it's for Levi, we don't have to be married for you to be in her life."

Jae-Hyun got to his feet to come and sit next to me. He

grabbed my hand and threaded his fingers through it. I stared at him, but he didn't look up, just kept his eyes focused on our interlaced fingers. "I feel like the answer to that should be obvious."

"It isn't Jae and you're talking in circles." I let out a sigh. I was getting more and more frustrated by the second. "Say what you want to say."

He finally looked up at me. "Why didn't you respond when I reached out to you?"

"What are you talking about?" I asked in confusion. The first time I had seen or heard from Jae-Hyun since high school was a couple weeks ago when he walked into that café.

"I tried to contact you six years ago. I tried texting, calling, I even went old school and sent letters. You didn't respond to any of it and I want to know why."

The immediate rage I felt even caught me off guard. It was like all the anger and resentment, the pain and grief over what we use to have all hit me at one time. I shot to my feet, balling my fists up at my side to keep from putting my hands on the man sitting in front of me.

I've had multiple dreams of strangling him after he disappeared and left me heart broken. Fantasized about beating him to a bloody and bruised pulp and it was taking everything in me not to fulfill that dream at this very moment.

"How fucking dare you!" Jae-Hyun got to his feet, mouth opened, preparing to defend himself but I didn't give him the chance. I couldn't hold back anymore. I reached up and used as much force as I could muster and slapped him as hard as I could. He stumbled back slightly, losing his balance and falling back onto the couch.

"You packed your shit and left one day out of the clear blue sky without so much as leaving a fucking note!" I was so angry I couldn't control the volume of my voice. I didn't care if his brat of a fiancée heard me.

Hell, I didn't care if his neighbors heard me. All I cared about was that he listened to ever single word I had to say. I've kept my feelings in check for years, but that was all over now.

"I find out I'm pregnant and I try to do the responsible thing and call the son of a bitch who was 50% of the human he put inside of me. You know what I got in return?" He didn't even bother making an attempt to stand up again, his eyes stayed glued to the floor, and he gently rubbed his rapidly reddening cheek. "A fucking disconnected dial tone, that's what I got."

"So don't you dare play the victim like I'm the reason you missed out on eight years of your daughter's life."

My chest was heaving, and I was incredibly out of breath when I finished talking. I rubbed my hands over my eyes trying to stop the tears I feared were going to fall any second. Jae-Hyun looked up at me, his eyes darting from side to side like he was looking at me but not quite seeing me. There was confusion on his face, but I couldn't understand why, what part of what I just said to him left any room for confusion?

"So, you never got any of my messages?"

Chapter 23

JAE-HYUN

A MILLION THOUGHTS WERE **running** through my head starting with the fact that Raylen claimed she never got any
of my messages and ending with the hope that maybe her
keeping Levi from me wasn't intentional.

Could I believe that thought? Maybe it was true that she
didn't get any of my texts or phone calls and maybe it's true
that she tried to reach out to me, and I never got any of her
messages either, but I remember every word of every letter
I ever sent her over those two years. Did she really not get
any of them?

I looked at her, really looked at her. Her chest was heaving
from all the shouting she had done. Shouting I probably

deserved, and there was a light sheen in her eyes like she was moments from shedding tears.

It broke my heart. After all these years I could never deny that I was still in love with her, and I never wanted to hurt her then and I wanted to do it even less now.

I believed her. I believe she tried to tell me about Levi when she first found out and I believed that she never received my messages. This was my fault, just like she said.

"Stop lying, I know you didn't give me a second thought after you left." She was wrong, all I did was think about her. "I was just a high school fling. You had your fun and then you left. I guess I never should've expected more."

All of that was untrue. I finally worked up the courage to get back to my feet. I reached out and grabbed Raylen, pulling her tightly into my arms, gently rubbing her back.

She tried to fight me at first, but I held tight. "That isn't true. My feelings for you were real and they still are. I didn't want to leave, but I didn't have a choice." Raylen stopped her struggling, but she didn't hug me back, she just kept her arms tight at her side. "It's a lot I haven't told you about my family and that's completely my fault. I want to tell you everything and I will, you have my word. Please just trust me."

It was like the tension had melted away. Almost instantly Raylen's arms wrapped around me. She squeezed me tight and suddenly my shirt was soaked with her tears. Her shoulders shook as she silently cried and I just held her to me, giving her all the time she needed.

I'm not sure how long we stood there just embracing each other but I would've stood there as long as she needed, I owed her at least that much.

I rubbed her back and tried to pull away slightly. "Will you at least stay the night?"

She chewed on her lip, and it seemed like she was unsure what to do. I figured in this moment it might be best to make the decision for her. I pulled my phone out of my pocket and checked the available flights. There was one that was set to depart in about three hours, plenty of time to get So-Hee to the airport.

I couldn't believe she actually came here. As much as she wanted to marry me, I know this decision wasn't hers alone, this was my parents doing. This is exactly why I didn't want to tell them about Raylen.

All I told them was that I didn't want to marry So-Hee anymore and that I had picked a new bride. Their response to that was to send So-Hee here, what was she supposed to do, interfere?

Raylen was the mother of my child, and I was so incredibly and deeply in love with her. That wasn't going to change just because they didn't approve of me marrying a foreigner. As far as I was concerned, Raylen was the only woman for me and nothing would change that, no matter what they had to say about it.

When Raylen finally spoke, her voice was rough, and it was obvious she had been crying. "Why wouldn't you tell me any of this?" She asked. That was the million-dollar question. I should've told her about my family's strict traditions years ago. Being the only male and even worse the oldest male in the family came with a lot of rules and regulations, ones that I should've told her about. To be fair, falling in love was not something I could've predicted to happen.

"I swear it wasn't intentional, I thought it would be better for you if I just left."

She pulled out of my hold so she could look up at me. Her eyes were red and puffy from all the crying she had done. My heart squeezed in my chest when I looked at her. I knew this would catch up to me, but I never would've expected it to happen this way. I wanted to explain everything to her properly.

"If you thought it was better that way, why even bother trying to contact me again, why come back? I take pride in my work as an author, but something tells me that wasn't the only reason you tracked me all the way to New York."

I smiled at her, reaching down and brushing a loose curl behind her ear. She leaned into my touch slightly, I don't even think she realized she was doing it. "I came back for you. I thought leaving you alone was for the best, but being away from you was unbearable. When my parents wouldn't stop bugging me about making good on this betrothal, I couldn't go through with it until I saw you one last time."

The constant nagging every day from my parents about

marrying So-Hee was getting increasingly tiresome. My father was getting up there in age and he wanted me married before I could officially step into the role of *daepyo*, head of the company.

He kept feeding me bullshit about wanting to make sure I would continue to embody the values of Yuu Corporation, family, and tradition. We both know it was just a control tactic. I had done everything my family asked of me since they kept good on their promise to force me back to Korea after graduation. I got my degree in business just like they wanted, I started from the bottom and worked my way through the company, busting my ass to learn the ins and outs of operations.

It took me almost seven years to become the *ee-sa*, the company director and another year to convince him to let me take over the U.S. publishing branch so I could come back and find Raylen.

I should've known that he had something up his sleeve when he agreed. I don't even know how he found out about Raylen and I getting married. That would be the only reason he sent So-Hee here. We weren't scheduled to get married until next year in Seoul and I would've gone through with it if I found out Raylen had moved on and was happy, but that wasn't the case. I had a family, and I wasn't going to lose any more time with them not for anyone, even my parents.

"I want us to be a family, that's why I wanted you to sign that contract. I knew no matter what I said, there was a good chance you would never forgive me for what I did. The contract was the only way I could be sure I wouldn't lose you completely." It was wrong of me to threaten her with her career and even worse our daughter, but I was desperate. She started dating that tool Luke, I had to put a stop to that as soon as I could.

Raylen nodded slowly, taking in everything I was telling her. "So, what now?" She asked.

I let out a sigh feeling like a weight had been lifted off my shoulders. I pulled Raylen in for another hug loving the feel of her in my arms, she always felt so perfect there. Rubbing her back gently, I gave her a kiss on the top of her head and giving her my honest answer. "We start our lives together, for real this time."

After one more squeeze, I pull out of her hold. "I'm going to take So-Hee to the airport, I'll be back in a little while. You wait here, take a nice bath and when I get back, we can stay in and talk." I rub her bare arms gently enjoying the feel of her soft skin. "We do still have a babysitter for the night."

I winked at her and enjoyed the shocking reaction of her cheeks reddening at my underlying meaning. Leaning in, I gave her a kiss on the cheek before leaving the living room.

So-Hee sat in the same spot I left her, gently rubbing her knee. She's been overdramatic her whole life, but this was a lot even for her. *"Let's go."* I said in Korean.

She looked up at me, her eyes red. I should feel bad that she was crying, but I didn't. she tried to hurt Raylen and I wouldn't allow anyone to do that especially her. So-Hee can thank my parent for sending her on this embarrassing mission to make one final attempt to get me to marry her. I never asked her to come here, I made that very clear when I told my parents I didn't want to marry her anymore.

"Where?"

"To the airport. I told you, you're going home." I didn't wait for her response, I didn't even help her get off the floor. I had to be tough with her, that was the only way she would get the picture that her and I would never be anything more than childhood friends who were forced into a situation neither of us wanted.

The drive to the airport was silent. Occasionally, I would hear So-Hee sniffle and out the corner of my eye, I would see her scrub at her face. She was starting to get to me. This sad, broken-down girl was not the same confident, funny and annoying girl who cared way too much about her make up to be scrubbing at her face like this, that I grew up with.

I had to keep giving her the cold shoulder at least until I officially married Raylen. I wanted So-Hee to go back to my parents and tell them that there was absolutely nothing left between us. That I had no feelings for her and that no matter her efforts, I followed through with my threat and I married another woman. It was the only way to get my parents to back off and accept that this was the way things were and they weren't going to change.

"Oppa why her?" So-Hee finally spoke.

"It doesn't matter, whatever I say to you won't make you feel any better." I really wasn't sure how she expected me to answer her question. The only thing I could come up with was why not her. Raylen was everything I wanted in a woman but that wasn't something that would make So-Hee feel better, so I stuck with avoiding the question.

"I can't go back and tell my family I failed." I could feel her eyes on me, but I kept my eyes on the road. We were about 20 minutes from the airport, the sooner she got out of this car, the better for everyone.

I could just start to see the flashing lights coming from the tops of the lookout tower at the airport when before I had any chance to react, So-Hee reached over and grabbed the bottom of the steering wheel giving it one hard jerk.

I grabbed her wrists and tried to pull her hands off the wheel, but it was too late. The car veered off into the next lane of oncoming traffic. Headlights flashed in my eyes, and it was like time stood still, my mind instantly went to Raylen and Levi. I was leaving them again. Would they even miss me or would they just go back to how they had been this whole time.

I heard So-Hee scream and when I looked to my right she was lifting her arms up to cover her face and brace for impact. I slid over in my seat and grabbed her, pulling her into me just as the steering wheel came rushing towards me and my head hit the windshield.

Chapter 24

RAYLEN

THE CHIME COMING FROM **my** phone is what wakes me up in the morning. That and the sun streaming in through the bedroom window. I rub my eyes and check the clock on the bedside table. It was eight in the morning. I don't even remember falling asleep.

My phone chimed again from the empty pillow next to me. When I grabbed it, I realized it was the alarm I had set to wake me up in the morning so I could be up before Levi and the babysitter got here. Jae-Hyun told me Levi would be back by 9 which brings me to my next question, where the hell was Jae-Hyun.

I sat up and tried to listen for any noise throughout the

rest of the house. Nothing. "Jae?" I called out but no answer. Did he not come back after taking So-Hee to the airport? What, did he decide the precious little princess needed to be walked all the way to the front door of her billion-bedroom mansion, so he hopped a flight?

I let out a frustrated huff and tossed back the covers. A chill hit my body causing me to shiver and reminded me that I went to sleep in nothing but panties and a bra. I was hoping when Jae-Hyun came back we could do a little more than just talk, but I guess he had other ideas.

Throwing my legs over the edge of the bed, I planted my feet on the nice plush carpeted floor and stretched one last time before I heard the doorbell ring. Shit. I shot up from the bed and raced to the huge walk-in closet.

Grabbing a pair of Jae-Hyun's basketball shorts out of one of the drawers and another of his oversized t-shirts, I tossed them on as I heard the bell again. Racing out of the bedroom door and down the hallway, I swung the door open just as Levi had her finger up to the bell poised to ring it a third time.

The pretty redhead standing behind Levi holding her bright pink backpack caught my attention. She looked incredibly familiar. "Momma, what took you so long?" Levi asked, distracting me from the babysitter.

I looked down at Levi and frowned a little at her appearance, her dark curls were all over her head and she was wearing the ugliest little blue jean dress and jacket combo I've ever seen with a pair of brown sandals. I sighed, lifting my hand up to scratch my head. The hair I get, I can't expect everyone to know how to maneuver the dangerous terrains of curly hair, Jae-Hyun probably didn't even send her with any of the products all over the bathroom counters. The clothes however, that was a whole other thing.

I've never even seen this outfit before, did he buy it just to send with her last night. How can someone who dresses so fashionably, willingly send his daughter out of the house dressed like this?

"Sorry bunny, mommy overslept." I smiled down at her, but my eyes went back to the woman behind Levi. I was hyper aware that she was there and the way she was looking at me was like she knew me too.

"Sorry, and you are?" I held my hand out to her. My action seemed to snap her out of whatever trance she was in, because she jumped slightly and quickly switched which hand she was holding Levi's backpack in so she could shake my hand.

"Sorry, I'm Mr. Yuu's assistant, Elizabeth." Now I remember, she was the woman trailing him that day in the café and the one who thought she had what it took to stop me from getting into his office the day he sent me that stupid contract.

Why would he choose her to babysit Levi, I thought he chose an actual service.

I couldn't help but admire her striking appearance. Fiery red hair, striking green eyes, huge boobs and a coke bottle body that could kill. She was like a modern-day Jessica Rabbit. I looked down at my own frumpy appearance, baggy shirt, and a pair of Jae-Hyun's shorts. There was probably crust in my eyes and I would bet my next five royalty checks my hair was a matted curly mess with barely any distinguishable curls left. That always happens when I carelessly go to bed without taking the proper steps to protect my hair.

Next to her I can admit it to myself, I was feeling a little inadequate. Anyone from the outside looking in would think Jae-Hyun would choose someone like her over someone like me. I tilted my head sideways, not taking my eyes off her. I wonder if anything has ever happened between the two of them.

I shake my head to try and clear the thought. That would be too cliché to be reality, the sexy boss sleeping with his equally sexy assistant.

"Momma, are you ok?" Levi asked. Her voice snapped me back to reality. I looked down at her and side stepped so she could come inside.

"Have you eaten bunny? Go put your things away and I'll make you breakfast." She nodded her head and reached for the backpack in Elizabeth's hand. She handed it over and Levi stepped through the doorway. She walked in but stopped just past the threshold. She looked around before turning back to look up at me. "Momma, where's Hyunny?"

That was a really good question and if anybody would have an answer to something like that, wouldn't it be his lovely assistant.

I looked up at Elizabeth just as her eyes were trailing up my body until they made it back to my eyes. She flinched a little when she realized she had been caught.

"Emily, right?" I heard her when she said her name, but something about the way she was looking at me when she didn't realize I was watching, didn't sit right with me. I was feeling a little petty and she was about to see the result of that.

I saw her jaw flex when she clenched her teeth, and I couldn't help the small amount of smugness I was feeling that such a small thing like a name slip up got to her. "Elizabeth actually." She tried to keep her tone neutral, but I could hear the irritation, nevertheless.

I waved my hand, brushing off her correction like I wasn't fazed by it because honestly, I wasn't. Something about her I didn't like, and if I had my way, I would never have to meet her again. "You wouldn't happen to have his schedule for today, would you?" I wasn't about to fully admit to her that I had absolutely no idea where he was right now, it wasn't her business and part of me felt like if I told her that, somehow, I loss.

Elizabeth gave me a strange look like she was confused that I would ask her such a question then her expression shifted, and I could've sworn it looked like she was smirking right before she covered it with mock concern.

"Oh no, Mr. Yuu informed me that he would be unavailable all today. I assumed to spend time with you."

Should I believe her, or was she full of shit? Something about the way she said it, a little too sugary sweet for my liking, makes me think I'm missing something.

I would've pressed her more, but I wasn't in the mood. I

had a child to feed, and I wanted to save all my annoyance for Jae-Hyun. After all he was the one so hell bent on me staying last night so we could *talk,* and I was fully ready to hear everything he had to say and then he just left me high and dry. Literally.

"Well thank you for dropping Levi off." She nodded her head and before she had a chance to say anything else, I closed the door in her face. Rude maybe, but like I said, I was feeling petty.

I peeked into the kitchen to see Levi sitting at the counter on one of the stools swinging her bare feet. She had kicked her shoes off at the door. Normally I would be angry at her because she knows I hate when she does that, but I hated those ugly little sandals so much, I was fully planning to toss them in the trash.

She had her back to me and her nose deep in a video she was watching on her tablet. It would've been so nice to spend this morning with the three of us together.

Jae-Hyun and I spending the entire night together, talking amongst other *activities.* Waking up in the morning to cook breakfast together while we wait for Levi to come home so we could spend the morning watching the sunrise and planning how we would spend the rest of the day.

That hasn't happened since Levi and I moved in. Jae-Hyun always had to be at the office early, so there was never time to have breakfast together, but he would always try his best to be back in time for us all to be together for dinner.

I headed further down the hallway, back to the bedroom to

grab a hair tie so I could put my hair up in a messy bun. I had to take a few calming deep breaths when I thought about the fact that Jae-Hyun was letting me down again.

This might not have seemed like a big deal, but after last night, I felt like we were making progress. Jae-Hyun was finally telling me the truth and then he just decided not to come home. What happened, did he spend the night with So-Hee or something? Maybe he never actually took her to the airport.

For all I know they could've had a nice long talk on that hour and whatever drive and decided that maybe it was in their best interest to get married after all. Regardless of the child he shares with me, he would much rather keep up with the family traditions he insisted that his family was imposing on him and marry the woman they picked.

So-Hee was gorgeous, anyone could see that. She had money and came from a similar background and culture as he did. He definitely could do much worse than her. Why would he pick the high school sweetheart he had years ago with the bad attitude and the emotional trauma?

Maybe he just wanted to do the honorable thing because of Levi. I shook my head slightly trying to clear all those depressing thoughts. I couldn't spiral like this. I told Jae-Hyun I would give him a chance to explain things and that's what I would do. Despite his past transgressions, in this moment, he was innocent until proven guilty.

I headed back into the kitchen with Levi, giving her a reassuring smile before I opened the fridge and began pulling things out so I could get started on her breakfast. I had lost my appetite, but there was no reason for the both of us to starve.

It had been hours since I heard anything from or about Jae-Hyun. It was now six in the afternoon. I had been pacing the floor in front of the front door for over an hour before the feeling in the pit of my stomach became almost too much to bear.

The first few hours after Levi came home, I was angry and anxious. I wanted to know where he had been the entire night and what was the reason he chose to do that instead of coming home to me. I even contemplated packing Levi and I up so by the time he did decide to come back, we would already be gone.

By noon I was feeling a little more forgiving, like maybe something came up and he had to deal with something at work that just had his full attention. Maybe he was so busy, he just had no time at all to call and let me know.

When 4pm arrived, I started getting worried. I called his phone a few more times, even sent a few texts asking where he was and if everything was ok, but nothing. I tried calling his office, but they said he hadn't been in all day, and no one had heard from him.

Now it was 6pm, the normal time he would've returned

home from work, and I was behind the wheel of the car with Levi in the backseat. I thought about checking a few hospitals and asking if he was there, but my brain was doing everything it could to make me reject that idea.

Jae-Hyun was probably just somewhere with So-Hee rekindling their love or something and he didn't have a phone charger. Or maybe he decided to just go back to Korea. There was no way he somehow landed himself in a hospital somewhere.

I said that, but the more the thought crossed my mind the more that was sounding like the most reasonable explanation.

All I could do now was retrace his steps. Jae-Hyun left home last night to take So-Hee to the airport, so that's where I was heading now. It was a long shot, because it wasn't like anyone at the airport could tell me if he purchased one ticket or two, but I was grasping at straws at this point.

I drove down the long stretch of highway. A few cars zipping by on the other side, but for the most part, traffic was clear, and the drive was smooth. I drove in silence, with the exception of Levi's tablet playing music from the backseat.

She had no idea where we were going, I didn't want her to panic by telling her Jae-Hyun was missing. All she knew was that we were on our way to meet him and for now, that was all she needed to know.

My palms were sweating like crazy as I tightened my grip on the steering wheel. The pit in my stomach seemed like it was only getting bigger and bigger by the minute. It was starting to feel like it might swallow me whole.

I wonder what I was more afraid of, Jae-Hyun abandoning us again, or him being hurt and lying in a ditch somewhere.

Traffic came to a standstill in front of us. The red brake lights in front of me pulling me from my trance. I slammed on the brake bringing the car to a jerky stop. Fuck, that was almost bad.

"Momma, what's wrong?" Levi asked from the backseat. I looked in the rear mirror to see she had dropped her tablet on the seat next to her and now her attention was fully focused on the long line of cars in front of us.

Her little curls fell in her eyes slightly as she strained her neck trying to get a better view but only able to move so much because of the seatbelt.

"I don't know bunny, there must've been an accident or something." I'm not sure how many cars were in front of us, but even from this distance, I could see flashing lights.

Traffic inched forward and with every passing minute, I became more and more anxious. The longer it took to get to the airport, the longer I would have to go before I could find out what happened to Jae-Hyun.

I was almost tempted to unbuckle my seatbelt and get out of the car to see what the holdup was, but I figured that wouldn't end well for me. After a few minutes of slowly inching forward, I saw a police officer up ahead in the middle of the road. He had the other side of the road completely blocked off with his cruiser while he waved our lane forward.

A few feet in front of him were the notable signs of tire

marks veering toward the left all the way over to the edge of the road where there was nothing but a huge ditch that went so deep if I got out of the car and stood near the edge of it, the trees down there would probably come to my hips. Considering I only stood at 5'4 that was saying a lot.

There was shattered glass and large chunks of car parts in the middle of the road. A tow truck could be seen near the edge of the ditch, trying to lift a car from down below.

So, there was an accident. My heart speed up as we inched past and I couldn't seem to take my eyes off the wreckage. I couldn't see the other car, but something about the one being dragged up the grassy hill, I couldn't seem to look away from.

It was a small black car, but it was crunched into nothing but a cube now. Whoever was in that car, there was no way they could've survived. The car spun in a slow circle when the tow truck managed to finally get it off the side of the hill and lift it into the air.

Something caught my attention, and I slammed on the brakes, almost making the car behind me slam into the back of me.

"Momma?" Levi called from the backseat, but I didn't turn around to look at her. I kept my eyes glued to the car. The bright red strip going down the middle of the all black metal heap was all I could focus on. Immediately flashes of the night Jae-Hyun picked me up for that banquet came to mind.

The sexy black car with the red strip in middle that had my jaw hanging on the floor, coming to the forefront of my mind.

Oh god no.

Chapter 25

RAYLEN

THE RINGING IN MY **ears** didn't stop long after I had passed the accident. The pounding in my head was getting worse the more the images of the crunched-up car flashed in my mind.

I was getting dizzy and nauseous all at the same time which resulted in me having to pull off the highway and park on the side of the road. My head pressed against the cool leather steering wheel as I tried to keep the bile from rising any further in my throat.

It wasn't true. I was making things up in my head, that had to be the case. That wasn't Jae-Hyun's car. He was perfectly fine off somewhere.

I wanted to believe that, but every time I tried to convince myself, there were those flashes again.

"Are you sick momma?" Levi asked. I almost forgot she was back there. My head snapped up and I wiped my face in case there were any tears that managed to slip from my eyes without me noticing.

I turned to face her and gave her my best reassuring smile. I couldn't let her know anything was wrong until I had confirmed there was anything to worry about and right now, I didn't know anything.

"Everything is perfectly fine bunny."

"Are we still going to see Hyunny?" I clenched my teeth. There was that bile again.

"Of course, baby, we just have to make a few more stops before we meet him." Levi and Jae-Hyun had bonded so quickly, and I was so happy and grateful for that.

When he came back into our lives, I was sure that he would hate me for not getting rid of her or not want anything to do with her. I thought they wouldn't bond, that he wouldn't feel that fatherly connection with her.

Imagine my surprised when he stepped into the role like second nature. It was a rocky start, but it didn't take long for him to get the hang of taking care of her. From the early morning school drop offs since she no longer had the car-pool group she use to when we were living in my apartment.

To the late-night fridge raids that both of them thought I didn't know about. To the little tea parties I've caught them having when Jae-Hyun thought I was too busy nose deep in my manuscript to notice.

Levi had turned into a daddy's girl overnight and I didn't want that to change now. I didn't want her to have the same heartbreak I did when he left us the first time.

I put the car back in drive and merged back into traffic. I had to get some answers and since I didn't know who I could call, I did the only thing I could do. I would check every hospital in the state if I have to. Starting with the one closest to the accident.

This was the third hospital I had checked and if he wasn't here, I didn't know what I would do. This was the hospital closest to my apartment and the one Olivia worked at. I thought about calling her first to see if she had heard any-thing about any patients in a car accident last night, but then I remembered she was on vacation visiting her parents in Ohio for the week. She wouldn't know anything. I even considered calling the twins to see if they had heard from him, but if they didn't, I didn't want to worry them until I knew for absolute certain that there was something to be concerned about.

I felt bad dragging Levi to all these different hospitals, but I didn't want to find a babysitter. I wanted her to be with me if I found out some information I didn't want to hear.

I walked up to the nurse in the powder blue scrubs and the

tight top knot bun standing behind the large round desk in the middle of the emergency room. Doctors rushed around with their long white coats flapping behind them. Alarms blared and I even heard a few people sobbing.

I've hated hospitals for I'm not sure how long, maybe it started when I almost died giving birth to Levi or maybe it was all the heartache that always came from whenever someone stepped foot in one. It didn't matter what my reasoning was, I was feeling my discomfort a lot more now than ever before.

Every hospital I stepped foot in today, my heart would race and for every nurse or doctor who told me they didn't have anyone who matched Jae-Hyun's description, I would breathe a tiny sigh of relief. The anxiety would still be there though because I would be no closer to answers.

"Excuse me." I said placing one hand on the desk to get her attention but keeping a tight grip on Levi's hand with the other one.

The pen in the nurse's hand immediately stopped its scribbling on the clipboard in her other hand and she looked up at me. She didn't smile and honestly, she looked a little annoyed that I interrupted her work.

I tried not to let the discomfort I was feeling from her stare intimidate me into walking away. I cleared my throat and tried again. "I'm looking for someone."

She sighed and rolled her eyes slightly. "Name?" She said flipping a page up on the clipboard.

"Jae-Hyun Yuu." My fingers twitch on the smooth wooden

surface of the desk as I watched her finger drag down the page to try and find his name.

After a minute, she looked up at me and shook her head. "Sorry, no one here by that name." It felt like that pit in my stomach had returned tenfold. There weren't any more hospitals in the area, he had to be here. Or what if he was still stuck in that ditch on the side of the road and they just hadn't found his body yet.

I clenched my teeth. No, I had to keep it together.

"Could you check again?" The nurse dropped her clipboard on the desk and folded her arms across her chest.

"That's the list of all our new patients and I'm telling you, the person you're looking for isn't on it." I took a few calming breaths. Weren't nurses supposed to be kind and helpful. At bare minimum not a total bitch. She acted like I was being hysterical, I was being as calm as I could possibly and would possibly be but clearly that was good enough.

I looked down at Levi with her big doe eyes expectantly. I crouched down so I was eye level with her. "Bunny can you do mommy a favor. Plug your ears and turn around." She looked confused but didn't question it. Levi lifted her arms, putting her fingers in her ears and turning around so her back was to me.

I got to my feet and looked the nurse right in the eyes. She narrowed her eyes at me almost like she was challenging me. "Look, I believe my husband and a family friend were involved in a car accident last night. I've checked two other hospitals before I came here."

I leaned further across the desk so I was as close as the wooden slab would allow me to be to her face. "You have five seconds to check if there was anyone brought in last night from a car accident, or my daughter is going to watch me get dragged out of here by security for smacking the shit out of you. You're choice."

The nurse's face twisted up like she was about to argue with me, and I was all about making good on my promises, so I prepared to do exactly what I just said I was going to do by taking the car keys out of my jean pocket and putting them on the counter next to me. Couldn't climb across with them restricting my movements.

Right when I thought I was about to have to spring into action, her face changed and one of recognition began to shine through.

"Did you say a car accident?" She asked. My shoulders relaxed slightly, and I eyed her suspiciously.

She sat down in the chair behind her desk and began typing something on the computer. The computer was tucked away in the little overhang of the desk so no matter how much I strained, there was no way I would be able to see what she was looking up.

After a minute or two, she looked up from her typing and looked up at me with a smile. To say I was shocked would be an understatement, I didn't even know this lady knew the equation to a smile.

"Thank god you came." She grabbed her clipboard again and walked around the desk to stand in front of me. "Follow me." I didn't hesitate, I grabbed Levi's hand, pulling it from her ear and followed the nurse down one of the many hallways.

She was walking so fast down the shiny tiled floor, it was a little hard to keep up with Levi in tow. She stopped in front of a room just as a red headed man with dark brown eyes who looked entirely too young to be a doctor came out. He had his nose buried in a metal clipboard with a pen tucked behind his ear, pushing back his red curls.

"Dr. Lenox," The nurse gestured towards me. "This woman is looking for two patients that were brought in last night from a car accident."

The doctor's head snapped in my direction at her explanation and his face immediately lit up. He held out his hand for me to shake. "Nice to meet you Mrs...?"

He waited for me to fill in the blanks. I grabbed his hand and gave it a little shake. "Clark."

He gave a nod and a small smile before looking back at the chart in his hand. "We're so glad you're here, we've had your husband listed as a John Doe for the last 12 hours."

My ears perked up at his words. "So, he is here?"

"See for yourself." Dr. Lenox took a step back and opened the door to the room he had just come out of for me. I waited back, giving Levi an opportunity to go in first.

The hospital room resembled the rest of the hospital. Bright white walls, even brighter fluorescent lights overhead. My eyes zeroed in on the hospital bed in the middle of the room.

White sheets covered most of the person laying in it and the white gauze wrapped around their head covered a good portion of their face, but even from this distance I could see who it was.

My gym shoes squeaked loudly on the polished floors as I raced over to the bed. My heart beating a mile a minute when I reached the bedside. I stood there frozen, looking down at Jae-Hyun's bruised and bloodied face.

There was gauze wrapped around his head and a huge bandage on his left cheek, a black eye over his right. The machines beeped steadily next to the bed signaling as bad as he looked, he was stable.

"What the hell happened?" I asked. I couldn't take my eyes off of him, but I was vaguely aware that Levi was standing right next to me. I wanted to reel in my emotions, so I didn't scare her. Seeing Jae-Hyun like this was probably already doing enough of that.

The doctor opened his mouth to speak, but I turned and stopped him before he had a chance to get a word out.

"Maybe we could speak outside?" I nodded my head in Levi's direction and he followed with his eyes. Understanding crossed his face and he nodded.

He left the room, waiting in the hallway for me. "Bunny, why don't you stay here and keep Hyunny company. You can tell him all about your sleepover, I'm sure he would love to hear that."

Levi looked up at me and I could see the tears ready to spill from her eyes. I reached down and gently rubbed her cheek.

"Don't worry baby, he's just sleeping. He'll be just fine."

I led her around to the other side of his bed and helped her climb into the small armchair right next to it. I gave her a kiss on the forehead and headed out of the room to meet the doctor.

I closed the door behind me, leaving just a tiny crack in it so I could hear Levi if she called me. "What happened?" I asked, folding my arms across my chest.

The doctor let out a sigh before looking me square in the eyes. "It seems your husband loss control of his car and collided head on with an oncoming vehicle in the next lane." My heart skipped a beat at the doctor's words.

That would explain that smashed up cube that use to be considered his car. "So, how bad are his injuries? Why is he here under a John Doe?" The fact that they didn't seem to know his name might explain why I was never contacted. That and since I wasn't really his wife, I wasn't even sure who was technically considered his emergency contact.

"Well, during the accident, he wasn't wearing his seatbelt, so he was ejected from the car." Bile began to rise in my throat. I could feel the tears threatening to come, but I tried to keep it together so I could listen to the doctor finish his explanation.

"He was thrown into some trees so along with a concussion he has a broken arm a few broken ribs and a broken leg. His injuries are surprisingly minor considering the circumstances."

I breathed a small sigh of relief, but a stray tear still managed to escape from my eyes. I wiped at it in frustration. I don't even know why I was crying, Jae-Hyun was alive and with no life threatening injuries so why am I crying?

"His car was so badly damaged during the accident, the police weren't able to get a vin number off of it to see who the car was registered to and his wallet and phone weren't recovered."

I nodded my head, feeling better about why it took so long for me to find him, but feeling even worse that I jumped completely to the wrong conclusion about why he didn't come home last night.

It took me so long to even realize something was wrong. Who knows long he would've stay unconscious not able to tell anyone who he was and just sitting in this hospital all alone.

There goes another tear.

"What about the woman he was with?" I asked the doctor.

He gestured toward the room right across the hall. I followed him over to it where he cracked the door slightly for me to see inside. I could see So-Hee inside.

Her head was completely wrapped in bandages, and she had tape on either side of her head with a long tube sticking out of her mouth and connecting to the machines next to her. Half her face was completely black and blue, and it was obvious her injuries were far worse than Jae-Hyun's.

"What's wrong with her?" I ask.

"The police think she hit her head on the dashboard which cause some brain swelling. That put together with the amount of time it took for first responders to get to her..." Dr. Lenox's words trailed off, and I was almost scared to let him finish.

"What?"

"She's in a coma and we're not sure when she'll wake up." I gasped, my hand flying to my chest. Oh god, what happened on that road last night?

Chapter 26

RAYLEN

FOR THE LAST TWO **days I** sat in this stupid uncomfortable chair next to Jae-Hyun's hospital bed, only rotating out when one of the twins came so I can make sure Levi was taken care of. He had been in and out of consciousness the whole time. For the brief moments that he had been awake, he was delirious.

The doctors had him doped up on a lot of pain meds. According to them he was really agitated and confused when he came in. They said they were worried he would make his injuries worse than they already were.

Olivia came straight from JFK yesterday and took Levi to her house for me. There was no reason for us to both camp out in this hospital. She had already missed three days of school this week and I felt bad having her sleep on the small, hard love seat in the corner of the hospital room. I didn't have anyone else to keep her so the relief I felt when Olivia came back to town was almost overwhelming.

After a very dramatic temper tantrum from Levi, she made me promise to call her the minute he woke up, which at the moment was an hour ago.

His groans of pain woke me up out of the uncomfortable sleep in the awkward position I had been sleeping in. Now the red headed Dr. Lenox was standing over his bed, showing him the pixilated images of his x-rays.

Jae-Hyun had 4 broken ribs on one side and one on the other. The bone in his left calf was fractured and so was the bone in his bicep on the same side.

He was out of the woods for any brain injuries, he would just be on a crap ton of pain meds for the next few weeks. The doctor even suggested some mild physical therapy in six weeks.

All the nurses and doctors keep telling me that he's so lucky to have made it out with just the few "minor" injuries that he had. Part of me felt the same, but another part can't help but look at him and wonder what part of this was "minor".

So-Hee still hadn't woken up and the minute Jae-Hyun had regained consciousness, he had asked about her. I couldn't bring myself to tell him that she was in a coma and the doctors couldn't tell when she'd wake up.

They told me there might've been a chance that he took

his seatbelt off to protect her and that's how he ended up getting thrown from the vehicle. She was strapped in, so she took the entire brunt of the crash.

Was I supposed to tell him that despite his efforts to make sure she came out of that crash with the least number of injuries, she instead came out with the most and that his efforts were pointless.

When the doctor finished his explanation to Jae-Hyun about his injuries, he scrubbed his face with his one good arm, making sure to avoid the bandage that was still taped to his forehead.

I could see the frustration written on his face and I wanted to relieve it. I also wanted to ask him what happened in that car, what caused the accident?

Was it just that he simply lost control of the car or did something else happened? I have no other reason to believe that anything other than him losing control of the car took place, it was just a feeling I was having.

I tried to put the thought out of my head and instead focused on my phone. I shot Liam a text, letting him know that Jae was awake and giving him a short rundown of what the doctor said. His response came seconds later, telling me that he would tell Danny and they would both be here in a couple hours. Dropping my phone in the chair, I got to my feet and walked to the side of the bed, placing my hand on Jae's shoulder.

"What about the girl that was in the car with me, how is she?" He asked. I really wanted to tell the doctor, that maybe it wasn't best for Jae-Hyun to know the full extent of her condition yet, after all he had just woken up, but there was no time for me to stop the doctor's words.

"She hasn't woken up yet, I'm sorry." The sympathetic look on his face didn't match the confused one on Jae-Hyun's.

"What do you mean *she hasn't woken up yet?*" Jae-Hyun looked at me for an explanation, but I just dropped my eyes to the ground. I couldn't bear to see his face when the realization finally hit.

I could feel Jae-Hyun's eyes on me, and it felt like he wasn't planning to look away anytime soon. I took a deep breath and finally looked up at him into those dark, pleading eyes.

Fuck. "Raylen, how bad is it?" I couldn't tell him, so instead I just looked at him and he knew.

Jae-Hyun's head dropped into his hand, and I could hear the shaky breath that erupted past his lips. Without thinking and before I knew it, I had my arms wrapped around him in a tight embrace.

I squeezed him as tight as I could without hurting his already injured body. I vaguely noticed when Dr. Lenox began backing away and heading toward the door.

The door creaked slightly when he opened it, but just before he slipped through it into the hall, he turned back to face Jae-Hyun.

"I also forgot to mention Mr. Yuu, we were able to contact your family." I felt Jae-Hyun's body stiffen in my hold. "I've been told they should be arriving shortly." Those were the last words he spoke before I heard the door click behind him.

I took a step back from Jae-Hyun so I could look at his face. The worry lines on his forehead were prominent. They almost distracted me from the slight redness in his eyes. Almost.

"Are you ok?" I asked.

He blinked a few times before he looked up at me with a strained smile. "Yeah, I'm fine." He wasn't fine. "I'm just worried about So-Hee that's all." That wasn't all.

I wasn't going to pressure him to tell me what was going on now. Instead, I decided maybe a little change of subject would be helpful. "I'm glad I finally get to meet your parents. Maybe I should have Olivia bring Levi so she can meet them too."

"No!" Jae-Hyun suddenly shouted. I jumped a little at his reaction. The instant guilt he was feeling at scaring me was evident, but so was the feeling I was having that there was once again something he didn't want me to know.

I sighed and tugged at the tight ponytail holder in my head. "We've talked about you hiding things from me Jae, so just spit it out."

Jae-Hyun leaned back against the pillows on his bed, scrubbing his face slightly with his good hand in frustration, leaving his normally fair skinned face slightly red.

"My parents don't exactly know about you." This wasn't surprising information to me. We were in high school the last time we were together and according to him, he knew at some point he would have to go home, so what would've been the point in telling them about me.

Not telling them about me now didn't hurt my feelings either. There wasn't anything to tell until I told him about Levi.

I shrugged slightly. "I figured, so what's the problem?"

He shook his head. "It's more than just me not telling them about you and Levi. Or about me not telling you that my parents were pressuring me to marry someone else."

"Ok so what is it?" While I waited for Jae-Hyun to finish with his explanation. I pulled my hair tie free, and my curls tumbled down my back. I slipped the band onto my wrist and shoved both my hands into my hair, giving my scalp a nice message.

I was so tempted to moan at the feeling. I had been so stressed over the last few days waiting for Jae-Hyun to wake up. It had made me literally sick to my stomach seeing him in this hospital bed unconscious. I lost count of how many times I had thrown up. It was like I couldn't keep anything down.

"I might have downplayed the amount of influence and money my parents actually have." Why Jae-Hyun thought I cared about him or his family's money I don't know, but I would entertain it if it at least got us one step closer to being completely transparent with each other.

"Your family is rich, so what?" I raked my hand one final time through my hair before dropping my arms to my side and taking a seat on the edge of Jae-Hyun's bed.

"I didn't tell you before, but I'm not just an editor at BY publishing, I'm the CEO of it. The company's mine." My head snapped in his direction, and I know my eyes had to be as big as saucers.

I don't know why I didn't put the pieces together before. All the long work hours and the fancy cars. How he was able to pay for the repairs to my apartment himself instead of letting the landlord deal with it.

Even the contract he made me sign that included us getting married, that wasn't the type of money or power a regular editor just had. I would know after all these years dealing with different ones.

"Why didn't you just tell me?"

"I didn't want you looking at me differently."

"And why would you think I would do that." It hurt to think that he had even the smallest thought that knowing he had money would change how I behaved towards him. I wasn't that kind of girl.

I lost count of how many times Jae-Hyun sighed in the last five minutes. I was starting to think it had more to do with him stalling to tell me what he needs to tell me, then actually being sad about it.

He wasn't getting out of this, whatever he needed to say, he should do it now before his parents get here and I find out anyway. If it was something bad, he should at least have the decency to warn me about it before I walk right into the lion's den.

"My family aren't just *rich,* they're generationally wealthy. Years ago, my great grandfather started the Yuu group and since it's only grown." I waved my hand so he would hurry up and continue.

"My father is in charge of the largest import export company in South Korea. He's invested in and acquired multiple other small business ventures including the publishing company I'm in charge of.

That's the reason I had to go back to Korea all those years ago, my father only wanted me over her to familiarize myself with western customs and then go back after graduation so I could prepare to take over for him."

I nodded my head as I listened to him talk. Ok, so they weren't just normal rich people, they were *mega* rich people with their hands in a lot of different pots. Suddenly the arranged marriage thing made 10x more sense.

But what still wasn't making sense to me was why Jae-Hyun seemed nervous for me to meet them, did he think I would embarrass him or something because he thinks I'm so unaccustomed to being around people of their "caliber" or was he just ashamed that he accidently impregnated a regular girl from the states?

"As someone in that position," he continued. "They had certain expectations for me when it came to who I would marry and start a family with."

Just like that I realized what he was trying to say. My eyes grew wide, and I placed my hands on my hips. "Are you telling me that in 2025, you have racist parents?" I might've said the word racist a little louder than necessary, but I couldn't help it.

I wasn't naïve enough to believe that just because we were

in the 21st century that this wasn't still a thing in the world, but for two parents that chose to send their son to a country full of people that don't look like him to be that backward thinking. It was a little off putting.

"No! Well... not exactly..." Jae-Hyun looked off to the side.

"Well then spit it out, I'm tired of these games Jae."

"My parents are very traditional. In my culture, it's normally expected that the oldest male or in my case the only male marry someone with the same ethnicity."

"Ok so, your parents want you to marry a Korean woman. How bad do you think they'll react when they find out you not only are planning on marrying someone black but that you already have a kid with one?"

This was all very dramatic, and it was honestly giving me a massive headache. It would've been nice if I could've met his parents without them already being biased against me. If that wasn't bad enough, based on how traditional and conservative Jae-Hyun was portraying them to be, I can't imagine they're going to be too happy about their illegitimate granddaughter.

Maybe I should prepare for them to have the same reaction Jae did when I told him. Hell, a better idea was to get it in my head that there was a very real possibility they wouldn't want anything to do with either of us all together.

"So, what do-" My words were cut off with the door swung open and in walked an older man and woman.

There was no question who they were, the man looked like an older version of Jae-Hyun with his dark almond shaped eyes and his slicked back dark hair except he had a small patch of grey at his right temple.

The woman looked a little different, she had light brown hair pulled back into a low bun at the nape of her neck. Her eyes were much wider than Jae-Hyun and his father and her skin was slightly tanner. She looked nothing like her son.

The moment they walked in, neither of them acknowledged me, instead both of their attention was focused on Jae-Hyun.

"I adeul-eun mueosingayo?"
(What is this Jae-Hyun?)

His father said gesturing his arm towards me.

My eyes traveled to Jae-Hyun who had his eyes dropped to the swirling patterns on the blankets across his lap. Jae-Hyun already had pretty fair skin normally, but this time he looked sicker than he did the day after his accident.

"Dangsineui abeoji-ga dangsinege jilmun-eul hasyeosseoyo."
(Your father asked you a question.)

His mother spoke. There was a long moment of silence, and it was so tense in the room, it was almost difficult to breathe.

I couldn't take it anymore, I needed to break the silence and if no one was going to speak to me, I would speak to them.

I walked around Jae-Hyun's bed, closing the distance between his parents and held out my hand for them to shake, but the moment I did, I regretted it. Isn't it customary in their culture to like bow or something? Was I supposed to do that, or would that be considered offensive?

I was flying blind here and Jae-Hyun wasn't helping at all. It was too late to turn back now. "Hello Mr. and Mrs. Yuu. My name is Raylen Clark, it's nice to meet you."

They both hesitated for a moment, looked at each other before looking at me. Finally, after what felt like the longest minute in the history of time, his father reached out his hand to shake mine. I breathed a sigh of relief. Good, I didn't offend anyone.

"We already know who you are Ms. Clark." His mother spoke. Her English was surprisingly a lot less broken than So-Hee's, something I was not expecting.

I turned to look at Jae-Hyun in confusion. He shared the same confused look but stared at his parents instead. Turning back to look at them, I waited for them to elaborate.

"Ms. Clark, I'm going to be blunt with you." His father said, folding his arms across his chest. "We've known about you since the beginning and we were hoping once Jae-Hyun returned home, that would be the end of your relationship with him."

The more they talked, the less their words were making sense. They knew about me since I was in high school, but Jae-Hyun told me they didn't know about me at all so what the hell was going on.

"We intercepted any communication the two of you tried to have over the years, including the message you sent telling our son that he was going to be a father." What the fuck.

"Our hope was that after a few years, he would forget

about this little affair he had." His mother chimed in. "Considering he is already engaged, it should have been a natural occurrence."

"*Geumanhaeyo.*"

(*Stop.*)

Jae-Hyun snapped but they ignored him and continued volleying all this information between the two of them before smacking me in the face with it. They knew about our relationship. They knew that I had tried to reach out to him to tell him when I found out I was pregnant with Levi and not only did they not tell him, but they destroyed any evidence of the message.

"I knew immediately why Jae-Hyun was so insistent about returning to this country and after some thought I allowed it."

"Why would you allow me to come back to the states and take over the publishing branch if you were against our relationship?" Jae-Hyun asked. I could hear the tightness in his voice. He was clearly trying to hold back and not yell considering these were his parents.

"After some thought, we realized that the child you two had together, still had our blood running through their veins." The look on his mother's face was making me incredibly uncomfortable and I was positive I wasn't going to like what she said next.

"We don't think you are good enough to marry our son Ms. Clark, however we do want his child to grow up in a stable environment, which we don't think she will get here. We want her to come to Korea to live with us."

Chapter 27

RAYLEN

I **DON'T THINK SHOCK would** be the proper word to describe what I was feeling right now. Anger, rage, the overwhelming sensation to slap the shit out of the person or in this case, *persons* in front of me. That sounded a little closer to where my mind was heading right now.

I wanted to keep my anger in control, you know, be respectful of the fact that these were Jae-Hyun's parents, and this would be their first impression of me, but Levi was where I drew the line. There was no way to hold that in and since they seem to have done some investigating on me, my reaction shouldn't come as a shock to them.

Closing my eyes, I took a deep breath and prepared for

the scene I was about to cause in this respectable hospital. I could hear Jae-Hyun behind me scrambling, he was probably trying to get to his feet so he could stop me, but I think by now he should know nothing was going to stop me when it came to our daughter.

"I don't know, nor do I care about whatever backwater traditions you want to impose on your son," I finally spoke, lifting my head so I could look Jae-Hyun's father right in the eyes. I wouldn't let this man, his wife or anyone else intimidate me for any reason. And for them to insult my motherhood after just now meeting me for the first time based off some invasive investigation they did was not going to fly.

"Ms. Clark-" His mother spoke. I could see the outrage in her face at me insulting their culture and I didn't mean for it to come out that way. I meant for it to be obvious that I was insulting their parenting because let's face it, they weren't winning any awards for it, and they started it.

I held up my hand to stop her from speaking, because at this point, I felt like they've more than put enough feet in their mouths. Her mouth clamped shut immediately. I think it was more of a shocked reaction than anything else.

"My daughter, however, is not your concern and never will be. Feel free to catch whatever smoking that you took to get here right back to your million-dollar mansion with your million dollar lives and leave me and mine alone." Before either of them had a chance to respond, I turned to face Jae-Hyun.

"I'm going to go talk to the doctor about your discharge so I can take you home." With his eyes the size of saucers and his mouth hanging open, he nodded his head. I turned and slipped past his parents and out the door into the hall, letting out the breath I had tucked right in the middle of my chest. I hope they got the message.

It had been three weeks since I confronted Jae-Hyun's parents in that hospital room and since then, they had begrudgingly gone back to Korea. Jae-Hyun never told me what they said to him after I left the room but based off the expression on his face when I returned with his discharge paperwork, I know they weren't singing my praise. Every time I tried to ask him about it, he always tried to change the subject.

After a while, I stopped bugging him about it. Whatever they said to him, it clearly didn't change his mind about staying with me and Levi. He still wanted us to plan the wedding and after So-Hee woke up a week later, he made arrangements for her to be transferred to a hospital in Korea after her recovery so she could be near her family.

I wasn't sure if he sent her away out of respect for me and the relationship we were trying to build, or if it's because of the guilt he felt every time he looked at her. He still hadn't told me what happened to cause the accident.

In these two weeks, Jae-Hyun was feeling a lot less pain,

but for the most part he was still bedridden. He had been working from home whenever he could, but considering he could only use one leg and one arm, there wasn't a whole lot he could do. It didn't stop him from trying though.

The twins had come over a few times to help out so I wouldn't fall too far behind on my writing schedule while I was taking care of him. Jae finally told me— after my constant prying about it— that So-Hee was the reason for the accident. I guess she couldn't accept the fact that her feelings for Jae would never be returned.

During that little revelation, Daniel even let slip that both him and Liam had met So-Hee one time when they flew to Korea to visit Jae and they both got the feeling that something was off with her almost immediately.

Of course I did the right thing and immediately told them it wasn't polite to say that about her while she was sick. Ok so *almost* immediately.

"Shit, how many did you buy?" I asked Olivia as she came racing into the bathroom and shutting the door behind her.

She was carrying a giant plastic bag filled to the brim with pregnancy tests. I had been sick and feeling really drained for three weeks now. I thought it was just a cold or maybe the stress I was feeling after the car accident, but it didn't seem like it was going anywhere anytime soon.

I thought about going to the doctor in case it was something serious, but before I did that, I needed to rule out one thing first. The most obvious thing.

It's not like Jae and I were being careful. Neither one of

us was using protection and it was never planned, it always just kind of happened. If I was pregnant, I wasn't sure how I would feel about it. We weren't even married yet and after the contract expired, I had no guarantee that Jae-Hyun would want to stay together.

For all I knew, he could want to stay in Levi's life and end the relationship with me. We never really discussed what would happen at the end of our contractual marriage.

"I got everyone they had on the shelf. We have to be 100% sure." Olivia looked more flustered than I was. Her long black waves that were normally somewhat tamed, were all over her head. She was wearing a navy-blue tracksuit and carrying the bag of tests close to her chest like she was making a drug transaction.

Honestly, it was a little funny. She was acting like this because she didn't want Jae-Hyun to find out what was going on before there was anything to tell. What she keeps forgetting is that Jae-Hyun could only move so fast with just one working leg.

"One test would've been fine." I said trying to hold back my laughter. I dig in the bag and grab one of the pink and white boxes, taking out the test and staring at the foil it was wrapped in.

Now that the test was in my hands, I was frozen. Something in me was telling me, no matter how many tests I took, they were all going to come back positive. I was going to have another baby with Jae-Hyun. I knew that in my heart.

Now it was just about confirming everything so I could tell

Jae-Hyun and we could figure out what it is we were going to do next.

"Will you hurry up, the anticipation is killing me." Olivia pushed me toward the toilet and then turning her back to me to give me some privacy. I sighed opening the toilet lid, ripping the wrapper, dropping my pants and placing the test underneath.

When I was finished, I put the cap back on the test and placed it on top of the sink before pulling my pants up and washing my hands.

Olivia went over to look at the test, immediately attempting to pick it up. I slapped her hand away. She snapped her hand back and looked at me like she was offended.

"Don't touch it Liv, it takes a minute for the results to come through." I put my hands on my hips and began pacing circles in the bathroom. I was beyond words anxious while I waited for the results.

"I thought you said it took a second for the results." I turned around to see Olivia still standing over the test.

"It does. At least two minutes." She shook her head no. I crossed the small distance in the bathroom so I was standing right next to her. I tried to collect myself before I looked at the stick.

When I did, there was two bright blue lines stared back at me. I don't think the lines were this vibrant when I was pregnant with Levi.

There it was though, clear as day. I was pregnant.

There wasn't a point in taking another test for confirma-

tion. As quickly as those results appeared, it had me wondering how far along I actually was. There was more than one
opportunity this could've happened.

I guess that really didn't matter now, what matter now
was telling Jae-Hyun. Would he be happy or angry that we
were having another child together? Afterall, he had a lot
of other things going on with his parents being against our
relationship and then of course with him not being able to
work like he wants to because of his injuries.

"So, what are you going to do?" Olivia asked. I hadn't realized I was just zoned out staring at the results until she said
something.

"What do you mean, of course I'm going to have it."

Olivia rolled her eyes at me. "I know that I mean what are
you going to do about Jae-Hyun? Is he ready for another
baby?" I had no idea how to answer that. "And if he isn't, are
the two of you going to break up again?" Another question I
had no answer to.

I ran my hand through my curls before grabbing the test
and shoving it into the pocket of the sweatpants I was wearing. I had a matching set with Olivia, but mine was a crème
color.

We hadn't had a girl's day in a few weeks, so we were going
to go out for mimosas and brunch, but I guess that was out
the window.

We could still go I just wouldn't have any alcohol, but we
both knew I would spend the whole time stressing about how
I would tell Jae-Hyun, so it was best to just rip the band aid

off now and not wait any longer.

I give Olivia a shrug and she took the hint that asking more questions wasn't going to help the current situation.

"I guess I should give you two some privacy. Do you want me to take Levi with me?"

I shake my head no. "No, she'll be nine soon, it's time I start including her in more adult conversations."

Olivia nodded her head then looked at the bag of pregnancy tests that she dropped on the floor. "What should I do with these?" She pointed at the bag.

I smirk at her. "Don't you need to restock your supplies."

She pulled back and punched me in the arm. It hurt but I could take it, I was use to her abuse. I grabbed my stomach and gasped. "Oh my god, precious cargo I can't believe you."

I feigned like I was outraged at her. She hit me when I was carrying her future god child, how could she.

Her face paled slightly, and she grabbed my arm gently rubbing it. I burst into a fit of laughter almost doubling over. Tears gathered in the corners. The look on her face was priceless.

When I looked back at her she gave me the most annoyed look. "I hate you." She shifted her weight to one side so her hip stuck out and she folded her arms across her chest.

"Love you too bitch."

Olivia and I spent another 30 minutes in the bathroom where she repeatedly told me I was acting like a pussy and that I needed to put my big girl panties on and tell my fiancé that I was carrying his *spawn*. Her words.

After pointing out how rude it was to call her god child that and then reminding her that I did in fact have a pussy she finally convinced me that it was now or right now. No other options, no putting it off.

I paced in the bathroom for maybe another 10 minutes after she left before finally working up the courage to walk out.

I headed down the hall into the living room where Levi and Jae-Hyun were curled up on the couch together.

Jae-Hyun had his broken leg propped up on the chaise part of the sectional with his broken arm resting on the armrest. His good arm was propped over the back of the couch with Levi comfortably curled into his side with her legs tucked under her.

He was in basketball shorts and a t-shirt with his feet bare and she wore a pair of hello kitty pjs. They looked so cute together enjoying their Saturday morning routine. They had been doing this for the last couple of weeks.

According to Jae-Hyun, the accident made him realize that he wasn't spending enough time making memories with Levi and he wanted to change that. The first thing he did when he got out of the hospital was announce to me that life was too short and that it was time.

That was all the warning he gave me before he sat Levi

down and told her the truth about who he was to her. He said he wanted her to get use to the idea of calling him dad although he had grown very affectionate to the nickname she had been calling him up until that point.

Levi being the little wonder that she was took to calling him by his new title almost immediately and they've been even more attached at the hip than they use to be. It warmed my heart to see him follow through with his word.

I never thought I would see this scene, my daughter doing something as simple as lounging on the couch with her father watching cartoons on a Saturday morning.

Jae-Hyun looks up at me and smiles when I round the couch to stand in front of them. "Hello beautiful."

He smiled brightly at me, and my heart skips a beat. Would he keep that same smile when I told him my news, or would it be a while before I saw another genuine smile from him.

I grab the remote off the glass coffee table in front of the couch and turn the tv off.

Levi groaned immediately. "I was watching that." I wasn't sure if I should laugh or be angry at her for the eye roll, but I would let it slide just this once.

"I need to talk to the both of you about something important." The smile disappeared from Jae-Hyun's face and he sat up a little straighter.

My heart was beating a mile a minute, but just like Olivia said, I had to rip off the band aid.

I dug in my pocket, wrapping my hand around the test, but hesitated to pull it out. Maybe I should've done something special to tell them. Maybe make the three of us a nice dinner or something. I was just about to back out when I heard Jae-Hyun speak.

"What's wrong?" I sighed. Nope no making stupid excuses like planning an elaborate dinner to prolong having to tell them. Tell them now.

I clutch the test in my hand and yank it from my pocket. I hold it up and watch as the immediate realization melted across Jae-Hyun's face. Levi looked between the two of us in confusion, but my eyes stayed locked on Jae-Hyun.

I was waiting for the smallest reaction. An eyebrow twitch. A clenched jaw. Anything.

Time seemed to stretch forever with nothing but silence between the three of us. Levi was the first to speak.

"What is it?" She asked. I finally broke eye contact with Jae-Hyun so I could look at her. I smiled softly at her.

When Levi was younger, she use to bug me all the time about wanting someone to play with. I hope she still felt the same way. I've heard that sometimes older siblings can resent their younger siblings for getting their parents attention. I didn't want her to feel that way.

I took a seat next to her on the couch and placed my hand on her leg. "This means I'm going to have a baby."

Her face brightened up instantly. "A baby?" she asked, and I nodded my head. Levi squealed and jumped off the couch. She jumped around and danced, fist pumping the air. I couldn't help but laugh at her.

In the corner of my eye, I could see Jae-Hyun staring me

down, but he still hadn't said a word.

"And how are you feeling about this?" I asked, turning to face him, and leaving Levi to continue her weird dances.

Jae-Hyun's mouth had been hanging open ever since I pulled that test out of my pocket. When I spoke, he finally snapped it closed and I saw his Adam's apple bob as he swallowed.

His eyes dropped low before they came back up to meet mine. This time though, instead of shock or fear in them, I could swear I saw the light sheen of unshed tears.

Jae-Hyun reached out and grabbed my arm pulling me closer to him. I slid across the couch to make it easier for him.

"Saranghae."

(I'm in love with you.)

I couldn't understand what he said, but the way he was looking at me, it couldn't have been bad.

"You're not angry?" I asked.

He shook his head no. "Of course not. Obviously, it wasn't planned, but it's not like we did anything to prevent this." He reached up and gently brushed his hand across my face.

"Now I get to be here for everything."

Chapter 28

JAE-HYUN

I **WAS GOING TO be** a father. No, that's not right. I was going to be a father *again*. Raylen was pregnant. When she told me, I probably didn't have the best reaction, I was too shocked to really react the way I should.

She was carrying my child and this time, I would get to be here for all of it. To help her through the entire pregnancy. To be there to see the first steps and hear the first words. All the things I missed out on with Levi.

I couldn't wait to tell Daniel and Liam about it. When I did they have me the *duh* face I had ever seen in my life like they had been expecting me to tell them a lot sooner that Raylen was pregnant with how much horizontal acrobatics they suspected we were doing after she moved in.

They weren't wrong to assume that, we had practically done it on every surface of this house, but I mean when you have a woman that looks like that walking around your home all day and night, I was just a man not a god.

Ever since she told me the news a week ago, I had been practically bouncing all over the house, failing miserably at trying to keep my excitement in check. I'm the one with the broken bones who's barely able to do anything by himself, yet I couldn't help hobbling around after Raylen to make sure she didn't do anything too strenuous.

Honestly, I was getting the feeling that I was starting to annoy her, but I couldn't help it.

It was Monday morning and she had just gotten back from taking Levi to school. It's been the same routine ever since I got in my accident. She would drop Levi off at school spend a few hours locked in our bedroom nose deep in her latest manuscript then around lunch she would come and check on me. Make sure I didn't need anything.

After that she was back in the bedroom until it was time to go pick up Levi from school. I felt like she was doing a lot all by herself and I even offered to get her some help, but all she said was this wasn't the first time for her.

I know she meant it to reassure me that she was fine but, it stung. It was a reminder that I wasn't there the first time she was pregnant which didn't help with how overbearing I was being with her.

I was in my office, staring at all the emails I needed to

address. My work was really piling up since I couldn't go back to the office yet. I had at least fifty manuscripts to review for potential buys, but the moment I heard the front door open and close followed by the door to the bedroom closing, my concentration was shot.

It had been a while since the two of us had any alone time together. We hadn't been to the doctor yet to verify when exactly she got pregnant. For all I know, the last time we had sex was when it happened.

That was weeks ago and if I was being truthful with myself, I was craving her more than my next breath.

The doctor's appointment we went to a few days ago confirmed that my bones were healing up perfectly. The doctor even told me that I might not need as much recovery time as they originally predicted, but I still needed to take it easy.

I can think of at least ten things I could do that don't require legs or two arms.

I powered down my computer. There was no point of even attempting to continue working, there was no way I was going to be able to regain my concentration.

I spun around, grabbing the crutch I had propped up against the bookcase behind my desk. I had gotten pretty good at getting around on this thing. A couple weeks of having to pee and not wanting to ask my future wife to help will make you learn anything extremely quick.

It also helped that I wasn't in that much pain anymore.

I took it slow, I didn't want to hurt myself, but I also only had one thing on the brain and nothing was going to stop me from getting it. It took some time to hobble my way out of my office, across the open space of the living room, and down the main hall until I was standing in front of the bedroom door.

I pressed my ear to the door expecting to hear the distinct sound of her nails typing away on her keyboard. Depending on how busy she sounded, I would consider leaving her alone.

I listened, but I didn't hear anything. Maybe she was sleeping?

I waited a few more seconds. If she was taking a nap, I wanted to curl up next to her. Just as I was about to reach for the doorknob, I heard a noise.

It wasn't the sound of her laptop like I expected. Instead, it sounded like a groan. I waited until I heard it again followed by a breathy sigh.

My heart skipped a beat. Fuck. Something was wrong, what if it was the baby. Without thinking anymore, I wrapped my hand around the cool material of the doorknob and turned it, pushing it open.

The door flew open and smacked the wall with a loud bang startling Raylen who sat in the middle of the bed leaning back against the headboard.

Her pants were missing, and her legs were spread wide. She had her fingers at her core. One hand massaging her clit and the other playing with her entrance.

Her hands stilled at the noise from the door, and she stared at me with wide eyes. Her mouth hanging open. From shock or the pleasure she was clearly experiencing, I wasn't sure.

I'm sure the expression I was throwing back at her mirrored her expression perfectly.

Out of all the things I was expecting to see when I opened this door, Raylen knuckle deep in a pussy that belonged to me was not one of them.

My dick shot straight to attention at the sight. The speed in which the blood traveled to my dick was so fast it made me a little lightheaded.

Raylen pulled her hands away and quickly snapped her knees together trying to cover herself.

It was too late though, I had already seen everything I needed to.

"I-I can explain." She sure can try, but honestly was there even a point.

I let my crutch slip from under my arm and fall to the floor and I gently and cautiously crossed the distance between the door and the bed, never taking my eyes off Raylen.

"Raylen." I'm aware the tone in my voice made it sound like I was giving her a warning which I guess in a way I was.

Her eyes stayed locked to mine and the reddening in her cheeks only deepened the closer I got.

When I reached the bottom of the bed, she opened her mouth to try and make an excuse for what she was doing. I didn't give her a chance.

I grabbed her ankles and pulled her to the bottom of the bed, ignoring the sharp sting in my still broken arm. She let out a yelp at the action.

I leaned forward so my body was leaning over hers. I rested my forearms on either side of her head so I wouldn't put too much weight on my broken arm, and my pelvis lined up perfectly with her glistening pussy.

"Here I am walking around for days on end feeling like I'm carrying the worlds bluest balls in my pants and you're in here doing this."

She reached her hands up and pressed the heels of her palms into her eyes. "I couldn't help it, it's this baby. The hormones are driving me crazy."

Raylen sighed and rubbed her eyes. "It wasn't this bad when I was pregnant the last time." I breathed a small sigh of relief at her answer to a question I secretly wanted to ask.

I was glad to know Raylen didn't having sex with anyone else while she was pregnant with my daughter.

I leaned down and pressed a soft kiss in the crock of her neck. Her whole body shivered, and her knees clamped tightly to my hips. "Why didn't you come to me?"

She pulled her hands away just long enough to gesture toward my body, eyeing the cast next to her head. "That's a stupid question, you're injured."

Raylen huffed. Was she frustrated because she didn't finish or was it because she got caught and now had to suffer through what I'm sure she deems an embarrassing conversation.

"What was I supposed to do, come to you and say *hey Jae I'm super horny. I know you're injured with several broken bones, but I really want you to fuck me senseless. You think you could help me with that?"*

More blood pumped into my dick. I was so turned on, I bet any minute now I was going to start soaking the front of my shorts with pre-come.

"That's exactly what you were supposed to do. You think I give a fuck about a few broken bones when it comes to you."

I was on edge now, speaking through clenched teeth. "I told you before, but I guess you need another lesson. This pussy," I reach down and cupped her core. Her entire body stiffens, her hands fly up to grip my shoulders and her eyes turn into slits. "Belongs to me."

I should be careful because she's pregnant and I don't want to hurt her, but I wasn't in the mood to be gentle today. Something told me she wasn't either.

The pads of my fingers rubbed over her clit roughly. Instead of complaining that it was too hard, or it hurt, her eyes closed completely and her back arched off the bed.

"Fuck" she moaned out. I smiled, pleased with myself that I can make her have such a strong reaction so quickly.

She wasn't making this much noise when she was doing it alone. It's clear I have a monopoly on her body. Nobody knew how to fuck her the way she liked it, only I do.

"When are you going to learn this lesson love?" She groaned in frustration when I pulled my hand away. I put my fingers to my mouth, using my tongue to clean the juices from the digits.

She always tasted like a sweet treat. Like a reward you

received when you did a job well done and a job well done, I do intend.

I let my saliva coat my fingers and without warning I slipped them past her tight hole. Raylen moaned out, tightening her grip on my shoulders.

I wasn't giving her any reprieve, the first couple strokes were slow until I found my rhythm then I began thrusting them in and out of her. Her moans grew louder and her grip on my shoulders tightened so much, her nails began to bite into my skin through the fabric of my shirt.

It was awkward to do this with my left hand, but she clearly didn't have any complaints.

"Does that feel good love?" She nodded her head.

"I can't hear you." I slowed the motion of my fingers, and she immediately began to squirm against my hand, trying to get me to move again.

"Yes." She moaned.

"Louder." I kicked back up the speed of my hand and she let out the biggest sexiest moan.

She was close to coming, but I wasn't going to let her until I was ready for her to. Her punishment for trying to have all the fun by herself, was following my lead.

"Yes!" She moaned louder.

I leaned into the side of her neck, pulling her earlobe between my teeth and biting down. Her body jolted like I had plugged her into an electrical socket.

I pulled back to whisper into her ear. "Do you want me?"

"I want you so fucking bad." I curled my fingers inside her, hitting that special spot before pulling out of her.

She groaned at the loss of contact, and I completely understood. I was suffering to, but it wouldn't be long.

I scooted off her and off the bed, stripping myself of my shirt and shorts in record time for someone with only one of each appendage. She watched every move I made closely, her eyes drinking in my entire body with every inch of skin I exposed.

It was making my dick ache to be touched.

I climbed back into the bed, lying next to her. Grabbing her hip at the same time, I tugged, pulling her on top of me in one fluid motion. Thank God I made the gym a regular thing for me, there's no way I would've been able to toss her body around this easily with one arm if I didn't.

She was planted firmly on my pelvis, her pussy lining up perfectly with my dick. She gasped at her sudden change in position but then the normally bright hazel and green eyes that I loved to admire when I look at her, suddenly darkened to a deep chocolatey brown.

She rotated her hips, so the soft head of my dick rubbed gently against her slit, her juices running down and drenching me. Fuck. I was going to drown.

"You want it," I smile at her. "Take it." She pulled her bottom lip into her mouth, biting down. She rotated her hips a few more times before placing her hands on my chest and dropping her weight onto my dick.

That tight warmth that always felt like home engulf my entire length in one smooth motion. My hand shot out and held a tight grip on her hip to stop her from moving anymore.

She was tight as fuck and so wet, she was leaking all over my thighs.

Shit is this what it's like to fuck a pregnant woman. If it was, I would make sure she stayed pregnant for as long as possible.

Raylen's body shuddered and I felt her muscles clamp down on me. She reached out and pushed my hand away, raising her hips up and dropping them back down into my lap.

I clenched my teeth when those tight muscles squeezed me on the descent. I looked up at her and she was staring down at me with a devious smirk on her face. Raylen knew exactly what she was doing.

Two can play that game. The next time she dropped onto me, I snapped my hips up, meeting her halfway. She tossed her head back and screamed out.

"Fuck! Do it again." She begged dropped her hips again.

"Come on love, I know you can beg better than that. Tell me what you want." Raylen swirled her hips and moved back and forth trying to rub her clit against my pelvis.

She let out a frustrated groan, but I wouldn't give her what she wanted just yet.

I grabbed the edges of her shirt that I realized was one of my graphic tees she got from my side of the closet and tugged it up as far as I could. She got the hint and pulled the oversized t-shirt up and over her head.

She wasn't wearing a bra so her titties were on full display for my eyes to feast on. I didn't just want to look at them though.

I slid my hand around her waist and pushed making her lean forward so those delicious looking brown nipples were dangling right in my face.

I opened my mouth and pulled one hard bud past my lips. I sucked hard, hoping it would leave a mark.

Her skin was so perfect and smooth, I wanted to do nothing but mark it up. Let every man know that she belonged to me and nobody else.

She moaned when I bit down on it slightly. The things Raylen enjoyed in the bedroom has changed in the years we were apart.

She use to love light kisses and gentle touches. Now the rougher I am, the wetter she gets.

"Jae" she let out a gasp when I bit down a little harder. I loved the sound of my name on her lips. "I need more." My hips stayed completely still as she continued to rotate her hips.

I slapped her hard on the ass and the vibrations from it caused my hand to recoil back. Fuck her ass was so soft and much bigger than it used to be. I almost wish I was fucking her from behind.

Maybe next time, this time I wanted her on top taking what was hers. I slapped her ass again, enjoying the feel of her pussy clenching around me when I did.

I let her nipple fall from my mouth just long enough to speak. "Beg me for it."

With one more frustrated twirl of her hips, she finally relented.

"Fuck Jae, fuck me. I want to come." That was all I needed to hear. I took a firm hold of her hips, careful not to jostle my broken arm too much.

I lifted her and slammed her down onto me, lifting my hips at the same time. "Yes!" She gasped. "More."

I repeated the action, again and again until I had her clawing at my bare chest. I pulled back from her chest so I could see her face. Her eyes rolled to the back of her head, her chest rising and falling rapidly, trying its hardest to keep the oxygen flowing.

Her pussy began to throb around my dick, and I knew she was right there, which was perfect because I didn't think I could last much longer.

I pulled one hand from her hip to reach between us. Giving her clit one pinch was all it took before she crumpled. Her body completely came apart.

She screamed out, her body shaking almost violently, and she squeezed me so tight, I was worried she would break me in half, but it felt so good.

I reached up to brush my hand across her cheek just as my orgasm hit. "*Yeppeuda.*" *(Pretty.)* Was all I could say before all the air rushed from my lungs.

My hips jerked as I emptied myself inside of her. Thank God we didn't have to worry about condoms anymore. Not like we worried about them in the first place.

With one final pulse of her pussy, Raylen breathed a sigh of relief and collapsed on my chest. I groaned when she put her entire weight on my still fractured ribs. I don't know how I didn't feel them before. Adrenaline is a son of a bitch.

Raylen gasped and rolled off me. "Sorry." She said, the guilt prominent on her face.

"It's fine." I snaked my arm under her head and pulled her close to my side.

We laid there in silence for a while just trying to catch our breath before Raylen finally spoke.

"Can you teach me?" My eyes had slipped closed, and I was close to falling asleep.

"Teach you?"

"Korean." I cracked my eyes open slightly and turned my head to look at her.

"Really?" She nodded.

"What do you want to learn?"

"Anything."

I turned my head back to look at the ceiling. "Let's start with something simple then." I could feel her eyes burning holes in the side of my face.

"*Saranghae.*"

(I love you.)

Chapter 29

OLIVIA

"CONGRATULATIONS!" **T**HE **THREE OF** us shouted popping the tiny confetti cannons at the happy couple. I still couldn't believe it, I was in the bathroom with Raylen when she took the test and I was still at a loss for words. The results showed up so quickly, it wouldn't shock me if later we found out there was more than one baby in there.

It happened so quickly for them, it had only been about three months since Jae-Hyun came back into her life, but now they were already on baby number two. Between all the drama with that weird contract he stuck her with and his hidden fiancée and even the car accident, not to mention an eight-year-old, when did they even have the time to do any smashing.

I stood on the other side of the island in the obnoxiously large kitchen while Raylen, Jae-Hyun and the twins stood on the other side. I tried to focus on the smiling, laughing couple, but my eyes kept drifting toward Daniel.

It had been almost a month since they both managed to corner me in Raylen's apartment. I hadn't told her about what happened, but I'm sure the guilty look that was written all over my face when her, and Jae-Hyun returned with the Chinese food an hour later as the two of us filed out of her bedroom said a lot.

Raylen had immediately went in on Liam for making them wait outside for so long before text Jae-Hyun and telling them to go ahead without him. The whole thing would've been suspicious to anyone.

I'm sure it told Jae-Hyun a crap ton if they hadn't spilled the beans themselves by the way he had been giving the three of us this stupidly sneaky look every time we were all in the same room. It was probably like the telephone effect, the twins told Jae-Hyun who told Raylen. Raylen was probably just waiting for the perfect time to use it against me like the little sociopath that she was.

I was going out of my way to avoid the both of them. The last time I saw either of them was that day at Raylen's apartment. I visited Jae-Hyun while he was in the hospital a few times to check on Raylen, but that wasn't really the time or place to talk about what happened.

Any other time Raylen had invited me to hang out here,

I had declined because in my mind, where there was Jae-Hyun, there was Daniel, and I wasn't ready to face him.

I still wasn't ready to face him, right now I was so incredibly uncomfortable being this close to him. I didn't have much of a choice this time though, I couldn't just decline my best friend's invitation to celebrate that she was pregnant with my new god child. I'm pretty sure that's a big no-no in the best friend handbook and the quickest way to lose your status.

Now I was standing here, awkwardly sipping on my glass of wine, and trying my hardest not to make eye contact with anyone.

"Who knew you had it in you Parker." Daniel laughed, clapping Jae-Hyun on the back. They had been calling him that since high school and I didn't understand the joke until recently when both Raylen and I found out that his last name was not in fact Park.

Why he trusted them with that secret and not Raylen, it wasn't my place to ask.

"Well since we already have one child together, I'm gonna go ahead and say I did." Raylen rolled her eyes at Daniel which only made his smile grow wider.

"Why don't we take this little celebration over to the couch, my *pregnant* fiancée shouldn't be on her feet that long." Oh I can see Jae-Hyun is going to be a delight for the duration of her pregnancy, good luck to her.

"Dude, I almost just threw up. Save all that gushy stuff for when the rest of us are not around." Liam rolled his eyes but turned his back and headed toward the couch. He took a seat on the floor and grabbed for the TV remote. "How about a movie?" He asked.

Daniel grabbed his beer off the counter and headed over toward the couch. He opted for sitting on the chaise, propping his legs up and crossing them at the ankle.

Jae-Hyun grabbed Raylen's hand and headed over to join them. I took another sip from my wine glass, fidgeting with it slightly. I hesitated to join them. If I sat on the far end of the couch, would it make it obvious that I was going out of my way to avoid him? If I tried to sit near him, would he get the wrong idea and read too much into it?

I shook my head trying to clear my thoughts. I was overthinking this entire thing. This is why it would always be a horrible idea to cross the line with someone in your friend group.

"Liv are you coming?" Raylen called for me. I looked up from my glass to see all four sets of eyes peering at me from over the back of the couch.

"Actually." I swirled the remaining wine in my glass in a circle. "I think I'm gonna head out."

"It's only 6 o'clock." Daniel raised an eyebrow at me.

"Y-yeah, I have an early shift tomorrow." I stammered out. I was a terrible liar, everyone in this room knew me long enough to know that fact. That didn't stop me from still attempting to get away with it.

"I thought you were off this weekend." Raylen has really been not keeping up with her best friend duties. Throwing me under the bus was definitely a big no no." I narrowed my eyes at her, and she caught on immediately clapping her lips together and turning back around to face the TV.

Daniel sighed and got to his feet, walking around the couch. The closer he got to me, the more anxious I got. "Can I talk to you for a second?" He asked when he finally stood in front of me. I looked over his shoulder at all the eyes staring at me.

"I don't think now is a good time for this." I nervously chewed on my bottom lip. Daniel reached out and grabbed my chin, tilting my head up so I would meet his eyes.

Those mesmerizingly strange eyes. They always took my breath away and made it really difficult to keep my focus.

"We talk in private, or we talk with an audience, but we will be talking." The look on his face was so serious, a side of him I had never seen before. It made my curiosity get the better of me. I knew he would want to talk about that day, but what would he say about it?

Did he want a repeat? Maybe he wanted the both of us to forget it ever happened because he realized how much of a giant mistake it was. Whatever he had to say, there was a good chance it would change everything. Was I ready for that?

Only one way to find out. I didn't take my eyes off him as I nodded my head. Daniel let go of my chin long enough to grab my hand and lead me out of the kitchen.

He led me down the hall all the way to the room that was once a guest room but had been converted into something more suitable to an eight-year-old. Now that we all knew this was much more of a permanent situation then we all thought it was going to be, Raylen and Jae-Hyun had begun bringing more of Levi's stuff from the apartment.

Princess posters now littered the wall, a huge mountain of stuffies sat in one corner, a huge, mounted TV sat on one wall and on the opposite, an adorable pink bed with a unicorn shaped headboard. That part was a little creepy to me.

Daniel closed the door behind us. Part of me was glad for the privacy, I don't think I want anyone out there to hear any part of this conversation. The other part was incredibly nervous because the last time we were alone, things did not go as planned.

"What do you want to talk about?" I asked. I folded my arms across my chest, and tried to act like I wasn't completely stressing about this conversation. I knew he could see right through me, but that wouldn't stop me from lying my ass off.

He took a step towards me, matching my stance and folding his arms, making his biceps bulge. My eyes dropped to them against my better judgement. I couldn't help it though, all I could think about was when they were wrapped around me and how I really wanted them to be again.

"Are we really going to play this game?" My eyes shot up to his. The smirk on his face told me he knew exactly where my mind was going.

I cleared my throat and turned my back to him. "There's really nothing to talk about."

"I think there is. You can't avoid me forever." The plush carpeting in the room muffled his sock clad footsteps, but it was like I could sense his movements and him getting closer and closer to me.

"Who says I'm avoiding you?" My voice sounded high pitched even to my own ears.

Daniel reached out and grabbed my arm, turning me so I would face him. I gasped when I collided with the rock-hard wall that was his chest.

"If you aren't avoiding me, why won't you look at me?" He asked. There go those eyes again. I think I could really drown in them. I hated the fact that after all these years, I had no defense against them.

I struggled to put some distance between me and his chest. "Daniel, I don't want to keep playing these games with you. That day was a mistake. We both know it, so we should both forget it ever happened."

He leaned in close and dropped his voice to just a whisper. "We both know you can't do that."

"You don't know what the hell I can do." I gave his chest one hard push, finally breaking free of his hold.

Not for long though. Daniel reached out and wrapped those long fingers around my throat, giving a gentle squeeze before yanking me towards him. My breasts pressed tightly against his chest, and I had to tilt my head back at an awkward angle just to look at his face.

He leaned in so his nose brushed against mine. His lips were so close that I could feel my mouth watering in anticipation. Why was I anticipating it, I needed to push him away. He wasn't going to kiss me, I wouldn't let him.

"I know a lot more about you then you think I do." I opened my mouth to argue with him, but that was all the invitation he needed. Daniel closed the rest of the gap, crashing his lips into mine and stealing my breath away.

I hated to admit it, but my body reacted immediately. My hands went from pressing into his chest to snaking around his waist, pulling him as close as I could get him.

Daniel pressed further, slipping his tongue past my lips. I felt like I was melting as he used my neck to tilt my head to the side, so he had a better angle to deepen the kiss.

The metal ball in his mouth gently messaged against my tongue. It made my knees quivered and a groan to escape me. I always forgot about his tongue piercing, but I'm not sure how, it completely fit the whole bad boy aesthetic he had going on. It made me wonder if he had secret piercings anywhere else.

I felt his hand slip around my waist, sliding down and grabbing a handful of my ass. Suddenly the rough material of my jeans felt uncomfortable and stiff. I was really wishing I could take them off.

Daniel took a step towards me, pushing me back until the back of my knees hit the edge of Levi's bed. The sudden contact caught me off guard and I tumbled out of his hold, falling onto the bed with a small squeak of surprise. He leaned down and placed both of his hands flat on the bed on either side of me.

From this close, I could see his lips were red and bruised and just a little swollen from how aggressively he kissed me.

"Still think you can forget." I was too dazed to respond, my jaw hanging slack. He took that as an invitation and chose that moment to reach up, threading his fingers into my hair, pulling it tight before he leaned in again. Before his lips could touch mine, there was a knock at the bedroom door.

I gasped and shot to my feet, pushing Daniel out of the way at the same time so I wouldn't crack my head on his jaw.

I turned my back to the door when it flew open a second later, furiously wiping at my mouth and trying to smooth any unrulily pieces of hair.

"Hey, are you two ok?" It just had to be Liam didn't it. In the corner of my eye, I could see Daniel trying to discreetly readjust himself in his pants. I would feel so flattered if I wasn't so mortified.

"Yeah, we were just coming up with some plans for the baby shower. Right Liv?" With one more aggressive swipe at my lips I looked over my shoulder at the two of them with a half-smile.

"That's right. What else would we be doing?"

Chapter 30

JAE-HYUN

"DON'T YOU THINK THIS **has** gone on long enough?" I sat in my office chair with my feet propped up on my desk with my fingers laced behind my head.

Liam sat across from me, his arms dangling at his sides and his head tilted towards the ceiling, eyes closed.

I had a meeting to get to in about an hour, but I would never turn down my best friend coming to see me on his lunch break, especially when he sounded so down.

This was something I couldn't do when I was back in Korea, but now that I officially had the global branch set up in New York, I was free to hang out with my best friends whenever they needed me to.

Right now, it was especially clear that Liam needed some-body to talk to. Somebody that wasn't his twin brother.

"That's such an easy thing for you to say." He said with a sigh. His feet were kicked out in front of him, and he was definitely wrinkling his pristine white button up shirt by sitting like that.

From the expression on his face, I doubted he cared that much.

"So, are you just going to keep this from them for the rest of your life? Daniel is your brother, you have to tell him at some point." I feel like this is the millionth time I've secretly had this conversation with Liam and every time that I have, he has gone out of his way to ignore me.

I know I'm the last one that should be giving relationship advice, but I feel like what I'm suggesting is the most obvious next step for him.

"Not forever," Sounds familiar.

"Then when."

"It's just not the right time to talk about something like this." I pulled my feet off my desk and sat forward, placing my elbows on the wood so I could get a closer look at him. I couldn't wait to hear what his excuse was this time.

"Please enlighten me on what is stopping you this time. Before it was *there was nothing to tell, Olivia didn't feel that way about either of you.* Last time it was *you wanted to make sure everyone was safe after the attack.* Which in my personal opinion was the dumbest excuse you have ever given me." Liam turned his head to look at me. I could tell he was about to argue that it wasn't a stupid excuse, but it in fact was.

"Raylen was the one that was attacked, not Olivia so whatever you were about to say is null and void and just that a fucking *excuse*."

Liam sat up straighter in his chair, turning fully so he would face me. "It's not an easy thing to blurt out. I wouldn't even know what to say." His head dropped into his waiting hands.

"How about *hey Daniel remember when we were in high school and you always wanted to hang out with Liv because you were in love with her. Well surprise, I guess we're identical in every way.*" The sarcasm dripping from my words probably weren't necessary, and I know I was probably being harsh with him. I don't mean to be, but this was something he confided in me before I went back to Korea after graduation.

I really thought while I was away, he would've gotten the courage to just tell them both the truth. Imagine my surprise when I came back to the states to see that nothing had changed. Daniel still hadn't told Olivia he was in love with her, and Liam hadn't told Olivia or Daniel the same thing.

I wanted my friends to be happy and that was never going to happen the way things were. He needed to tell them both the truth, the sooner the better.

Liam lifted to his head to look at me with a deadpan face. "Don't be a tool."

"Don't be a pussy. It's time Liam, you have to tell them both. Ideally Daniel first" Liam slouched back in his seat.

"Why do I even come to you about stuff like this when I already know what you're going to say." I smirked and lifted my hand up to run my fingers through my hair.

"Because you like seeing my face almost as much as you like seeing Olivia."

He snorted and rolled his eyes. "Yeah, I really don't think that's the answer."

We sat there in silence for a while me shuffling through the papers on my desk, trying to prep a little before my meeting and him with his eyes still glued to the ceiling. That is until something occurred to me.

"Why did you bring this up again, did something happen?" I asked.

I saw a smile crack then, but he didn't look at me. I hated when he had that look on his face. It looked a lot like a school yard kid that knew a secret about someone that no one else knew. It was the same look he had on his face right before he told me that he found out Raylen was in New York. He had plenty of time to tell me that little tidbit, but waited until I came to town for a visit before he sprung it on me.

It was safe to say I kicked both of their asses when I found out they knew where she was for over a month and didn't tell me when they knew I was looking for her. I kicked it again when I found out Levi existed. Not because they knew about her because it seems Olivia kept that piece of information from them, but because they cost me another month I could've been getting to know her for their stupid practical joke.

"Tell me." I said through clenched teeth, bracing for whatever he was about to tell me.

"Why don't you ask Daniel." I groaned and got to my feet, stacking the papers on my desk into a neat pile before shoving them in the vanilla envelop and then into my briefcase.

I got to my feet and grabbed my suit jacket off the coa-track behind my desk. Slipping it on, I looked at Liam who still hadn't moved from his spot in the chair. He continued looking at the intricate patterns on the ceiling.

"Don't tell me, but whatever happened is clearly eating you up inside and it's only going to get worse if you don't tell them the truth." The amused look on his face disappeared and he nodded his head absentmindedly. He probably heard part of what I said, but honestly, I doubted he heard the whole thing.

I couldn't imagine what I would do in his situation. To be in love with the same woman that your brother was in love with. Not just a regular sibling bond, but an identical twin. Someone you shared a womb with for nine months.

Knowing that same twin had been in love with one person since he was old enough to know what a crush was. And aside from random hookups hasn't had any kind of relationship with anyone because of that same woman.

To be in love with that same woman for almost the same amount of time and have to listen to your other half consistently talk about her and their feelings for her and never have the courage to say anything. I honestly don't think I could do it. It had to be pure torture, it was like having to choose between yourself and yourself, because as much as they hated to admit it and worked their asses off to prove how different they were, Liam and Daniel were the same person. Liam choosing between his feelings and Daniel's feelings would ultimately break him in the end, but he couldn't continue to go on like this.

"I bet you and Raylen have a lot of fun when you have conversations. You acting like a know it all and her pretending like you're not annoying as hell." I let out a snort. If only he knew how wrong he was. I might act like a know it all, but Raylen has vocalized several times that I annoyed the hell out of her.

I grabbed the briefcase off my desk and headed to the door, leaving Liam behind. "Get out of my office Liam and go talk to Daniel." I called over my shoulder.

"While I'm there I'll talk to him about your baby shower." He called after me. I stopped in my tracks at his words. A baby shower? I groaned. Seriously?

Chapter 31

RAYLEN

FOR THE LAST FOUR **weeks**, Jae-Hyun has been having these super secret whispered conversations on the phone. Whenever I asked him about them, he would try to change the subject. The most I could get out of him was that it was a secret. What the hell did that mean. I think the two of us have had enough surprises over the last few weeks to last a lifetime.

At one point after dropping Levi off at school, Jae must've not heard me come in because he was on the phone again, but this time the person he was on the phone with was on speaker phone.

I could hear one of the twin's voices on the other line.

Which twin, I wasn't sure. Both of them sounded very similar to me especially when you're eavesdropping from the hallway.

I tried asking Olivia about it later, but she was very insistent that she had no idea what they were up to. Whether or not I believed her, I wasn't sure. Maybe it was my brain being so worked up between worrying about everything being ready for the baby and this wedding that according to the contract was suppose to happen well before I give birth. All that is to say, I haven't been able to really focus on anything else, which includes figuring out if my best friend was keeping things from me.

Olivia has definitely been acting strange lately. I know something happened between her and at least one of the twins, which one I wasn't sure. I had always known they were both obsessed with her. You would have to be blind not to notice that. It was obvious.

I was trying to give her space to tell me when she felt comfortable enough to do so, but my impatience was getting the better of me and I was so ready just to force it out of her.

I didn't know if all this secretive business with Jae-Hyun and the twins had anything to do with that or if it was something else, but it was all driving me up the wall.

Now I was sitting in the driver seat of my car in the driveway at home. Jae-Hyun had sent me out on some bullshit errand claiming that he desperately needed me to pick up some files from his office and he would stay behind with Levi.

Why he wanted his pregnant fiancée to drive all the way

across town in the middle of the day to go get these extra special documents instead of him, I don't know.

When I got to the office building, I was supposed to meet up with his pretty red-headed assistant Elizabeth, and low and behold she wasn't there. Really strange right?

When I called to tell Jae, he claims Elizabeth ended up bringing the papers to the house and that I didn't need to go get them at all.

Something in my stomach was telling me I should ask him more about his relationship with that assistant of his. Something was definitely off. I felt it the day she dropped Levi off and even the day they walked into that café together. The puppy dog look she gave him that day as she trailed closely behind him. Even the disgusted look she shot me when she thought I wasn't paying attention when she brought our daughter home.

She looked shocked to see another woman at his home and it made me wonder, did she know Levi was his daughter. Did he tell her Levi was just a family friend and she was just ok with doing a favor for him?

The biggest question I really wanted to know, all those late nights at the office, did anything ever happen between the two of them.

I'm not blind, the woman was sexy as hell. If I swung that way, I would definitely be all over her, so as a healthy man with two working eyes and one working dick, I'm sure the idea had at least crossed his mind.

The thought of those ideas crossing his mind, made other

ideas cross mine. For instance, why was he so insistent on me driving almost 45 minutes away to his office and having to drive 45 minutes back. Did he invite her over while I was gone?

He wouldn't do something like that to me right? Especially not with Levi in the house. I took a deep breath and tried to calm my racing mind. Spiraling like this wasn't going to do me any favors. If I had questions about the relationship Jae had with his assistant, I have to be an adult about it and just ask him.

I closed my eyes and took one final breath before I opened the car door and got out. Walking up to the front door, I pulled the keys out of my pocket and hit the lock button for the car and fumbled around for the key to the door.

I didn't get a chance to put the key into the lock before the door was yanked open and Jae-Hyun stood in the doorway. He had the biggest and goofiest smile on his face. It was contagious, his smile made me smile.

"What took you so long?" He asked. I eyed him suspiciously trying to figure out what's with the personality switch.

"Your office isn't exactly around the corner. Couldn't you have found a house closer to the city." With the new baby on the way, maybe a bigger house would be in order. At least while we're all staying here. If our marriage only lasted until the contract was over, we should all at least be comfortable and not feel like we were standing right on top of each other.

It was only two bedrooms here, I had no idea where we would put the baby when they got here.

One of the things we talked about when Jae came home from the hospital, was that he got this house for us, but that was before he knew we already had a child together and realized that maybe we would need something a little bit bigger.

"We could always shop for one together." Jae winked at me and then stretched out his arm for me to grab his hand. I hesitantly reached out and interlaced my fingers with his, not taking my eyes off of him. He was definitely up to something.

"What's going on?" I asked. He pulled my arm slightly, leading me into the house and closing the door behind me.

He didn't say a word as he grabbed my purse from my shoulder and the keys out of my other hand and placed them on the table by the door. What the hell was going on?

Jae pulled me further into the house until we stopped in the huge archway that led into the living room where a crowd of people were waiting for us.

My jaw drops and a small gasp escaped my lips. There were pink, blue and white balloons littering the entire room. The couch and the small dining table we had, had been removed, replaced by a long white carpet down the middle of the room that led to a archway made out of a combination of white flowers and white balloons.

Against the wall behind the archway, there was a light up sign on the wall that read, *Will you marry me?* in swirling letters.

I clamped my free hand over my mouth and looked at all the eyes staring back at me. The twins were there, so was

Olivia and Jasmine. Levi and I even recognized a few people from Jasmine's office. A few of the other hands behind the scenes that always made sure there were no hiccups when it came to any of my manuscripts hitting the shelves.

"What is all this?" I asked when I was finally able to get my words and my mouth to work together to form words. I looked at him and the look he gave me back made my heart skip a beat.

Jae had given me a lot of different looks over the last couple months, but I don't think he's looked at me like this since we were in high school, when we both believed we could conquer the world together.

Still not saying one word, he pulled me further into the room and down the aisle made by the white carpeting. When we stood under the archway, he turned to face me fully, grabbing my other hand in his.

I watched his shoulders shake as he took a deep shaky breath. He closed his eyes and just let the words flow. "Things didn't start off the best between the two of us. At least not the second time around." I nodded my head because that was the understatement of the year, but I didn't interrupt him.

"We both had our secrets and we've been working towards being completely honest with each other." Jae let go of my hands and turned around to grabbed a small stack of papers from Liam. He held it up for me to see. The contract.

He turned the papers horizontally and right before my very eyes, ripped the flimsy material in half, tossing them off to the side. "This relationship might've started off transactional, but I want you to know, that I want this. This isn't about our daughter or your being pregnant. I want to marry you because I love you and my feelings haven't changed since the first day I met you."

He reached into the back pocket of his jeans, at the same time dropping down to one knee.

I watched as he pulled out a black velvet box, opening it to reveal the most beautiful ring. It had a thick diamond encrusted silver band on it and in the middle sat a huge light blue diamond. My eyes immediately began to water.

Was this really happening? Was this a sincere proposal or was this all for show. A big spectacle making everyone around us believe that it was real.

I looked into those eyes, those beautiful dark eyes that always made my heart skip a beat and I knew the truth.

A lumped formed in my throat and I was trying my hardest not to look like a sappy ass wuss in front of all of our friends by bawling my eyes out, but I couldn't help it. Once the first tear fell, there was no going back, the flood gates open.

I'm surprised my body didn't go the extra mile and produce an obnoxious amount of snot to go along with all the sobbing I was doing.

Jae smiled at me and pulled the ring out of the box. "I got an aquamarine stone instead of a diamond to represent Levi and her birthday. I wanted her to be a part of this as much as possible." The crowd around us let out a synchronized 'Awww.'

That was it, there was no going back. There was no hiding or running away from my feelings anymore. I love him. I loved the way he treated me, like I deserved to be praised and worshipped whenever the opportunity presented itself.

The way he defended me and our daughter to anybody who dare try to harm us in any form. The way he treated Levi, like they hadn't spent the last eight years apart, he included her in everything he did, like she was an extension of himself which in a way I guess she was. Like he had been there for everything, and he couldn't love her any more even if he had been there for all those missing milestones.

I loved him. I wanted to be with him, contract be damned.

"Raylen Clark, will you marry me?" Unable to get the words out, I nodded my head and held out my hand for him to slip the ring on.

The crowd around us cheered and popped miniature confetti poppers when he slipped the ring on, and it fit perfectly. He got to his feet and walked into my waiting arms. I wrapped them tightly around his neck and let him lean in for a kiss.

"Congratulations!" I heard Olivia shouted at me. I pulled out of the kiss but kept my arms wrapped around his neck so I could look at her. "Happy baby shower too." She waved her arm toward the kitchen island that was stacked high with presents. My head snapped toward Jae who hadn't taken his eyes off me this whole time. That goofy smile still plastered on his face.

"I love you." He said and kissed my cheek.

"I love you too." And man did I ever.

Chapter 32

JAE-HYUN

WHAT'S THE SAYING AGAIN, **back** to the scene of the crime. That's exactly what it felt like standing in front of *Trust* again. I haven't been here since the night Raylen told me about Levi. Looking at the tacky building with all the neon blue and pink lights made me feel sick to my stomach.

That night was also the night I monumentally fucked up by sleeping with my assistant. I tried to push it to the back of my head because I couldn't fully get over how guilty I felt about it, but that was hard to do when we had to work together every day.

I could've just fired Elizabeth or at least gave her a raving recommendation and referral to another position so we wouldn't have to see each other as often, but not only would that be extremely unethical and I'm pretty sure illegal, I can't deny the fact that she is one hell of an assistant.

We've work together for years, starting when I first took over the literary division of the company back in Korea and extending to her willingly following me all the way to New York.

Us still working together is part of the reason why I haven't told Raylen about what happened, that and the overwhelming terror I felt at how she might react.

Still, at some point I was going to have to tell her the truth. Not only did Elizebath still work with me, but now that Raylen had signed with my company, she would be constantly working with her too. The level of anger she would feel if I told her now would be 1000x less than what she would feel if they formed a working relationship.

A slap on the back brought me out of my head and back to reality. "Hey man, you ready for tonight?" Daniel threw his arm around my shoulders and gave me a squeeze. When I looked at him, he had a goofy looking smile on his face.

I don't know why I let these two idiots talk me into this, it was an incredibly stupid idea. I would much rather be at home with Raylen and Levi cuddled up on the couch watching movies while I rubbed Raylen's belly than be here around a bunch of drunk people. She was almost 7 months pregnant, which meant she was huge and needed mine and Levi's help to do a decent amount of things around the house. I didn't like leaving her.

She had been so stressed with the wedding planning for a wedding she insisted on having before the baby gets here, I wanted to be there to take any stress off her plate whenever I could.

The twins always cause so much commotion when they went out, the women flocked to them and in turn me. I was far from unattractive, but I've mastered the art of fading to the background when I needed to. The twins either never learned to or never cared too I wasn't sure which.

"Oh come on, don't make that face. This is supposed to be a fun night. You've been stuck in that house since you got engaged. All you do is go to work and sit in the house all day." Daniel rolled his eyes and pushed me towards the entrance of the club.

Next to me I could hear Liam snort a laugh in agreeance. They weren't wrong, but I didn't need to do anything else. I had fun being at home with my family. Playing dress up and tea party with Levi and relaxing and talking with Raylen. What else did they expect me to do stay out drinking and partying all night.

Unlike the two of them, I had the woman I wanted so I didn't need to find mental peace at the bottom of a shot glass.

"This is stupid." I level him with a straight face, reluctantly allowing him to push me closer to the club.

"It's not. This is your bachelor party, can you at least try to be excited about it Parker. Liam and I worked very hard on it."

I scoffed. "Worked hard on what, navigating to a club we were just at a couple of months ago?"

Liam stopped in his tracks and turned to face me, slapping me in the chest. "That is not the point." He sighed running his fingers through those light brown locs. "What my younger brother is so terribly trying to get you to understand is," He side eyed Daniel who rolled his eyes in return. "You've been through a lot over the last couple of months between settling into New York, finding out you have a daughter and then now having another on the way."

"Don't forget the part about the psycho fiancée that tried to kill him." Daniel chimed in a little too excitedly if I might add.

"Oh yeah," Liam agreed in a huff. "How could I ever forget that part. Point is, you're finally getting to marry the girl you've been in love with since we were in high school and then you two can finally start your lives together. Before that you should have at least one night of fun with your best friends." I looked back and forth between the two of them. I knew they were both just trying to look out for me. I also knew they were both absolutely right. I needed to unwind a little, at least one last time before I got married, and what better way than to get drunk off my ass with my friends and go home so I can fuck my sexy ass fiancée into oblivion.

That thought alone brought back memories of a couple months ago when I caught Raylen pleasuring herself because she didn't want to bother me with the 'task'. Her pussy was so wet that day and the sex was out of this world.

Now that Levi was home more often because she was on break from school, it was incredibly hard to find any time for just the two of us to have a little mommy and daddy adult time.

I was hoping that would change tonight.

"A little drinking and maybe a little harmless flirting never hurt anyone." I chose to ignore Daniel's comment because there was no point of addressing it. We all knew there was no way in hell I was flirting with anyone but the sexy curly headed goddess I had waiting for me at home. Those two can go wild though.

I lost count of the number of shots I had taken tonight. It was somewhere north of eleven. By now I feel like I might be getting dangerously close to suffering from alcohol poisoning. Call it the competitive side of me, the twins, Danny specifically always insisted that he could drink me under the table.

Every time without fail, I knock him on his ass, but he still keeps on trying. I threw back another shot as the crowd that had formed around us for our little competition cheered. I held the shot glass over my head upside down shaking it in triumph. Behind me, Liam doubled over in laughter, barely being held up by the sexy brunette whose ass he had firmly pressed against his crouch.

It could be the liquor, but she looked suspiciously like Liv. I guess Liam had a type. He couldn't have the real thing, so he chose second best.

Behind me, Danny was slumped in the booth. One hand was wrapped tightly around a bottle of tequila and he was just barely holding up his head.

I turned to grab the bottle from his hand with the mindset of I could still force down a few more shots before I called it a night and went home to drill my woman into the mattress, that is until I felt a hand snake around my waist and up under my shirt.

My body immediately stiffened, and I tried to turn around to see who's hands were on me, but whoever it was pressed themselves tighter against me, making it damn near impossible to turn around.

If the delicate fingers that were slowly sliding higher up my chest was anything to go by, it was definitely a woman. I grabbed their wrist forcing the hand still and yanked it from my body. I spun out of their hold and came face to face with the bright green eyes of Elizabeth.

Speak of the fucking devil and they will appear. I fully blame this bout of déjà vu on this stupid fucking club that I will never be setting foot in again after tonight.

I immediately let go of her hand like I had been burned and took a step back. She took a step forward closing the gap between us once more and stood on her tippy toes so she could get close enough to say something to me over the loud music.

"Do you want to dance?" I pulled back from her with a frown and shook my head no. What the hell was she even doing here?

She reached out and grabbed my hand again, threading her fingers through mine. When I looked up at her face, she poked out her bottom lip and gave me a little pout. She dropped her head slightly, drawing my attention to her perky breasts that were barely contained by the skintight strapless dress. The sides of the dress were cut out, so the whole thing resembled an hourglass that just barely covered her tits and her pussy.

She pulled my arm slightly, trying to lead me back to the dance floor. I looked behind me to see Liam preoccupied with the Liv look alike. He had her bent almost completely in half. His hand on the middle of her back holding her in place while she grinds her ass against his dick.

Daniel had his eyes closed and his head leaned back in the booth. He was clearly done for the night.

I looked back at Elizabeth when she pulled my arm again. I took a step towards her before finally sighing and letting her lead me to the dance floor. The bright smile she gave me when I finally relented made me sick to my stomach.

This was a bad idea. I shouldn't be doing this, all I was doing was leading her on. There was no way what happened that night was happening again. She knew about Raylen and the fact that I was getting married, so I don't know what she's planning.

She found the two of us a spot right in the middle of the

dance floor. She turned so her back was to me, grabbed both my hands and pulled them around her waist. She pulled me close enough to snuggly tuck her ass against my dick and pressed into me.

I had to suppress a groan with the first shake of her ass against me. Fuck I hated to admit it, but that felt great.

When the tempo of the music blasting through the speakers sped up, so did the rotation of her ass on my dick. Those last two shots I took were finally hitting my system, slowly quieting the alarm bells going off in my head.

Part of me knew this was a horrible idea and if Raylen ever found out about it, I think she might actually kill me, but the other part couldn't help but enjoy what Elizabeth was doing. The thumping music the copious amounts of liquor racing through my body, leaving every inch of me warm and tingling.

All mixed together with the beautiful woman in front of me rubbing her ample body against me. I could feel myself getting harder with every passing second.

I closed my eyes and enjoyed the feel, but just as quickly as it was there, it was gone again. I opened my eyes to see Elizabeth facing me. She wrapped her arms around my neck and before I had chance to react, she leaned in and placed her lips on mine.

I put my hands on her hips trying to push her away, but she took that as motivation to try harder. She opened her mouth and slipped out her tongue, licking my lips and begging for entry. I wouldn't give it to her though.

I might be drunk off my ass, but those alarm bells came back full force when she put her lips on me. I kept my lips pressed firmly together and tried again to push her away, this time much harder.

Maybe much harder then was necessary if the fact that she now sat on the dirty club floor with her legs spread for everyone to see was any indicator. The crowd around us stopped and stared at her and part of me felt extremely guilty for pushing her that hard, another part wished I had pushed her harder and much sooner.

She knew that I was in a relationship and that I was getting married soon. Drunk or not, it was clear by the fact that I could see straight up her dress at her bare pussy, that she came here with a specific type of intention in mind.

This would be the end of our relationship. There was no amount of legal jargon or lawsuit that would make me keep her in my company or anywhere near me and my family after this.

She looked up at me expectantly, like she thought I would apologize, or something but I didn't. I didn't even help her up, I just turned on my heels and like the horny coward I was feeling like, fled the club.

Chapter 33

RAYLEN

THE FIRST THING **I did when** I heard the crash was clutch at my stomach. Well, you know after I clutched at my chest to make sure my heart didn't jump out of it. I sat up in bed and looked around, trying my hardest to get my eyes to adjust as quickly as possible to the darkness that surrounded me.

When they finally did, I surveyed the bedroom, but nothing looked out of place. I was still in the room alone, with the moon streaming in the window to my left. The bedroom door hadn't been opened and I didn't hear anyone shuffling around in here.

I must've just been having a bad dream. I took a few deep

breaths, trying to calm my racing heart before I laid back down and tried to get comfortable again.

This baby had been giving me so much trouble over the last couple of weeks kicking the shit out of my ribs, so sleep has been a rare commodity for me. Tonight, was probably the first night I've had some decent sleep in a while, who knows if I'll be able to get it back.

The moment I closed my eyes, another crash had me jerking back into a sitting position, effectively causing a cramp in my side.

I definitely wasn't dreaming that time, which meant someone was in the house. Reaching over, I grabbed my phone off the nightstand next to the bed and hit the power button. The screen lit up revealing this adorable candid shot of Jae with Levi in the park. He pushed her on the swing with a huge smile on his face and she had her head tossed back with a tight grip on the two metal chains. Her eyes closed, mouth open, nothing but pure joy on her face.

The time at the top read, *3:36*. I had no missed calls or text messages from Jae or anyone else. He told me he was planning to stay the night at Daniel's apartment, so he didn't risk waking me and Levi up stumbling through the house in the middle of the night.

Tossing my legs over the side of the bed, I grabbed the handle to the nightstand and pulled it open. Jae kept a small safe inside of it that would only open to either his fingerprint or mine. Inside he kept a gun. He use to tell me all the time how he never felt like he needed one when he was back in

Korea, not to mention they're illegal there, but here in New York, he wanted to make sure he was always able to protect his family.

I hated guns especially in the house where there was an eight-year-old roaming freely around, but I felt a little better about it when he showed me how the safe worked. I heard the satisfying click of the latch releasing on the door and a few moments later, my hand wrapped around the rough, cold metal of the grip.

I slid further forward until my feet touched the plush carpeting, keeping my eyes on the bedroom door. My heartrate kicked up another notch when I heard a litter thump that sound like that it was right outside the bedroom followed by the door handle jiggling.

I got to my feet and lifted the gun ready to take out anyone who walked through that door. Jae had taken some courses on how to use the gun and showed me everything I needed too. As someone who grew up in the states, sad to say this wasn't my first-time handling one, that's why I absolutely hate them.

Hate them or not, my daughter was out there and I needed to do whatever I had to do to get to her. The door slowly creaked opened and a black shadow came tumbling in with a thump. I raised the gun higher, but it wasn't until I heard the audible groan that I lowered it again.

"Jae?" He groaned again. I breathed a sigh of relief and set the gun on the nightstand before rushing over to him. I flicked the light switch on the wall and stared at his body sprawled out in the middle of the floor.

I rolled my eyes. Typical, of course he didn't do what he said he was going to by staying at his friend's house tonight. Instead, he somehow found his way home at the risk of scaring the crap out of our daughter and almost winding up with a bullet in him.

I lightly tapped him in the ribs with my bare foot, bringing another groan to his lips. I shushed him and looked down the dark hall to see Levi's bedroom door was still closed. My shoulder's slumped. Good, I didn't need her seeing him like this.

Jae reached out and grabbed my foot, lifting his head enough to place a kiss on the inside of my ankle. "I missed you." I would've thought it was sweet if his speech wasn't so slurred, instead all it made me do was roll my eyes again.

I pulled my foot out of his grip and squatted down as best I could with this huge belly I was sporting, so I could be as close to eyelevel with him as I could be. I looked at his unfocused glassy eyes and it took everything in me not to burst into a violent fit of laughter.

I've never seen Jae drunk before, in the time that I've known him, he barely ever touched alcohol. Even when we were in high school, we would go to parties together, but he would always only sip beer. He always told me it was because he wanted to make sure I had as much fun as I could and that required at least one of us to be somewhat sober.

Now, I was starting to think it was because he just couldn't handle his own liquor. How many shots did it take to knock him on his ass like this? I couldn't help but wonder how bad the twins were if this was the state he was left in.

I grabbed his arm and tried to help him get to his feet. He couldn't stay here in the doorway like this.

"Jae, come on you have to get up." He groaned again but tried his best to put his feet under him. He failed a few times, but eventually he was able to stand straight up. I took a step back so I could see his face once I was sure he was stable on his feet.

The glassiness in his eyes had cleared just a little and for a second he looked like he was completely sober. Before I had time to react, he turned and closed the door. At the same time, he reached out and grabbed my arm, spinning me and pressing my back against the door.

I gasped at the sudden movement. He pressed his hands flat against the wall on either side of my head and leaned in so close I could smell the strong sent of alcohol on his breath. He was definitely wasted.

"I missed you." He said again. I lifted my hand and gently brushed his unruly hair from his forehead.

"I missed you too." I stood on my tippy toes and pressed a kiss to his lips. When I opened my eyes to look at him again, he shook his head no.

"No," He said. One of his hands dropped from the wall. Slowly he trailed the back of his hand down my side until he reached the top of my thigh right below the hem of the thin night gown I was wearing. Being pregnant always made me run hot when I sleep, even when it was cold outside. I could barely bring myself to sleep in any clothes at all at night.

When Jae got to the hem of the gown, the direction of his hand switched direction and began traveling back up my thigh. It took him no time at all to reach the sensitive folds between my thighs.

"I *really* missed you." The first rub of his rough fingers against me, had me grabbing onto his shoulders so my knees didn't give out. I let out a surprised gasp and closed my eyes enjoying the feel. "No panties tonight?" Panties were yet another thing that fell into the 'uncomfortable' column when you had a bowling ball for a stomach, and you just wanted some sleep.

He grabbed my wrist moving my hand from his shoulder and instead placed it against the front of his jeans, right over the outline of his hard dick. Another side effect of a drunk Jae-Hyun, he was hard as a rock, and I couldn't help but wonder what made him like this.

My thoughts were cut short when he let go of my wrist and instead place his hand around my throat, giving me a slight squeeze. The rush I felt instantly at the action, had more moisture pooling between my legs. I could practically feel it running down my leg as he doubled his efforts, now putting most of his focus on my clit. He leaned his face in, gently brushing his nose against my cheek.

"Do you still like it rough when you're pregnant. I've been pretty gentle with you lately." His voice sounded so rough in my ear and the way his warm breath brush against my cheek sent a shiver down my spine. It was the pregnancy hormones

I swear. For months, the slightest touch, hell even a look from him would have me swimming in my own panties.

"I hope you do because I don't think I can be gentle tonight." He pulled back from my face and I opened my eyes to look at him. He looked so focused. His grip on my neck tightened again, almost to the point that it was too tight, but that just made it even better. Without warning, he shoved two fingers inside. My back arched towards him, and my mouth fell open in a silent scream. The grip he had on my neck was too tight to allow any words.

"Nod your head so I know you understand." I followed his command immediately. Whatever he wanted me to do as long as he didn't stop his assault on my body.

Jae let go of my neck and spun me around so I was facing the wall. He grabbed both of my hips and pulled me so I would arch towards him and have room for my belly without feeling squished. His hands slid up my back, lifting my night gown as they went.

I heard him fumbling with the buckle on his belt before hearing the very unmistakable sound of his zipper. He leaned forward so his chest was flush against my back. I wish I could feel his bare skin. The rigid outline of those abs against me, the thought alone was enough to make my mouth water.

Jae had been hitting the gym a little hard lately more than likely because he couldn't do much during his recovery time. He kept cracking the joke that now that he was going to be father of two, he didn't want to get a dad bod. Something about wanting us to start on number three as soon as I gave birth, and he wanted me to still find him attractive. I really don't think he had anything to worry about in that department.

"Try not to scream." He said with a moan before he licked the shell of my ear. My legs quivered. Fuck, he was barely touching me, and I feel like I could explode already.

That was the only warning he gave before I felt the spongey mushroom head of his dick slice through my body. The force knocked the wind out of me, and I was gearing to do the exact opposite of what he just told me not to do and not only wake up Levi but the entire neighborhood.

He knew immediately what was about to happen because he reached up with one hand and shoved two fingers into my mouth. The same two fingers he just had inside me.

"Suck" He commanded. "If you bite me be prepared to suffer the consequences of your actions." Shit. If he kept talking like that, I was going to drown him.

The brat in me wanted to bite him just to see what these mysteries consequences he was bragging about were. The other part was trying to focus on not waking our daughter up. His hips snapped forward, burying him balls deep inside of me. My teeth grazed his fingers, the urge to clench them strong. I opted for sucking on them instead, tasting myself on his fingers.

"Good girl." He praised.

He was relentless. His thrusts brutally hard and fast going deep. I don't think he's ever fucked me this aggressively before and I was loving every second of it. I want to scream out his name, tell me how much I loved everything he was doing, but I had to keep in the back of my mind that I had to stay quiet.

I braced my hands against the wooden door, trying my hardest not to faceplant into it. He was going too hard, I was struggling to stay upright. His grunts and groans behind me were like wicked music to my ears. That mixed with the wet sound of skin slapping against skin was like the perfect symphony.

"Fuck." He groaned. I could hear his teeth grinding even over all the noise we were making. Jae pulled his fingers from my mouth, and instead dropped them back between my legs, landing right on that sweet spot.

My hips jerked at the contact, and I could feel his grip on me tighten. "I'm close." He let out a puff of air like he was shocked that he had gotten to this point so fast. I wasn't. Jae had an astonishingly high stamina level, but everyone's drops when they're drunk and as sober as he seemed at this moment, I knew that liquor was still running rampant through his bloodstream.

He took his slick fingers and circled my clit gently at first, teasing me to the point that a whimper slipped past my lips.

Jae took my whimpers as motivation to plow into me even harder. At this point he was pretty much ramming me into the door. The wood groaned and squeaked. I even think I heard the hinges rattle. I was going to be so deliciously sore in the morning and it would serve as a reminder of the way he handled me tonight.

His finger moved from circling my clit to gently messaging it. When I started rocking my hips in time to his rhythm begging for more, he gave it a quick squeeze and release and that was all it took for me to shatter.

"Oh, thank god." He groaned out his relief before I felt his dick jerk inside of me and then he flooded my insides. His body instantly went limp and the only thing that stopped him from crushing me between him and the door, was the hand he placed next to my head to keep himself upright.

"I'll never get tired of fucking you." I heard him whisper. The feeling was mutual.

Chapter 34

RAYLEN

"DUH ISANG IYAGIHAL GEOSHI *eopseumnida!"*
(There is nothing left to talk about!)

I had been hearing Jae-Hyun yelling from his office for over an hour now.

At first, I thought it was a work thing, but then after thinking about it I realized I've never heard him yelling when it comes to anything work related.

The car accident was months ago and since then, Jae had returned to work all of a week and a half before he went back to working from home again. He wouldn't tell me why he had started working from home again. He claimed he wanted to be near me, the baby and Levi.

His excuse was invalid, Levi spends most of the day at school, I work in the bedroom and according to the doctor as of today I was only 28 weeks and safely out of my second trimester.

Over the last few days Jae-Hyun had been receiving phone calls that he always insists on taking in his office. The phone calls always end in screaming.

Every time I ask him about it, he tells me it's nothing to worry about which of course only makes me worry more.

I creeped outside the office door trying to listen in, but he was speaking Korean and I couldn't understand a word of it.

"*Maeumeul bakkugi anheul geoyeyo.*"

(I wont change my mind.)

That was the last thing he said before I heard the distinguishing sound of his cellphone hitting the wall. I jumped at the sound and turned to leave.

It probably wasn't the best idea to be listening in on his conversations even if I didn't understand what was being said. He told me not to worry about it, so I didn't want him to know I was in fact worrying.

I wasn't fast enough though. "What are you doing?" He asked. I turned to see him with his arms folded across his chest, leaning against the door frame. I didn't even hear him open the door.

"Oh, I was just coming to see if you were hungry?" Years of being a writer made the lie fall from my lips like it was actually the truth.

"Then why were you leaving?"

"Heard you on the phone, didn't want to interrupt." I gave him a shrug. It wasn't a complete lie. I did hear him on the phone, and I didn't in fact want to interrupt. The only part I left out was the fact that I didn't interrupt because I was hoping I would eventually figure out what he was talking about.

Jae-Hyun eyed me suspiciously, but as much as he liked to pat himself on the back, he hadn't quite mastered figuring out when I was lying and when I wasn't.

He sighed and dropped his arms to his side. "I know you were listening." Or maybe he did. "Maybe it's a good thing you were."

I cocked an eyebrow at him. He wasn't annoyed at me. "Meaning?"

"I wanted to talk to you about the wedding." Another thing Jae-Hyun had been pretty hush hush about these last couple weeks was this wedding. He insisted on planning this whole thing by himself and wouldn't give me not one detail about anything.

I let him do it because I had enough stuff on my plate between the baby and my deadline only being a month away. Not to mention, I figured he might want to incorporate a couple traditions from his culture into the ceremony and since I knew nothing about that, I figure it was best to leave it up to him.

Olivia was not happy about it though.

"Finally, I thought I was going to find out the day of when it actually was." Jae-Hyun reached his hand up and nervously rubbed the back of his neck.

Suddenly it seemed he had lost the ability to make eye contact with me. I sighed rubbing my eyes, this wasn't going to be good.

"Jae, the longer you take to say it, the madder I'm going to be when you do so just get on with it. I have work I need to finish."

"*Sibal*"

(*Fuck.*)

He threw his hands in the air in frustration before slapping them back to his side. "My parents aren't coming to the wedding. They don't approve of the marriage."

I guess I shouldn't be surprised, this was something any-body could've guess after our interaction at the hospital.

After I basically told them to go fuck themselves after they offered to take my daughter from me because I'm just such an unfit parent. Oh, and let's not forget after they admitted to knowing about Levi from the very beginning and kept the truth from him this entire time. Let's just say that was probably the fastest their pilot had ever gotten their private plane back in the sky.

I couldn't expect them to come to my wedding after how "disrespectful" I was to them. To be fair, they started it.

I leveled him with a deadpan look so I could tell him how uninterested I was with them being in attendance in the first place. "Jae-"

"They're also still insisting that Levi would be better off in Korea with them." He interrupted me. The way my mood switched from annoyed and uninterested to full blown rage was enough to make me a little lightheaded. These pregnancy hormones were really whooping my ass.

"What is it with your family and always wanting to be in control of something they have no right to." I had my hands on my hips now. "I thought that was just one of your sick, weird traits, but now I'm finding out that bullshit is hereditary."

I hadn't even realized I had been pacing during my rant until I felt a sharp pain in my side and immediately stopped in my tracks. I grabbed at my belly as the world tilted on its side slightly. One arm shot out to brace myself against the hallway wall.

"Raylen." Jae-Hyun rushed up behind me, one hand circling around my waist and landing on top of the hand I had on my belly, the other rested comfortably on my hip.

I took a couple deep breaths and kept my eyes closed waiting for everything to right itself. I hadn't felt any morning sickness so far unlike when I was pregnant with Levi. I could barely work I was so sick. In this moment, I was feeling a strong sense of déjà vu from that time.

Jae-Hyun pushed me forward, trying to get me to walk. He led me down the hall and toward the living room, depositing me in the middle if the couch.

He crouched down in front of me, taking both of my hands in one of his and using the other one to lift my chin up so I would look at him.

"Talk to me Raylen, how are you feeling?" It took me a second to be able to open my eyes fully. The first few attempts resulted in me almost throwing up right in Jae-Hyun's face, but finally the nausea began to fade, and I could look into those deep brown eyes.

The pale look on his face made me feel guilty for making him worry. This was the first time he had to deal with a pregnant me so I couldn't expect him to know that this wasn't out of the ordinary and nothing to really put up alarm bells about.

I pulled my hand out of his grip and gently rubbed his face reassuringly, giving him a small smile. "I'm fine."

"What about-"

"The baby is fine too Jae, I just got a little too worked up." His head dropped and he let out the breath I know he had been holding for the last ten minutes unsure of what was going on.

There was a long moment where he didn't do anything but just stare at me, but when he finally opened his mouth, I don't think I was expecting him to say what he did.

"I think we should move up the wedding."

"Why?" I thought maybe this would make him want to push it out even more.

Originally, he was hell bent on having the wedding before the baby was born, but he change his mind after he tore up the contract because I told him I didn't want a maternity wedding dress. Now all of sudden he wants to move it up, not further back.

"This wedding is only going to cause you more stress, I

think we should just get it over with now before you get any further along." Get it over with? Well, that's a lovely way to think about our wedding. Would make any woman fall head over heels in love with him at this very moment wouldn't it.

"I was thinking maybe next week." I could feel my eyes ready to bug out of my head and he must've noticed because he rushed out the rest of his little speech. "Before you say anything, there's still time to make everything perfect. It could just be something small with friends and family."

He was rubbing his hands together nervously and unlike him, I was a pro at telling when he was keeping something from me. Usually, I'll give him the opportunity to tell me on his own, especially after having had multiple conversations about him keeping secrets, but I wasn't in the mood to pacify him today and this was our wedding he was talking about.

"You're hiding something from me Jae-Hyun." He opened his mouth to protest, but I spoke over him. "Tip, never interrupt a pregnant woman." His mouth snapped closed immediately. "Tell me what it is now, or their won't be a wedding, I could care less about the contract."

"What makes you think I'm hiding something?" I put my fingers to my temples rubbing them gently. This headache was intensifying by the second.

"Another tip, don't lie to us either."

Jae-Hyun clenched his teeth. This was a losing battle, the sooner he realized that the better. Suddenly he shot to his feet.

"Fine... It's my parents."

"Yes yes, I heard you they don't want to come to the wedding. They hate me blah blah blah." Jae-Hyun shook his head, the nervous look still prominent on his face.

"That's not it." He waved his hands. "I mean it is, but that's not what I was going to say."

I sat quietly waiting for him to continue. "My parents told me they were the reason I never got any of your letters over the years. That was why they knew about Levi, and I didn't." There goes that headache again.

I didn't think I could not like his parents any more than I already did. I thought maybe they would have their redeemable moment. You know like how it is on tv.

The misunderstood parents don't approve of who their child wants to be with, but eventually they come around and eventually accept the inevitable and maybe even come to like their child's partner.

Nope, leave it to the people who made their son come to America with a different last name just so no one would know he had any connection to them. Leave it to the same people who knew he had a child out there and didn't so much as tell him let alone let him come back to us to break that cliché.

The same ones who would prefer him to marry someone who shares the same race over someone he actually wants to be with just because they wanted him to and for no other reason.

These are the same people who wanted me to just willingly give my daughter over to them for them to raise her to only embrace half of who she is.

After all that, why am I surprised that they intercepted any form of communication Jae-Hyun and I could've had over the years just because it didn't benefit them. If it wasn't for his insistence to come back to the states, he would go the rest of his life without knowing she ever existed.

The more I thought about it, the funnier it is actually. In a way, they did the same thing I did. They in some roundabout way, thought they were protecting their child by keeping things from him, the same way I did by not telling Levi who Jae-Hyun was when he came back into our lives.

"They said they wouldn't come to the wedding and if I go through with it, they'll disown me." For a second I was so caught up in my own thoughts, I had forgotten Jae-Hyun was even talking. I tuned back in around the time he started talking about his family cutting him off.

I didn't care about his money, my daughter and I were doing just fine without, despite what his parents think. The tone in his voice is what caught my attention. I thought he would sound angry and frustrated that his parents were reacting this way to his decisions as a grown man, but he sounded hurt. I didn't like it.

I would've preferred if he was angry, not because I wanted him to hate his parents or anything. It would be great if his parents could be part of our lives, know their granddaughter and this baby I'm carrying now, but I didn't like him sounding so defeated. It hurt me, *physically* hurt me.

"What does that mean?" I asked. If they disowned him

because he married me, they wouldn't really cut off communication with him, would they?

"Just what it sounds like," he said with a sigh. "If I marry you, they want nothing to do with me or our family."

I got to my feet, trying my hardest to ignore the dizziness that was trying to take over me and grabbed his arm. He grabbed my wrist trying to stabilize me when I stumbled slightly. "What about the baby? Do they care that we are having another child? Don't they have any interest in getting to know either of your children."

He rubbed my arm gently, but he didn't meet my eyes. "I hadn't had a chance to tell them. It wouldn't matter anyway, they made their position perfectly clear. Marry you and I'm cut off."

Chapter 35

RAYLEN

"WILL YOU STOP WITH **the** whining, you're worse than Levi and you're making me nervous." Olivia and I stood in Jae-Hyun's bedroom, well I guess it was *our* bedroom now. She stood in a floor length gold ballgown covered in Swarovski crystals.

It was a gorgeous dress with puffy long sleeves and a deep plunging neckline. Her hair was swooped up in a tight bun at the top of her head with a few wispy waves falling around it. She looked gorgeous honestly. Well except for the sour look on her face.

"I won't let you be in any of my wedding photos with that stupid look on your face." I was growing increasingly frustrated with my own hair and every time I looked in the mirror, I didn't like what I saw.

I stood in front of the floor length mirror in an all-white ball gown. It was princess style, extremely poofy at the bottom with a faux strapless corset at the top. It would've been nice if the corset was more than just for show, but considering I now had a baby bump, it really wasn't much I could do about that.

There was a powder blue sash tied around my waist that tied in a bow at my back. The gown was beautiful and perfect with its intricate flower design covering the skirt of it. It was my hair that was the problem. It was always my hair that was the problem. Leave it to curly hair to be a nuisance when you really need it to come through for you.

I turned toward the mirror again only to see the diamond studded tiara once again sitting lopsided in the middle of my head. My curls preventing it from sitting properly in place. I groaned in frustration and ripped the stupid headpiece from my head, tossing it across the room and onto the bed.

"Fuck it." I said smoothing down the curls that went in all different directions when I yanked the tiara off.

"No, I won't fix my face. This is too soon." Olivia had been sitting on the edge of my bed for thirty minutes angrily staring at me while I got ready. She had made her displeased feelings about the wedding being so soon very vocal multiple times. It wouldn't change anything though.

I wasn't happy it was this fast either, I wanted it to be in a few months, so we had more time to make sure everything was exactly how the both of us wanted. The few family members that still speak to me, weren't able to be here because of how fast it was happening. The same for Jae-Hyun's family, although he seemed much less upset about that fact then I was about my family.

"Will you get over it, it's happening." Olivia huffs throwing her arms down and slapping the mattress.

"Yes, but why is it happening so soon? You couldn't have waited until after the baby was born?" I wanted the same thing, but I didn't want to tell Olivia my doubts now. She would only push me to tell Jae-Hyun to call it off.

I didn't know what his plan was, or what his family disowning him had to do with him wanting to move the wedding up. I wanted to trust him, but right now it was feeling more like he was being a stubborn child, doubling down on his decision because mommy and daddy told him not to.

What else was I supposed to think, he never includes me in his plans and no matter how many conversations we've had about him opening up more, he still manages to have more and more secrets up his sleeves.

That really wasn't something I wanted hanging over my head before we got married even if it was supposed to be a contractual marriage, we're still supposed to be able to trust each other.

I chewed on my bottom lip while my mind raced, effectively ruining the thick layer of gloss I had put on a few minutes prior. Maybe I should try talking to him before the ceremony started. There was still another hour and not many guests had arrived.

We had opted to have the ceremony at home since it was so last minute, luckily the backyard was huge. Big enough to fit the thirty or so people that were able to attend.

I heard a gasp coming from behind me. My head snapped in Olivia's direction only to see her staring at me with wide eyes.

"What?" I asked.

"You didn't want this wedding, did you?" Fuck.

"Of course I did, what are you talking about?"

"Bullshit." She got to her feet. "You do realize you're standing in front of a mirror. I saw that look on your face." I rubbed my hands together nervously. I hated that she could read me like a book. One of the downsides of knowing each other for so long.

"Ok fine." I surrendered, turning to face her. "I wasn't exactly the happiest when Jae told me he wanted to have the wedding so soon, I would've preferred for it to be after the baby was here."

"So why the hell are you standing here in a wedding dress right now." Olivia threw her hands up in frustration. Nobody was more frustrated about this entire situation than I was. I didn't have a legit answer to her question, but I was going to get one.

"Hold that thought." I held up my finger to her before turning and heading to the door and out into the hallway.

With the bedroom door closed I couldn't really hear much of what was going on in the rest of the house, but the moment I stepped out into the hallway, I could hear soft music playing over the loudspeakers out in the backyard.

Walking into the living room, the large black framed double glass sliding doors that led out into the patio were wide open, letting the workers Jae-Hyun had hired walk in and out of the house freely.

The house was bustling with people between the staff and the few guests that had arrived. Some of them looked at me and smiled when they saw me in my wedding dress. Some even tried to stop me so they could offer me their congratulations and while I appreciated the sentiments and didn't want to be rude, I was on a mission, and I couldn't let them slow me down.

I searched the entire house, and I couldn't find Jae-Hyun anywhere. He had told me before, that unlike the American tradition where it was bad luck to see the bride before the wedding, in Korean weddings, it was common for the bride and groom to wait for the ceremony to begin together so that they can walk down the aisle together.

He told me he would meet me in our bedroom thirty minutes before everything was supposed to start, that was supposed to be twenty minutes ago. The ceremony started in ten minutes, and I couldn't find him anywhere.

My only other option was to check outside, but enough of the guests had seen me in my dress and I wasn't sure I wanted the rest of them to see it before I walked down the aisle in it. What choice did I have though, there wouldn't be a wedding if I didn't talk to Jae-Hyun first.

I walked through the glass doors out onto the patio, and I didn't see him there. Everything looked beautiful as the workers scrambled to finish the last touches before the ceremony began.

Bypassing them, I headed around toward the front of the house, he had to be here. His overbearing and helicopter fiancé bit hadn't ended like I was hoping it would after my first trimester was over. If anything, he was even worse now.

That being said, I knew he wouldn't have left the house without saying anything to me. There were thick bushes surrounding the sides of the house, keeping it slightly cut off from the back yard. I would've walked right passed them like I normally did, except this time I heard the distinct voice of Jae-Hyun shouting in Korean.

I almost missed it because the music from the speakers drowned out most of the sound in the general area, but lately I had been so attuned to everything that is Jae-Hyun, I think I would've heard his voice in a loud crowd of people.

I stepped closer to the bushes so I could hear what was being said clearer or at least figure out who he was talking to.

"Wae yeogi wasseoyo? Jae saenggak-i byunhaji anneundago malhaetjanayo."

(Why did you come here? I told you I wasn't changing my mind.)

I heard his voice say. Jae-Hyun had been helping me learn Korean just like he promised, but I hadn't gotten that far and it was even harder to make out what they were saying when he was speaking so fast.

"Dangshin-eun iseongjeogiji anayo."

(You are not being rational.)

I recognized that voice immediately. After the way that voice tore apart my parenting ability in Jae-Hyun's hospital room, there's no way I would forget it. *"Dangsin-gwa ttal-eui mirae-reul saenggak-hae boseyo. Igeon non-ni-jeo-gi-ji anayo."*

(Think about you and your daughter's future, this is not logical.)

Jae-Hyun's mother spoke.

"Jeon-eun geunyeo eopsineun mirae-ga eopseumnida. Geun-yeo-neun je a-i-reul an-go issseumnida."

(I don't have a future without her. She's carrying my child.)

There was long stretch of silence that made me even more frustrated that I couldn't understand what he said. Whatever it was, it must've stunned her into silence.

I took another step closer to the bushes, straining to hear more of the conversation, but making sure not to get any stains on my dress.

"Myut nyeon jeon-gwa gateun sil-su-reul jeong-mallo jeo-jeul geongayo?"

(Are you really going to make the same mistake you did years ago?)

"Uri gajogeun silsuga animnida.
I gyeolhonsigeul jiji-haji anneundamyeon wae yeogi osyeon-nayo?"

(My family is not a mistake. Why did you come here if you don't support this wedding?)

"Dasi han beon jeongsin charil su inneun gihoe-reul deurigo sipeosseumnida.

Sohui-wa gyeolhonhal sigan-eun ajik nam-a issseumnida. Geureochi an-eumyeon deo isang bo-ho-hal su eopsseumnida."

(We wanted to give you another chance to come to your senses. There is still time to marry So-Hee like you're supposed to. If you don't we cant protect you anymore.)

That sounded like his father's voice. How lovely for both his parents to grace us with their presence at our wedding.

I have to say, the more they tried to make their presence in our lives known, the more they were pissing me off. Every time they were around, they made Jae-Hyun so angry and completely different from the man I know him to be.

I wouldn't completely be upset about them cutting him off and going back to Korea, at least then the four of us can live in peace without all the drama tied to them.

"I'm going to say this in English, so you know how serious I am." I heard Jae-Hyun speak. I leaned in closer, hanging on his every word.

"I don't care about the company or marry So-Hee. I will be marrying the mother of my children right here today. If you don't like it, there is nothing stopping you from leaving." I put my hand to my chest as I continued to listen to him talk.

"If the company is so important to you, feel free to continue running it. I have no intention of moving back to Korea to take over unless it is what my *wife* wants." My heart skipped a beat at the emphasis he put on the word wife.

"That company means nothing to me now. As a matter

of fact, after your little revelation at the hospital where you admitted to knowing I had a daughter and instead of telling me, you hid it from me, I took matters into my own hands."

Now my ears were on high alert. I had been wondering what Jae-Hyun was up to in his office for the last few weeks. Even though he had been working from home, he use to at least take a few breaks throughout the day to spend time with me, but for the last two weeks, he had barely left that room at all.

I thought maybe he was just planning for the wedding, and that's where all his free time had gone, but there was clearly something else going on and now I was going to find out what it was.

I leaned in even closer and immediately regretted that decision when I lost my balance and fell through the shrubbery. Eavesdropping in the grass in four-inch heels when you're weighted down by a huge belly and an even bigger dress probably isn't the smartest thing to do.

I closed my eyes when I fell, fully expecting the ground to be where I landed, but it wasn't. Instead, I landed on the hard, ribbed chest of my husband to be. I opened my eyes to look at him and the look on his face told me he knew what I was doing and that we would be having a nice long talk about it later.

He masked his expression as he helped me to my feet and then turned his sights back on his parents.

"My beautiful bride loves to make an entrance doesn't she."

"*Igeoseun sajjeogin gajok daehwa-imnida.*"

(This is a private family conversation.)

His mother said eyeing me with distaste. I didn't need to speak Korean to know she was talking shit about me. Every day I liked this lady less and less. I've never put my hands on someone's parents before, but these pregnancy hormones were really making me wonder why I haven't put them on her. She should really tread lightly.

"She is my family, so she has every right to be a part of this conversation." Jae-Hyun fixed the powder blue tie around his neck that matched the sash around my waist and grabbed my hand squeezing it tight.

"I spoke with the board and there are a few members who have grown tired of your outdated traditions. They feel as if you are holding the company back and were much more eager than I expected to jump ship." His father's face immediately scrunched up.

"Out of the twelve members that make up your board father, seven of them have agreed to invest in my company." I couldn't understand any of Jae-Hyun's business talk but based on how quickly his father's face had turned red, whatever he had done was not going to be good for him.

"That's impossible." He said through clenched teeth. "Those men have been with me almost since the beginning."

"Well maybe that's why they feel it's time for a change. I should be thanking you father, you're overwhelming interest in my personal life has made you neglect your business and in return has provided a wonderful wedding present for me and my wife."

Jae-Hyun took a step forward pulling away from me and folded his body in half, giving his parents a very deep bow. "Thank you, father." He stood up and leveled them with a cold stare. "Now you both are more than welcome to stay, but if you will excuse us, we have a wedding to get to." He reached back his hand for me to grab, and I did immediately, letting him lead me out of the shrubbery and back around to where the guests were starting to file into the seats that lined the aisle we would walk down.

The conversation he had just had with his parents completely let all the wind out of my sails. I didn't need to talk to Jae-Hyun about anything anymore. He was willing to completely severe ties with his family for Levi and me, I didn't need to question anything anymore.

This wedding wasn't just him throwing a temper tantrum. Jae-Hyun wanted this wedding because he loved me.

Chapter 36

JAE-HYUN

THE MUSIC PLAYED LOUDLY **through** the speakers, the bright sun shone overhead and at least thirty pair of eyes were on us. I held out my elbow for Raylen to grab. I could feel her shaky fingers through the thin fabric of my white button up as she snaked her hand around my arm.

Glad to know I wasn't the only one nervous in this moment. I feel like I had been doing a pretty good job at hiding my emotions up until this point. I tried to keep my mind focus on the business dealings I had been quietly working on so my mind wouldn't spiral thinking about this day.

Now here I was almost completely soaking my shirt in sweat with how nervous I was. In this cool 69-degree weather, I shouldn't be sweating at all. That's what she did to me though.

I've wanted to marry Raylen since I was 17 years old and now finally, nothing was going to stop me from doing just that.

I looked down at her meeting those gorgeous, sparkling eyes and she smiled at me. The look on her face told me she was confident in her decision to go through with the wedding despite the jitters I could feel radiating all over her body.

That look made my heart skip a beat. I took a deep breath and faced forward, leading Raylen down the aisle.

Ahead of us, the priest stood ready to perform the ceremony. To my left stood Raylen's best friend Olivia stood holding a bouquet of white roses in one hand and the small hand of our little princess Levi in the other.

Levi was dressed in a smaller version of the same dress Raylen was wearing. A white princess style dress with floral detailing on the skirt except the sash tied around her waist was gold instead of the powder blue Raylen wore. She had her hair swooped up into an intricate curly bun that I'm sure Raylen was responsible for since I had yet to master anything that had to do with my daughter's hair and a white floral crown on top of her head.

Our little flower girl looked adorable as she smiled back at us.

Most of my family were still in Korea because the wedding was so last minute, but the few work friends I made here in the short time I had been back were more than happy to step in as witness. Of course the twins acted as my groomsmen because I could never decide between the two of them who would be the best man. They both wore black suits with white shirts underneath. Gold colored neckties were around their neck to match Olivia's dress.

I tugged my arm forward slightly, letting Raylen know it was time to walk. I took my first step, and she matched me perfectly. Our walk down the aisle was perfectly in synched, and I tried to focus on looking straight ahead instead of at everyone watching us, so I didn't trip and drag her down with me. Who knew the white rose petals that littered the path could be so slippery, especially in grass. I did notice that my parents were nowhere in sight, I guess they were going to be heartless till the very end. Their loss, I had a new family now, one I wasn't planning on ever letting go. I had no regrets.

Before we knew it, we had made it to the golden archway trimmed in blue ribbon and stood in front of the priest. I turned to face Raylen, giving her a chance to pass her bouquet to Olivia before grabbing both her hands.

"Friends and family thank you all for being here to witness this blessed event," The priest began when I gave him a head nod to let him know we were ready. "We are gathered here today to celebrate Raylen Levi Clark and Jae-Hyun Yuu in holy matrimony."

The priest turns to look at Olivia. "May we have the rings please." Olivia digs out her ring from the little satin pouch tied around her wrist and passes it to Raylen. I turn to face Liam as he passes me his ring as well.

I looked to the priest, who gave me a head nod letting me know to go ahead with my vows. "With everything going on lately, I never had time to actually write my vows, so I was just going to be honest.

I grabbed Raylen's hand and slipped the thick diamond encrusted band onto her finger. I knew she wouldn't want something super loud, she preferred things that were on the simpler side.

She looked at the ring and smiled before bringing her eyes back up to meet mine. I held her hands and took a deep breath, speaking from the heart.

"When I met you that first day of junior year, I thought you were the most beautiful girl I had ever met. I also thought there was no way in hell you would ever give me a chance." The priest cleared his throat at my choice of words, and I shot him an apologetic look. This is what happens when you don't plan out your vows.

"Imagine my surprise when the beautiful artsy girl who preferred baggy, comfortable clothes over the latest fashion trend. Who preferred to sit in the corner and read a good book over going to parties. Who would rather be invisible then have all the attention she unknowingly got, was interested in a guy like me."

"I waited for the day you realized that I wasn't good enough for you." I chuckled. "I'm still waiting for that day."

"When I left you back then, I regretted it every day and now that I have you back in my life, I don't ever plan on letting you go again. I'm in love with you Raylen, I always have been."

Raylen smiled at me, the tears flowing freely from her eyes. She pulled one of her hands out of my grip just long enough to dab her face slightly and then put her hand back in my grip.

She took a deep breath and then blew it out. "I guess it's my turn." She joked and a few of the guests giggled along with her.

I felt her squeeze my hand slightly before she began to speak. "For a really long time, I hated you." She spoke. I flinched slightly at the comment, not because this was new information to me, but because I always felt guilty for not having the backbone to stand up to my parents and tell them what I wanted and what I wanted was to stay with Raylen.

"That was wrong of me. I should've believed in what we had. I should've held onto the hope that maybe there was another reason you weren't in my life anymore."

"I knew the type of man you were and still I had so little faith in you. I'm sorry for that. "When you came back into my life, I thought it was a cruel joke from God, reminding me of what I had lost and would never have again, but you showed me that he was giving me another chance at the happiness I deserve."

"I want this. Past all the drama and all the hurt, I want to be here with you and no one else. I..." Raylen's words cut off and her eyes locked onto something over my shoulder. Suddenly her eyes grew the size of saucers and she screamed.

Behind her, I saw Olivia's face mirror Raylen's as she reached down and grabbed Levi, yanking her out of the way.

Raylen tightened her grip on my hand with one of hers and used her other hand to grab my arm and pulled. I stumbled forward, but instead of falling into her, she sidestepped, and I landed on the ground.

The crowd around us erupted into screams of panic. It took me a second to realize what was going on, that is until I turned around and saw the man standing over Raylen's body. She was crumpled into a pile on the floor, bright red blood staining large portions of her dress.

The blonde-haired blue-eeyed asshole I had to throw out of Raylen's apartment a couple months ago, stood with blood splatter on his face and a huge knife in his hand. He looked down at Raylen's body in disinterest, his chest still heaving from the act of stabbing her.

I sat there on the ground, frozen, unable to believe what Iwas seeing. Luke looked up, his eyes locking with mine. He stepped over Raylen's body, coming straight for me, the knife he was caring poised to deal the same damage to me that he just did to her.

He pulled his arm back and swung it with as much force as he could muster, but before it could touch me, I rolled out of the way, and he stumbled forward from the force.

I got to my feet as quickly as I could, preparing for him to come at me again. In the corner of my eye, I could see the guests and the priest had run towards the house, leaving me, Raylen and my groomsmen outside with Luke.

The two men who stood beside me on a day that was supposed to be the happiest of my life just like they had every other monumental moment, began surrounding Luke. They both looked like they were gearing up to jump him, but unsure of how to approach without getting hurt by the huge knife he was swinging around.

I clenched my teeth as I watched him find his balance and then turn back to face me. He wiped his face with the back of his hand, causing Raylen's blood to smear across his cheek.

"Just the man I was looking for." He said with a smirk.

My eyes darted to the side where Raylen still laid in a crumbled bloody pile behind him. I saw Olivia running in our direction from the house, but I didn't see Levi with her. I could only hope that she was safely with the other guests, and she hadn't completely seen what he did to her mother.

I watched Olivia stop just behind the wall of men that was surrounding Luke. Her eyes falling on Raylen. I knew she wanted to get to her, but it wasn't safe yet. I had the same mindset.

This entire time Raylen hadn't moved a muscle and my heart was beating a mile a minute imagining the worst-case scenario. I needed to get to her.

"What are you doing here?" I asked him, not taking my eyes of Raylen. I needed to see her move, even if it was just an inch, a twitch, something.

"Well, I never got my invite to the happy occasion, so I figured I would ask you why that was in person." He took another step towards me, and I matched his movements, taking one back.

"Leave Luke, before we call the police."

He gave a shrug and then wiped the bloody blade on the jeans he was wearing, leaving behind a bright red streak. It was so much blood. My jaw clicked from how tightly I was clenching it and my palm ached slightly from my fingernails digging into the skin with how tightly I had them balled up.

"What do I care, the two of you have already ruined my life." He waved the knife over his shoulder at Raylen.

"What the hell are you talking about?" I hadn't thought about the guy since the day in Raylen's apartment.

"I know it was you that reported me to the medical board after our little disagreement at that bitch's apartment." He was absolutely right, it was me. I reported him to the director of the hospital and the medical board. I should've reported him to the police too, but I was trying to be nice. I was regretting that decision heavily at the moment.

"Because of you, I got fired and I lost my license." The corners of my mouth twitched as I tried to hold back the smirk that so desperately wanted to present itself. Serves him right for what he did to my woman, I should've caved his skull in.

"What happened was completely your fault, Raylen wasn't yours to claim and it's clear you can't take rejection well." From the corner of my eye, I could see my Liam and Daniel slowly tightening the circle around Luke. He was so wrapped up in his evil villain dialogue, I wasn't sure he even noticed they moved at all.

That was perfect, I just needed to keep him distracted long enough for them to make their move.

"She was mine, and if you hadn't shown up when you did, she still would be." I scoffed at that. Raylen had been mine since the day I met her. Years and thousands of miles apart, wasn't going to change that.

"You think that's funny?" He asked taking another step towards me. The moment he moved the twins took two steps towards him. He was letting his rage get the best of him and he had no idea he was doing exactly what I wanted him to. I folded my arms across my chest and stared him down with a smirk on my face.

"I think it's funny that you thought one little date was going to change the fact that no one can make her squirt the way I can." That did it.

Luke's face twisted up into one of pure rage and he lunged at me. I sidestepped his knife and when he tilted past me, I kicked out my leg landing a blow right to the back of his shin. He yelled out, falling forward.

Before he hit the ground, he turned back swinging the blade out and slicing at my shirt. The small nick to my side made me wince and I stumbled a little. Luke thought that was his opening and tried to get to his feet so he could come at me again.

He didn't get the chance though, the twin's sprang into action, lunging at him, grabbing both of his arms. Liam held one of his arms back and Danny twisted his other wrist until he groaned and lost his grip on the knife, dropping it.

I grabbed at my side and lifted my hand up to see it stained in red. Fuck, that hurt.

"Hold him down." Daniel shouted while Luke flailed about trying to get them off him. The guests began trickling back outside to get a better look at everything going on now that the danger was contained.

"Did someone call 911?" One of them shouted.

"Raylen!" I heard Olivia shout from behind me. My head snapped in their direction. She still hadn't moved an inched. I darted toward them moving Olivia off to the side so I could better assess her wounds.

There was so much blood, but I couldn't see where it was coming from. She looked so pale I was almost scared to touch her because I didn't want to make it worse.

"What about the baby" Olivia cried next to me. When I looked at her, she was pointing at a spot on Raylen's stomach, just above her hip and that's when I saw it. There was a big gaping wound there gushing blood.

Oh god no.

Chapter 37

JAE-HYUN

"27-YEAR-OLD FEMALE. STAB WOUND to the right iliac region." One of the paramedics said as they raced us through the emergency doors down a long white hallway. Doctors swarmed us trying to get a better look at the damage to Raylen. "We were able to stop the bleeding, but the victim is 27 weeks pregnant." *Victim.* They called the woman who still hadn't had a chance to be called my wife the *victim*.

The doctors and nurses buzzing around me while I tried to keep up with how fast they were rolling her through the halls never even registered to me. My mind was so focus on keeping my eyes on her, like the moment I turned away something worse would happen.

We made it into a small, enclosed room with a glass door on one side, a bed in the middle and a boatload of machines surrounding it. I remembered being in a place like this after my accident.

I didn't like the fact that our lives consisted of so many hospital visits recently.

The doctors wheeled Raylen in, and I tried to follow behind, but a nurse grabbed my arm and pulled me back.

She was a short older woman, on the heavier side with blonde hair slicked into a bun at the nape of her neck.

I was just about to snatch my arm away from her so I could follow Raylen when she spoke. "I'm sorry sir, we need you to wait out here while the doctors work. You have to give them space so they can treat her."

I wanted to pull away, but something about the look on her face had my feet firmly planted. Like she was silently telling me if I went in there and caused a commotion not only would I risk them not being able to save her or our baby, but I would also be thrown out and I wouldn't be able to be there if something happened.

So, I did the only thing I could do, I took her silent advice and waited in the hall, watching. It was so many people working on her at once, I was wondering how so many people could fit in one room but at the same time I was grateful that it looked like they were giving her the attention she deserved.

One of the doctors called out for them to get an OB in there. Another worked on getting her hooked up to all the different machines positioned behind the bed. Doctors and nurses ran in and out, grabbing supplies, cutting away her dress and assessing her injuries.

All I could do was stand there and watch the chaos.

I was completely zoned out, not able to focus on anything around me but what was happening to Raylen.

More than an hour had gone by with me just standing in the hall, my eyes just locked on her, before I finally heard all the machines around her quiet down. She was finally stable. While I stood there, multiple people had come up to me but I couldn't get myself to focus on them.

Liam and Danny had come to check on me but after several attempts to talk to me with no response, Liam patted me on the back and told me they was here for me before they ducked into the waiting room. Olivia came back to stand next to me in the hall, wait with me for a while, telling me that surprisingly my parents were taking care of Levi.

I wasn't sure how to feel about that after what happened before the ceremony started, but I couldn't focus on that right now. What was more important was that Levi was safe and she didn't have to see her mother like this.

Eventually Olivia left me by myself to my own thoughts and feelings, that is until a doctor stepped in front of me.

She was a short woman, standing about a foot shorter than me. She had long dark hair pulled back into a low ponytail that she kept draped over one of her shoulders. She looked like she could be of Indian descent, and she wore a look of pity on her face.

That look made my heart hammer in my chest. She had

been the last one in to check on Raylen. Looking at the monitors and the long sheet of paper one of the machines was spitting out before jotting something down in the notes on her clipboard.

My eyes dropped to the stitching on the lop left of her white coat. *Obstetrics.* So, she was here to keep an eye on our child. Was the look on her face her way of telling me that we lost the baby?

"Mr. Yuu, there's something I need to discuss with you. Would you mind joining me over here for a second. She gestured toward the right of Raylen's room, further down the hall.

My feet remained planted. I knew I should follow her, listen to any and everything she had to tell me about Raylen and our baby's condition, but everything in me was telling me I should stay where I was.

Like if I looked away from Raylen for even a second, something bad would happen.

The doctor reached up and gently touched my arm. I looked down at her and realized this was her way of trying to reassure me that leaving Raylen for just a second would be ok. I took a deep breath and almost like I was a robot, my legs stiffly followed her.

The doctor led me two doors down to another room with one wall acting as a giant glass window, including the door. It gave the impression of being in a fishbowl and I wasn't sure I liked it. It made me feel like all eyes were on me while the doctor delivered whatever devastating news she needed to.

When we walked in, there was a giant wooden table in the middle. Honestly it looked like it belonged in a conference room and not in the emergency department of a hospital. This must be where doctor's take the families of patients to tell them the horrible news.

I pulled out a chair and sat down, the doctor closed the door behind us and took a seat across from me.

She placed both her hands on the table, interlacing her fingers. I couldn't bring myself to look at her and I wasn't sure I was mentally prepared for whatever she was about to tell me. It couldn't be worse than what I was imagining in my head right?

She cleared her throat before she started talking. "As you know Ms. Clark-"

"Yuu" I said cutting her off. I lifted my head slightly so I could look at her. Her face twisted up into one of confusion and I knew what her next comment was going to be. I wasn't delusional. I know that we never completed the ceremony, which meant technically Raylen was not my wife.

I didn't care though, everything was perfect before Luke showed up and I wouldn't let anyone, not even this doctor take away from the moment we shared.

Understanding shone in her face and she nodded her head sightly. "My apologies. Mrs. Yuu is only 30 weeks into her pregnancy." I nodded my head letting her know that I was listening and that she could continue with whatever horrible news she had to tell me.

"Since she hasn't regained consciousness, I need you to be

the one to make the decision." I lifted my head slightly so I could see her better.

"A decision about what?" She looked a little shocked by my question, but I didn't know why. No one had said anything to me since they wheeled her into that room. I was completely in the dark about everything except the fact that those machines that are connected to her are still beeping.

"I'm sorry, I thought someone had come and informed you." I saw her hands tense up on the table like she was squeezing them for dear life. "Where Mrs. Yuu was stabbed, the knife has put a small hole in the amniotic sac surrounding the baby.

"If the hole had been any bigger, we would've had to remove the baby as soon as she was brought in because the infection it would cause can kill her."

I tried to swallow the lump forming in my throat as I listened to her words. I couldn't fully understand what she was saying. I know English isn't my first language, but I would like to think I was pretty fluent in it. Except for right now, everything she was saying was getting jumbled in my head and I couldn't figure it out.

"So," I started but the lump in my throat was getting bigger by the second. "The decision you want me to make is..." I trailed off hoping that she would provide more clarification.

"Mr. Yuu, I'm asking you who would you like us to prioritize in this situation. If we take the baby out now, there is a chance it won't survive this early. If the baby stays in, the infection could kill your wife."

I couldn't hold it anymore, at her words the tears just slipped from my eyes, racing down my cheeks and there was nothing I could do to stop them. My head dropped to my waiting hands. They wanted me to decide something like this. How the hell was I supposed to do that?

I had to make a choice between saving our child or saving the woman I love, was it even possible to decide something like that?

Whatever I chose, the other would hate me in the end and I don't think I could live with myself regardless of the choice I made. If I chose to save Raylen and let our baby die, she would never forgive me. I know she wouldn't because I wouldn't be able to forgive myself.

If I chose our child and let her die, I would have to live with the knowledge that at some point in the future both of my children would look at me and ask how their mother died and I was expected to respond and say what? That I killed her, or at least my actions did.

If I hadn't reported Luke, if I had just kicked his ass and thrown him out of Raylen's apartment that day, he wouldn't have spiraled and followed Olivia to my house. He wouldn't have tried to attack me, and Raylen would never have thrown herself in front of me.

Everything was my fault, just like it was years ago. If I had just stood up to my parents and told them I wanted to stay in the states. I didn't want to leave Raylen, we could've been together this whole time. We could've raised our daughter together.

No, those things didn't happen, I always picked the wrong moments to try and act like the hero and I had done it again. This time, it was about to cost me everything.

I wanted Raylen to make this decision and whatever she decided, I would be willing to live with. I don't think I can make it by myself.

"I'm going to give you some time to decide, but please keep in mind you don't have a lot of it. If we wait too long, both could die." The doctor got to her feet and left the room, leaving me with my thoughts.

I could hear the sound of rushing water in my ears. It was so loud, I couldn't think. I looked around but I didn't see any water nearby, there wasn't even any sinks in this room. My head was feeling light and suddenly I was extremely cold.

I looked down at my hands and realized they were shaking. What the hell is happening? I tried getting to my feet but the moment I tried to stand, my legs gave out and I fell to my knees.

I leaned forward and placed my palms flat on the grey carpeted floor. The floor spun and then it hit me. It wasn't rushing water that I was hearing, it was all the blood in my head rushing to my feet.

This must be what it felt like to be in shock. I thought I experienced it the night Raylen told me that I was a father, but now that I'm looking back on it, that might've been more anger than anything.

This was completely different.

There wasn't the immediate feeling of passing out or the

overwhelming sense that you were going to throw up like you see in movies. No, this was a very subtle change in the location of my blood supply.

I was cold and shaky, and I had the feeling that if I tried to talk to anyone, I would somehow forget how to use my tongue. I was completely at the mercy of my body and maybe that was a good thing. If I passed out right now, I wouldn't have to think about what the doctor just said to me. I would have to make this decision. Then again that wouldn't make the situation go away, if anything it would make it worse for Raylen and our baby.

I didn't want to make anything worse for Raylen, I wanted to make life easier for her, but it seems like at every turn I was doing the opposite.

I wonder what her life would be like if I didn't enter it when I did. She would probably still be one hell of a writer, taking the world by storm one word at a time.

She would probably have found another man, one who could prioritize her the way she needed to be prioritized. A man who would choose her over his family without a second thought.

They would have a beautiful family together, a bunch of children, maybe even a cat and live a happy life, never wanting for anything.

Or maybe we would've met eventually. Well into our adult years, I would read one of her manuscripts and fall utterly in love with it. Meet her for a business meeting and fall just as immediately in love with her as I did her writing.

We would date, marry and have our own huge family and live here away from mine. That's how I wish our story would've turned out, but unfortunately, here we are. Raylen and our baby clinging to life and here I am falling to pieces when I needed to be the one keeping it together.

I took a few more deep breaths, trying my hardest to get myself together and not succumb to the darkness trying to creep its way in and take me under.

Once I was sure that I could safely make it to my feet and not tip over headfirst into the thick oak of this conference table, I stood up. Slowly putting one foot in front of the other, my feet feeling like they had lead weights around my ankles.

I made it to the conference door. Through the glass I could see the doctor speaking to a nurse outside of Raylen's room. They had their noses buried in her chart, probably trying to decide what to do if I couldn't make a decision.

What they didn't know was that I made one, it was the most obvious decision. An answer I should've given her the moment she laid out my choices for me, instead of trying to make this about me and my own grief.

I opened the door and trudged towards her. Her head lifted when I got close, but she didn't say a word, just silently waited for me to tell her what I wanted. So that's what I did.

"You do whatever possible to save them." She opened her mouth to argue with me, but I didn't want to hear it. I didn't care about the facts or the statistics or whatever long medical explanation she was about to give me.

This wasn't a normal situation, and we weren't normal

people. The woman I love and the child we created together were the exception to whatever the hell she was rearing up to say to me.

"I don't care what has to be done, do it."

Chapter 38

JAE-HYUN

I CAN'T REMEMBER THE **last** time I was able to close my eyes and fall asleep. I shifted uncomfortably in the rock-hard hospital chairs in the lounge, clutching a cup of coffee in between my hands.

If I wasn't mistaken, I had been in this hospital for more than 48 hours. I honestly couldn't remember. All the days are starting to blend together. I didn't have my phone, I think I dropped it during the ceremony. Too busy worried about the knife wielding psycho who just impaled my wife and was coming at me next.

I needed to check on Levi, she must be scared out of her mind. I knew she was with my parents, but I had yet to decide if that was a good thing or a bad thing. My parents were great businesspeople, but they were in fact shitty parents. They did a horrible job raising me, and I was nervous to think of what kind of job they were doing to my daughter, especially knowing how they felt about her and her mother.

I had seen Olivia one other time since her original visit to let me know Levi was fine and where she was. When she came that second time, she offered to get me a change of clothes and swap shifts with me so I could get some sleep, but I declined in the politest way I could at that moment, letting her know there was no way in hell I was leaving Raylen's side until she left this hospital.

Liam and Daniel had stayed by my side without complaint this whole time. They two were still wearing their suits from the wedding, sitting next to me in uncomfortable positions, trying to get some sleep.

They hadn't said a word since that first day, just silently offering me their support, whatever happens and occasionally getting me fresh coffee.

Olivia had made them the same offer of getting them a fresh change of clothes but they also declined. When Daniel noticed the deep worry lines on her face, he tried to lighten the mood by telling her, maybe our collective smell would wake Raylen up.

I couldn't bring myself to laugh right now, but the joke did it's job of getting Olivia to at least crack a small smile at him.

When the exhaustion was finally starting to get the better of me last night, that's when everything went to shit.

I had just closed my eyes, thinking that I could just sleep for an hour or two and everything would be fine but my fear of taking my eyes off Raylen and something bad would happen came true immediately.

Alarm bells began going off, over the loudspeaker I could hear a robotic sounding voice calling for a code blue. I got to my feet and tried to race towards her side, but the nurses wouldn't let me in her room. I could see her body convulsing through the window. I felt sick to my stomach and honestly if I didn't feel compelled to stay in that one spot, I would've found the nearest trashcan so I could throw up the empty contents of my stomach.

I hadn't eaten in I'm not sure how long, so who knows if anything would've came up anyway. Too busy arguing with my parents and trying to make sure everything with the wedding was perfect.

Her body tossed and turned, and I had to watch while two fully grown male nurses held her down. I wanted to go in and help her, soothe her but I knew that I couldn't.

"Mr. Yuu, it's time for that decision." The doctor came out to speak to me. The look on her face left no room for argument, but I had already given her my decision and I was going to stick by it. She would save my wife and our child, no matter what it took.

I didn't say anything in response, I just stared at her. I wasn't sure what expression I was giving her, my emotions so all over the place, but whatever look I gave her was enough for her to realize she wasn't getting another answer out of me.

She sighed and turned on her heels heading back into Raylen's room. She flagged down a few more helping hands and they got to work on her.

Raylen's convulsing had stopped, but the machines around her were still going crazy. I took a step towards the room trying to get a better view at what was happening. My hope to keep an eye on what they were doing went out the window when a group of nurses surrounded Raylen's bed and wheeled her out of the room.

They raced her bed down the hall and to a waiting elevator. I wanted to follow, but one of the nurses stopped just long enough to let me know they were taking her up to surgery and I couldn't follow.

Now here I was with nothing left to do but sit in this waiting room clutching this cup of coffee that Liam had brought me. I couldn't bring myself to drink any of it. Every time I tried to take a sip, it just tasted like sand in my mouth.

It's been maybe two hours since the nurse told me that, and the only reason I even knew was because I couldn't take my eyes off the clock on the wall opposite of me, just ticking away. The noise was annoying, like nails on a chalkboard because it just reminded me that even though it felt like time both stood still and flew by at the same time, the day was moving along just like normal for everyone else in the world.

I wondered how much longer I was expected to sit here twiddling my thumbs. I had no idea what they were taking her into surgery for. No one explained anything to me. Were they going to attempt to fix the hole and keep the baby in longer, or were they planning to just attempt to deliver the baby early?

I told the doctor I wanted her to save them both by any means necessary, but what exactly did that mean?

In a perfect world, it would be a simple situation where they were able to patch up the hole that was made by the knife and both the baby and Raylen would be fine until it was time to deliver in a couple months, but there was nothing simple about this. I don't even think what I was hoping for was a possible outcome. I had no knowledge of medicine and even less knowledge of the female body.

I just had to hope that the doctor was as good at her job as she claimed she was and could save my family.

No sooner did that silent prayer leave me, the doctor walked into the waiting room. My eyes immediately locked onto her, and I was looking for any signs of if she was going to tell me some good news or some bad news before she even opened her mouth.

I needed to mentally prepare myself, but for what, happy news or another devastating blow to add to everything else. I got to my feet setting the coffee cup on the small wooden end table next to me. The twins matched my movements, standing up next to me, holding their breaths just like I held mine.

Nervously I rubbed my hands on my dress pants. The doctor approached me, and it wasn't until she got closer that I realized she had blood smeared all over her scrubs and she looked haggard like she was exhausted.

Was that Raylen's blood all over her? God, was there any left in her body?

"Mr. Yuu," she said with a sigh. She didn't just look exhausted, she sounded exhausted too. "I'm glad I found you."

I nodded my head absently. I wasn't sure what else I was supposed to do, but the days I had been stuck in this hospital, it had felt like my skin was crawling, like I constantly needed to be moving. I wondered a few times if this was how Raylen felt when she had to sit by my bedside after the accident.

Constantly wondering if I would wake up or not.

I stared at the doctor and the moment her face split into a smile, it felt like my knees were ready to give out. She closed the distance between us and placed a gentle hand on my arm.

"Would you like to meet your daughter?" Those words sounded so beautiful they didn't match her appearance. It made the whole thing feel like a dream. Like I would wake up any second and realize I had fallen asleep in the hospital chair and the doctor was still in that room working on Raylen and the baby.

I heard the twins breathed a sigh of relief next to me.

If I was dreaming, I hope I never woke up. I wanted her words to be real.

She tugged my arm slightly and it brought me out of my thoughts. I followed her out of the room, that coffee cup I was nervously clinging too completely forgotten.

"We'll wait here for you." I heard Danny shout after me.

The doctor took me up an elevator to the fifth floor. When the doors slid open, there was a golden plaque right in front of me on the wall that read, *Labor and Delivery*.

"We were able to get the baby out, but I just want you to be aware, so you're not alarmed when you see her." She led me down the hallway, past all the patient's rooms to a big glass wall all the way at the end.

"She is incredibly small, and we were worried that her lungs wouldn't be developed enough to survive. Babies born this early, run a few risk and have to be monitored very closely. To our surprise, her lungs were a lot further along than we expected." She nodded her head to the window and took a step back so I could take a look.

Inside the room, there were maybe 20 or 30 babies, but my eyes immediately fell on one in particular. The name *YUU* in bold letters on the front. She was two rows deep, wrapped tightly in a pink blanket with a matching pink hat.

She was incased in a huge plastic incubator with a tube coming out of her nose and another coming out of one of the arms they left free of the blanket.

She was so pale and tiny, but she looked just like a smaller version of Levi.

"She will have to stay in the incubator for a few weeks until she is a little more developed, but other than that, your daughter is a fighter." Fuck. There go those tears again. I couldn't help it. I had another daughter and against the odds, she was here and according to the doctor, she was healthy.

I was reluctant to pull my eyes away from her, but I turned toward the doctor. "How is Raylen?"

The doctor smiled again. "She made it through the surgery like a champ, there were no lasting injuries. She should be fully healed in a couple weeks." The doctor reached down and grabbed her vibrating pager off the waistband of her scrubs.

"As a matter of fact, I think she might be waking up soon if you want to go and see her." I nodded my head immediately and let the doctor lead the way.

"She's so beautiful." The nurse wheeled the incubator right next to Raylen's bed. She had woken up a few hours ago, but the doctor wanted her to get some food in her stomach and run a few tests before she saw the baby.

Now finally she was able to lay eyes on our beautiful miracle baby.

"She looks just like Levi." She said excitedly, turning to look at me. I nodded my head in agreement.

I wasn't entirely sure which one of us Levi looked like more. I liked to think she was a healthy blend of both of us which means so was our second daughter.

It had hit me the moment I saw her behind that glass window that I was now the father of not one but two little girls. It made me want to live my life completely different.

I thought I was being overprotective when it was just the three of us. Just the two most important women in my lives, but now with this new addition, my protective instincts were going into overdrive.

I was almost tempted to do something completely outrageous like whisk the three of them away where no one could get to them, that way I knew they would be safe. Raylen would never let me do something like that, but it was a satisfying thought.

"Ok mom and dad," The nurse crooned. "Have we picked out a name for baby?" I lifted my head to look at Raylen, expecting her to already have something picked out. Wasn't it usually common for pregnant women to already have a few names bouncing around in their heads.

We never got around to finding out the gender in person, but I was sure Raylen had a few picked out for either. At least that's what I thought, until I looked up and found Raylen staring back at me expectantly.

My eyes bugged slightly. "Why are you looking at me?" I asked.

She laughed and leaned back in her hospital bed. "Why else. The nice nurse asked you a question."

I turned my head to look at the nurse to see she was patiently waiting on my response as well. My eyes flicked back to Raylen. "I don't understand."

Raylen reached out for my hand, and I immediately gave it to her. She gently rubbed the outside of it. "You missed out on a lot of stuff when it came to Levi, including something as simple as picking out a name, so I'm giving you a chance to do that now."

The way she smiled at me. A look that was so warm, like the reason behind her getting attacked and landing in this hospital bed had nothing to do with me. Like I was someone she could never hate completely.

I noticed it a couple months ago when I came back into her life. When she looked at me, behind all that rage and pain she was feeling, in her eyes I could see it just as clearly as I could see it now. Raylen loved me.

Just like me, she probably never stopped after we went our separate ways. I regretted how much time we missed out on because of my actions but I said it before and I would say it as many times as she needed to hear it, I would spend the rest of my life making up for my past actions to all three of my girls.

Nothing and no one was going to keep them from me ever again.

"Are you crying?" I heard Raylen's voice. I couldn't help the laugh that slipped through. I rubbed at my face with my free hand.

"Can't a man bask in the beauty of the women in his life."

Epilogue

RAYLEN

TWO YEAR LATER

And that's when I knew love and happiness can find you in the most unexpected of ways.

I breathed a sigh of relief when I hit the final period on the draft of my newest novel. I reached my hands high above my head and gave a nice stretch. God that felt good. I looked out the window at all the tall buildings surrounding me.

Why was this scene so peaceful, maybe because it reminded me so much of home. The tall buildings, the long line of cars on the streets just trying to make it to their destination. The billboards tacked on the side of buildings, flashing ads 24/7 even in the dead of night. I never needed a lot when it came to a place to settle down.

I didn't need beaches or palm trees like I thought once upon a time. I was a city girl through and through, the city was always where I would find my harmony.

After Ra-Mi and I were finally discharged from the hospital, Jae strongly suggested that we make a change to our lives. He wanted us out of the states so he could raise his daughters around the other half of their culture.

I was skeptical at first about moving to South Korea, after all I had never so much as visited another country and now, he wanted me to move there. I wanted to be fair though, I raised Levi in the states for most of her life, it was good for her to be around her Korean heritage, I wanted her to learn, Ra-Mi too.

Since making this move, I've never regretted it. This country was beautiful and vibrant and surprisingly a lot more accepting to other ethnicities than I thought they would, if his parents were anything to go by. We were happy.

As far as Jae's parents, in the last year, they had completely abandoned their prejudice towards me. According to them, anyone who was willing to step in front of a knife for their son was worthy of being with him.

So, all it took was almost dying to get their approval, noted. They were also thrilled that I was embracing more of their culture between Ra-Mi's name and moving to Korea, they've been acting like the best grandparents in the world, spoiling the girls rotten.

I was grateful. I never wanted to keep my family away from

them, but I also didn't want to expose them to anyone who thought of them as less than or unworthy and so far, that hadn't happened.

A scream ran through the house followed by a chorus of giggles. "Hey, that was my sandwich." I couldn't help it when the corners of my mouth twitched up at the noise. There was never a dull moment when it came to the three of them.

Pushing back my chair I got to my feet and headed out of my office. Jae had found us a nice penthouse apartment. Four bedrooms, two bathrooms. He said he thought I might like an apartment better than a house because of the view and he was right about that.

I heard another scream followed by someone being shushed. "You're going to disturb momma."

"Too late mommy has been disturbed." I walked into the open plan kitchen. Jae-Hyun stood on one side of an island in the middle of it. His arms spread out in front of him, palms flat on the marble countertop with an empty glass plate in front of him.

On the other side Levi and Ra-Mi crouched down. Ra-Mi holding a chicken sandwich in one hand and gripping tight to Levi's hand with the other.

Just like the day she was born, Ra-Mi looked like a lighter, slightly chunkier version of Levi. She wore her hair in two curly Mickey Mouse ear buns and a blue jean overall dress with a white top. Jae-Hyun had told me that her name meant someone who would blossom in their journey through life, when I look at her now compared to how fragile she was the day she was born, I knew that was true.

Levi sat next to her in her school uniform a grey skirt and I white button up top with the school logo stitched above the right breast pocket.

"Oooh." Levi said pointing at Ra-Mi who was still holding the incriminating evidence. Levi ever the instigator.

Ra-Mi turned her head and took a bite of the sandwich before shoving her hand behind her back trying to hide it. I tried to keep a straight face and keep up the charade that I was mad, but I couldn't help it. The laughter burst from my chest and when I looked up, Jae-Hyun was eyeing me suspiciously.

"You traitor." He said and took off running at me. I screamed and ducked behind the counter next to the girls. He was right, in stand offs like this, I more often than not sided with the girls which is why he's been consistently bugging me about giving him a son.

Jae-Hyun rounded the island, but before he could get us, I shooed the girls and the three of us took off running toward the door on the other side of the living room that led out to the wrap around balcony we had. Jae-Hyun was hot on our heels.

"It's our sandwich now daddy." Levi shouted reaching for the doorknob. I loved hearing her call him that, it made my heart fill with so much joy. It made everything I had to deal with over the last two years and even ten years ago all worth it.

Now I had my family, my girls and my husband the love

of my life. Someone I couldn't imagine spending this life without. Who would've ever thought it was all thanks to that stupid contract.

Acknowledgements

Thank you to all the KDramas that have helped inspired me all these year. Shout out to my friend/ writing peer for always letting me bounce ideas off of you day and night no matter how much I got on your nerves.

Bestie I didn't forget you, sorry for all the anticipation filled now months and all the future months to come. Thank you for always being supportive.